Shapeshifted Peace

Passaconaway's Pacification of Settlers

Shapeshifted Peace

Passaconaway's Pacification of Settlers

by

Stephen W. F. Berwick

Parisburg Publishing

Copyright 2012 by Stephen W. F. Berwick

Line drawings and Photos by Stephen W.F. Berwick:

pp. 11, 12, 13, 14, 86, 90, 113, 116, 117, 118, 127, 128, 135, 139, 149 & 203

Other books by Stephen W. F. Berwick:

Land of the Shapeshifter (2011)

Shapeshifter's Peace – Passaconaway's Path to Peace (2011)

In the Shadow of Agiocochook – Stories from the Land of the Shapeshifter (2011)

Parisburg Publishing

www.parisburg.com

www.parisburgpublishing.com

ISBN-978-1-61918-005-5

Acknowledgments

Deep appreciation and heartfelt thanks to so many people who have assisted me along the path toward the finalization of the manuscript, offering encouragement and kindness and insights when I most needed it: Valerie J. Laker, S. David Siff, Ruth Kevghas, Peter Brodeur, KJ Finnemore, Nancy L. Heath, Mark Ball, and, as always, my beloved parents, Rosemary and Nelson Berwick for helping me to "keep it real" and not take myself too seriously.

Dedication

To my paternal great-great grandparents:

Minnie Bell (Berwick) and Ueo Isaac Switser/Sweetser (above)
Alma Nelson (Blake) and John Frederick Simpson
Margaret-Anne (Elliott)and Joseph Harris
Letitia (Thurston) and James Lent

To my maternal great-great grandparents:

Marguerite (Duchesney) and Francois Houle
Archange (Vaillancourt) and Jean-Baptiste Richard
Delima (Grandmaison – a.k.a. Jessie Big House) and Edmond Haule
Marie (Touchette) and Moise Prive

Contents

ABENAKI PRONUNCIATION

Generally speaking, the consonants and vowels are similar to English but are spoken with less stress than English.

Aw	Sounds like "ow" in "now"
"8" or "ô."	Sounds like "aw" in "dawn"
Kw	Sounds like "Qu" in "Quiet"
W	Sounds like "Oo" at the beginning of a word

Preface to Shapeshifted Peace

Shapeshifted Peace takes up where *Shapeshifter's Peace* left off. The story begins with an overview of European reasons for colonizing as well as the "legal" documents that authorize the colonization.

Next are introduced some of the key English players in early New Hampshire history; men such as Rev. John Wheelwright and Captain Jonathon Danforth. Then come events such as the accidental death of Reginald Jenkins; the marriage of Passaconaway's daughter that led to Whittier's romanticized version of the wedding "Bridal at Penacook." From there we are observers of the Great Chief of the Penagok Confederation's uneasy peace with the English settlers and the death of the Great Chief at over 120 years of age and the assumption of duties by his son, Waolinasad.

In terms of historical dateline, the story takes place from 1621 to 1664 when Passaconaway is believed to have died. This is a pivotal period in American history. Although there is peace, the peace is like a lid on a boiling pot. Many of the wars that later occur are based on what takes place during this time and, in comparison to Passaconaway, rather the short chieftainship of Waolinasad.

Shapeshifted Peace also introduces a number of my English ancestors who had a hand in shaping the course of events in New Hampshire. Among them are my 10th great-grandfathers Jonathon Danforth, Jonathon Heard, and Abraham Drake as well as 10th great-uncles Thomas Paine, Peter Coffin and Major Richard Waldron (Walderne).

In Chapter 2 I introduce Wheelwright's Deed. In recent years much discussion has ensued regarding the historical authenticity of this document. Whether or not the document is authentic is beside the point. The fact is that even if Passaconaway and other leaders signed the document with their totem symbols, the fact is that the spirit of the document was destroyed almost as soon as the ink dried. Native peoples would not give up hunting, fishing and trespass rights even if they would have been safe from "Tarratines" or Mohawk incursions. If they signed the document, it is almost a given that they did not understand the legalese or the true intention of the crafters of the document which was to take away their rights to the land and legitimize English claims to the land. Also, I feel it important to remind readers that this work is an interpretive account of historic events, i.e. fiction. I am first and foremost a poet and writer, not a historian, anthropologist or ethnologist. I am also a romantic and my writings tend toward romanticism, which I employ to open hearts and minds to alternative ways of thinking.

As I've mentioned in previous works, perhaps some will say my view of history is skewed toward the Penagok. As a descendant of both European and Native ancestors as well as a Buddhist-Animist, I try through my writing to be attuned to the ancestral voices in me. So far in the march of American history the European version of the story of what took place in what the Abenaki called "N'dakinna" has long been heard; the Native voices have yet to be heard. It is my hope that *Shapeshifted Peace* will help long silenced voices to be heard.

Pebonkik
Amariscoggin
Ômanosek
Gôdag Wajo
Bemijijoasek
Tawakwtegok
Mskwamagek
Asepihtegw
Passaguanik
Wiwninebesaki
Adelahiganek
Nôwijoanek
Winnimsquam
Beskeodanak
Pesgatakwa
Seninebik
Penagok
Gôwizawajo
senigok
Bagôntegw
Annahooksett
Ktsipontegok
Massabesik
Passaguanik
Namaskik
Menonadenak
Natticook
(Nutigok)
Skawôhigan
Morôdemak
Nansawi
Pawtucket
Naumkeag
Shawmut
(Bastan)
Patuxet
Gwenitegw
Morôdemak
Nôbagw

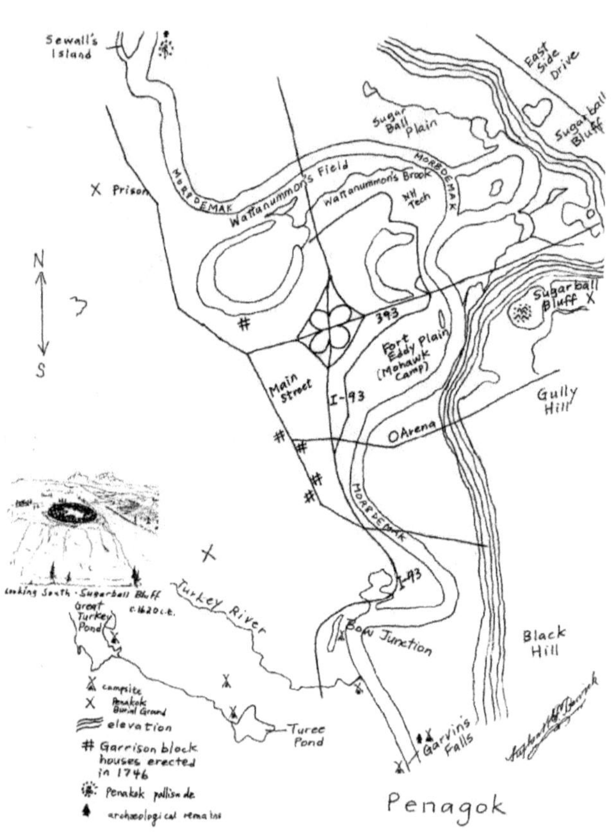

Sewall's Island
East Side Drive
Sugar Ball Plain
Sugarball Bluff
MORĒDEMAK
Wattanummon's Field
Wattanummon's Brook
MORĒDEMAK
NH Tech
Prison
N
S
393
Sugarball Bluff X
Fort Eddy Plain (Mohawk Camp)
Main Street
I-93
Gully Hill
O Arena
MORĒDEMAK
looking South · Sugarball Bluff c.1620 c.e.
Turkey River
I-93
Great Turkey Pond
Bow Junction
Black Hill
campsite
Penakok Burial Ground
elevation
Garrison block houses erected in 1746
Penakok pallisade
archæological remains
Turee Pond
Garvins Falls
Penagok

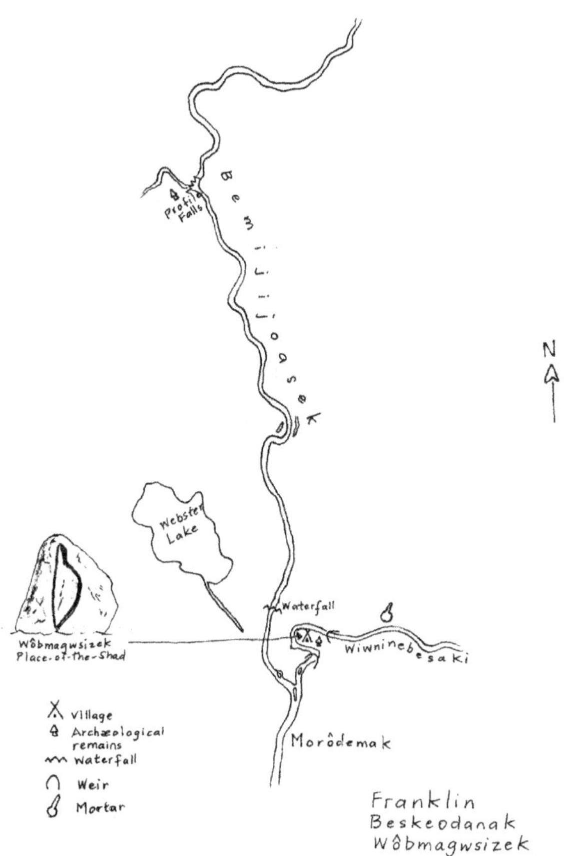

Bemijijoasek
Profile Falls
Webster Lake
Wôbmagwsizek
Place-of-the-Shad
Waterfall
Wiwninebesaki
Morôdemak
N
Village
Archæological remains
Waterfall
Weir
Mortar
Franklin
Beskeodanak
Wôbmagwsizek

Indian Head

Deep in New Hampshire's White Mountains,

High above the National Forest

Where it juts out from a cliff,

A face believed by Abenaki to belong to a stone person

Who'd long ago been smashed by the Great Maker

For destroying his creations

And by others to be the profile of Chief Pemigewasset

Who awaits the return of his Mohawk wife

From the land of her people.

"Who is that?"

A boy asked his father.

"Indian Head. Face of one of those who've disappeared"

The father answered his son's inquiry.

"Where'd they go?" the boy responded.

"Oh, I guess they just died off"

Responded the tan face father.

Many years have since passed

As I now recall those, my father's, long ago words,

And ponder how easily history

And facts

Can cloud

An Indian's head.

1

PENAGOK

In dreams

To life's possibilities

The heart awakens;

While awake

Heed dreams

For without them

Lost in schemes

Life's meaning.

(a)

The Great Creator, Nawawas, continues to sleep. Nawawas, who is also known as "The-One-Who-Comes-Among-Us," has yet to awaken and continues to dwell in the land of dreams. When the Great Creator awakens, so believed the ancient Abenaki, everything in this illusionary world of reality that was, is and would otherwise be, all that we have believed to have experienced, seen, heard about, will disappear with not even a trace to remain.

The early medôlinôwinnoak (persons-of-medicine) believed that "true" reality existed only in dreams: the dreams created by Nawawas. Glimpses of the true reality can be seen in visions gifted to us by our animal spirit protectors and our ancestors who surround and guide us in our journey through life. That which occurs in the dreamtime is lasting and eternal, as it exists in the eternal mind of Nawawas. In dreams we can glimpse Nawawas who is in everything as all of us are one with Nawawas.

Dreams. As with all beings, I have entered the land of dreams every night and at times during the day. Among my dreams is a dream of a land where a wide river flows through an alluvial intervale. The river is called the Merrimack (Abenaki: Morôdemak); the intervale is called Concord (Abenaki: Penagok). The Merrimack River at Concord is deep and bends nearly back on itself as it flows beneath the high sandy bluff where an ancient palisade stares down over the valley below. The bluff gave the name to the intervale: "At the Place of the Falling Bank" for the soft, sandy bluff gives way under foot. Here people have lived since the stone people were destroyed and replaced by the ash tree people.

Further upriver, I see in my dream a small island where tall white pines that reach over two hundred feet high and have a circumfrance of eight people standing shoulder to shoulder, stand sentinel above gravel and sand beaches. In the island's interior and along both banks of the river are cornfields. This is the Great Chief Passaconaway's island where he keeps his lodge during the planting season and where he returns during the harvest. The air here is redolent with the scent of the oak leaf tannin hued river, wet sand and pinesap and alive with the sound of the animal people.

As my dream progresses I am in the White Mountains where I see a sharp stone face jutting from a cliff side. The stone face seems to ponder all that has happened and all that will happen in the land of reality. Across from the stone face that I knew most of my life as the Old Man of the Mountains and who the Abenaki considered, until he fell, to be one of the first ones – the stone people - I observe a solitary raptor wing the thermals, traversing the bluest of mile high skies as it soars above the intemperate granite ledged summits.

As the dream progresses sunlight filters through the glacial carved notches, sprinkling gold specks atop silver-hued waterfalls and streams that rush toward the rivers and from there to the sea. I return in my dream to Concord and see in my dream under the eternal gaze of these White Mountains, a proud and ancient people welcome newcomers to share Wôbanaki, the Land that Greets the Dawn.

My dream continues.

As my spirit soars far above the trees, mountains, rainbows and rain clouds, beyond the stratosphere and ozone, feeding off the cosmic dust that coats the universe, my dream takes me to the bears who make up the constellation Ursa Major. Among the bears are five who sit on Sky Council: Fire Eyes who is the chief and story teller; Scorching Tail; Gray Ear; Great Heart; and, Matted Fur.

Fire Eyes, like all Bear People who sit on Sky Council, is deep in wisdom and compassion. Fire Eyes got his name from the intensity and seriousness of his flaring gaze when he relates stories. It is said that through his eyes you can see down to the fire inside his belly; fire which is also the spark of life and which lies at the center of everything and everyone. It's the same fire that lies in the center of flint which when hit against another object, sparks. It is the fire of the first spark that created all universes. Fire Eyes, the Chief of the Bear People who hold Sky Council, receives his authority from consensus and respect of the others.

In addition to Fire Eyes there is Scorching Tail who got his name because he sits too close to the council fire where he singes his stubby tail. Scorching Tail is a deep thinker and is noted for his undiluted sarcasm and ready wit.

Then there is Gray Ear, whose analytical skills were called upon by the others in reaching consensus on important decisions. He received his name due to the two gray smudges on the fur over his cheekbones just below his ears.

Great Heart, whose pupils seem always to be swimming, is a bear whose heart aches at the suffering humans create for themselves. She was also younger and more inquisitive than the others.

The last of the five Bear People who sit on Sky Council is Matted Fur who rarely spoke but who, although as comely as a dustball, is greatly respected for his intelligence and keen scent of the situation.

My dream continues. With bright eyes flashing across galaxies like twin suns lighting the darkness of the void, Fire Eyes begins to relate all that had occurred to the Penagok after the arrival of the Pilgrims and Puritans to Wôbanaki, the Land that Greets the Dawn.

Ursa Major by Johannes Hevelius c. 1611-1687 Danzig

Fire Eyes glances around him and then clears his throat:

"Happiness left the Land that Greets the Dawn with the arrival of the English settlers. For the Penagok it was the beginning of the end. Millennia of traditions, stories, belief systems… in short, a way of life would be systematically eradicated by those newly arriving on these shores. All that had been revealed to the Penagok's Great Chief Passaconaway in dreams and all that the One-Who-Likes-to-Sleep-So-Well had forewarned him about had occurred and would come to pass. Ever since the shooting star pierced the night sky above Penagok, striking deep into the heart of its people, the world they knew was changed forever."

Fire Eyes continues:

"The Great Chief, who was one of the greatest shapeshifters in the history of the Penagok people, spoke to his council at Penagok and urged the Shapeshifter's Peace with the English. The council agreed and peace did come to the land. But soon the Penagok learned the price of that peace for how could lopsided peace that favored the settlers and hobbled the Penagok and other Native peoples lead to happiness? Along with peace came more disease and more death to the Penagok and other native peoples. The winters that followed the Pilgrims' arrival at Patuxet and later the Puritans who arrived at Naumkik (Salem, MA) and Shawmut (Boston, MA), filled the Penagok people with sadness, a deep sense of loss, and foreboding. The sense of loss would follow their descendants for hundreds of years to come. The only thing the Penagok people could count upon was their Great Chief and Person of Medicine, their shapeshifter, Passaconaway, the Child-of-the-Bear."

Eyes arrowed across the galaxies and settled on the figure of Passaconaway as the Great Chief himself begins to relate what occurred after the Pilgrims' landed at Patuxet.

Listen and I will tell you how after convincing my people to make peace with the English, that we Penagok kept that peace even when the English proved they did not want peace and had no intention of maintaining peace. They wanted land: not just some of the land but all of the land. Listen as I relate how the English took our lands causing my peoples' anger to grow until peace was no longer possible. Listen as I relate how I came to know the ways of these strangers who came like demons in the night, pretending friendship when all they wanted was our death.

Within my heart I continue to cry the tears that will not fall from my eyes. My heart cries for all my peoples' tears that dried behind eyelids that would not release water. Although it has been almost 350 human years since I last walked atop the sandy bluffs at Penagok all that transpired there is forever a part of me. Forever a part of me and my people until Nawawas awakens.

The bear council members focused their eyes on the human plane as Passaconaway continue:

At first we Native peoples all over Wôbanaki felt pity for these people who came like refugees on floating islands from far across the great water to live on our lands. They seemed like children. They came hungry and at first were unable to grow enough food to feed themselves or to adapt to the land. They were starving. It stirred our hearts to pity. Some of my people thought the strangers must have left their own lands far away across the Great Water because the strangers didn't know how to grow corn, vegetables or hunt. We reflected over their sad plight.

"Maybe there had been a great battle with an enemy," said some, no doubt thinking of our own recent battle with the Mohawk that occurred just after harvest.

"They are refugees."

Others thought:

"Maybe the Great Creator sent the strangers to our lands in order for us to teach them how to live."

"Teaching them how to live" was a natural way for Penagok to think, after all, it was our way to help strangers and to share. Grandmother land's bounty was for all to share equally. This had been our way since the beginning time.

Others were more cautious:

"Maybe they have been sent by the Ice-Hearted Ones to destroy us," said others.

"Not too far from the truth," *snarked Scorching Tail.*

The Bear Council members shook their muzzles in agreement.

Yet, I knew. The white men had been coming along the shores of Zobagw for many generations before mine. I had heard stories about these strangers from my grandfather. He told me how the strangers terrorized those who lived along the coast.

"Grandson, these people are like demons that come in the night and take people away from the land of the living. Be wary of them," he had said to me.

"Keep an eye on the sea. If you see a white bird in a tree floating closer and closer to you, leave immediately. It is an ill omen and will mean the strangers are coming. Nothing good comes of it."

He had been correct. These white men were met with fear and suspicion by some peoples because the white men took Native peoples prisoner and brought them far away across the great water. No one knew why the strangers took them away from our shores. They had no reason to make us prisoner as we never made war on the white men. Like many things that would come in the future, their actions made no sense to us.

"They are not like other humans and do things for no purpose," said some of my people about the actions of the white men.

"Not even the Mohawk do what they do," said others.

The Mohawk had been our enemies for some time and were called "Maneaters" by us because they were believed to eat their enemies. They called us "Adirondacks" meaning "Bark Eaters" because in times of famine we eat the inner layer of white pine bark to sustain us. Even my grandfather did not know when the animosity with the Mohawk had begun. A few years before the strangers arrived at Patuxet, the Mohawk struck us at Penagok. We pushed them back.

"They are like ghosts who come on floating islands that stink and take away our people," said yet others about the white men.

Scorching Tail notes:

"They were taken to become slaves by one of Captain John Smith's men as they sailed along the Gulf of Maine. He figured the Spanish would give a good price for them."

The other bear council members agree.

Passaconaway continues:

A few who were taken away from our lands did return. One, Tisquantum, went to Patuxet to help the English survive. It was believed; however, by many of us that the mind of Tisquantum, whose people had died of the disease brought to our lands by the Europeans and at whose village, Patuxet, the English chose to live, had been changed by his time among the English:

"His mind is twisted," said Chief Massasoit against Tisquantum, who didn't trust him.

"He is always trying to make trouble for the people," said his lieutenant of Tisquantum's penchant for arousing suspicion among the Native peoples.

Chief Massasoit explained to me:

"Tisquantum attempts to pit the English against our people! When I ask him face-to-face he says:

"'I do not make trouble'

"But his actions speak differently. I believe it's his desire to survive that makes him a traitor and spy for all sides. I have asked Hobamok to keep a close eye on him and to follow him wherever he goes to make sure that he creates no more trouble for us."

The concerns around Tisquantum's behavior were a sign of things to come. The Great Spirit had told me why the English came this time to stay. I had seen signs of what was to come. I knew that there would be many more of our people who would act like Tisquantum.

The first sign of what was to come happened long before the strangers came. The first sign came when the sky became dark at midday and was followed by a great fiery arrow that shot across the darkened sky. Next came the sound of the Great Spirit's voice carried by the wind. I didn't know why the strangers came to our lands only that we were warned by the Great Spirit not to make war on the strangers. Still, for three days after they arrived, out of fear for what my terrible vision of the future revealed to me, I went to Patuxet and hid in the swamps, trying to rid the land of the English strangers. I failed.

Fire Eyes interjected:

"The intentions of the English settlers became more clear to the Penagok as winter passed. Soon the Penagok knew for themselves that what Passaconaway had warned them about regarding the English settlers was true."

"Didn't his people believe his vision?" *asked Great Heart.*

"Oh yes," *Fire Eyes continued:*

"Visions were important as were dreams. They gave insight into the true nature of things. Visions and dreams were to be followed, but the Penagok were never a people to follow the leader. They had listened and respected Passaconaway, but their independent nature always induced them to see things for themselves before believing it. To the Penagok a leader, no matter how respected by the people, could lead for a time, but each person was their own leader in the hills and mountains and along the riverbanks of the Penagok lands. The Penagok did not know the word 'settler' nor understand the concept. To them, the Native peoples of the 'Dawnland,' the land was grandmother who provided the people with everything they needed to survive. Penagok life revolved around the land and the seasons. During the planting season the Penagok stayed at their villages and planted their crops; during the fishing season they traveled to waterfalls and the ocean; during autumn they returned to their fields to harvest the earth's bounty; and, during the time of snows they stayed at their winter camps. This was their way of life as it had been since the beginning. But in the end, all would change. The land and sky would remain the same, but man's impermanent nature was different and would change all the old ways."

(b)

Fire Eyes begins to relate how those from the "Old World" colonized the "New World".

"Among the first Europeans to see 'the new world' were the Norse. The Grœnlendinga saga ('Greenlanders Saga') tells how Bjarni Herjólfsson was sailing from Iceland to visit his parents during the summer of 985 or 986 when he was blown off course by a sudden storm. His parents, as luck would have it, had decided to visit Greenland; however, no one in Bjarni Herjólfsson's crew had ever been to Greenland. While trying to regain his course to Greenland Herjólfsson noticed forest covered hills located to the west. Although he felt the land looked hospitable, he didn't take the opportunity to explore since he wanted to see his parents. Upon arriving in Greenland and later in Norway, Herjólfsson reported his sighting of this new land that he believed had never before been seen."

"So Herjólfsson sighted North America, but he never went back to explore or try to land?" *inquired Great Heart.*

"No. That was left to another Norse explorer. The Grœnlendinga saga relates the story of how in 1002 or 1003 Leifr Eiríksson followed Herjólfsson's route. He also founded a Norse settlement at Vinland."

"Where was Vinland?" *asked Great Heart.*

"It's believed to have been on the northern tip of Newfoundland at L'Anse aux Meadows."

"Yes, but the Grœnlendinga Saga indicates it was Þorfinnr Karlsefni who actually tried to settle Vinland in 1010," *adds Scorching Tail.*

"Yes, but Eiríks saga rauða (Saga of Erik the Red) relates the events that led to Leifr Eiríksson's discovery of Vinland. The first land he went to was probably Baffin Island because the land there is as he describes, covered with flat rocks. He called this land "Helluland" (Land of the Flat Stones). Next Eiríksson came to a woody flat land that also had white sand beaches."

"Let me guess, he called it 'White Sand Beach Land,'" *remarked Great Heart.*

"No. He called in Markland, meaning 'Wood-land'."

"Could have guessed that one," *winked Scorching Tail.*

23

"Where was Markland?" *asked Great Heart.*

"Since he sailed from north toward the south, passing Baffin Island first, it was probably Labrador since he eventually ended up at Newfoundland," *responded Fire Eyes.*

"Don't forget Karlsefni," *reminded Scorching Tail.*

"Ah, yes! Karlsefni arrived at Vinland with 160 settlers who went with him in order to live there. He also came with his wife, <u>Guðríðr Þorbjarnardóttir</u> who gave birth to a boy in Vinland between the years 1005 and 1015. The child was called <u>Snorri Guðriðsson</u>. Snorri became the first child of European descent known to be born in the 'New World,'" *replied Fire Eyes.*

"Did they stay in Vinland?" *asked Great Heart.*

"No. They left because of hostilities between the Norsemen and the people referred to in Norse as '<u>Skrælings</u>' which were the natives of northern Newfoundland," *said Fire Eyes.*

"Sign of things to come," *said Matted Fur.*

"The Native peoples of North America were to be left alone for another 482 human years before hooligans and ne'er-do-wells once again moved into the neighborhood," *remarked Scorching Tail, moving his tail away from the council fire and then adding:*

"There went the neighborhood!"

"Not far off the mark," *agreed Fire Eyes, adding:*

"It wasn't until 1497 when John Cabot and later European explorers came to North America that Native Americans were once again in contact with Europeans. Then for a hundred human years prior to the French and English settlers' arrival, the English, French, Basque and other Europeans trade and fished along the coast of North America some taking Abenaki hostages off the coast of Maine."

"That made them popular," *remarked Scorching Tail.*

"Agreed. But those who traded and fished did so seasonally, arriving in the spring and leaving in late summer. The French had tried and failed to establish successful settlements on Sable Island and St. Croix Island and then tried again and succeeded in Acadia and Quebec. Acadia and Quebec were growing communities but the French didn't push the Natives away from them. The English did," *said Fire Eyes.*

"The English came to conquer the land and make it theirs. Passaconaway knew this," *added Scorching Tail.*

"How did the French view the Native peoples?" *asked Great Heart.*

"I thought the French and English viewed the Native peoples the same."

"No," *responded Fire Eyes.*

"The French, under King Henry IV and Samuel de Champlain, looked upon the Native peoples as equals and as people with souls. They considered the Native peoples to be intelligent and able to reason like all other peoples. They had just not seen the light as illuminated to the human soul in the Bible, they reasoned. The English, on the other hand, felt the Native peoples were incapable of reasoning and were savages who did not have souls."

"I thought King Louis XIII, who followed King Henry IV, was cruel and ruthless," *noted Great Heart.*

"Not really ruthless," *added Fire Eyes.*

"Did he carry on the policies of Henry IV and Champlain toward the Native peoples?"

Fire Eyes responded:

"Louis was cruel but it was, to an extent, in response to his overbearing mother. He eventually put her in the background. Louis didn't change things very much. There was also conflict between the French and Native peoples; however, it was nothing compared to the English and the Native peoples."

"Didn't King Louis also want to take advantage of the Native peoples by taking their land?" *asked Great Heart.*

"It was different with the French. They weren't interested in making slaves of people or in taking the land. They were more interested in the fur trade and converting the Natives through peaceful means to Christianity. Overall, it can be said, the French treated the Native peoples as close to being equals as you could get during that time," *replied Scorching Tail.*

"There was also quite a lot of intermarriage with French men who took Indian women as consorts," *added Matted Fur.*

"Consorts only because the Jesuits wouldn't allow them to marry 'heathens,'" *noted Scorching Tail who added:*

"Some of these women did marry, though, but were given Christian names, French surnames and lineages that went back to France. Some lineages actually belonged to the priests themselves."

"True. More than two hundred human years from Passaconaway's time the blood of many Native peoples will be mixed with that of the French. In the centuries to come many of this mixture of people will migrate from what was once New France into the land that would become northern New England in the United States," *said Fire Eyes.*

"Anyway, the long and the short of it is that unlike the English, the French didn't look upon the Native people as 'beasts,'" *said Scorching Tail.*

"But didn't the French call all Native peoples 'sauvage?'"

"Yes, but the word, during the 16th and early 17th century only referred to someone who lived in the woods, a son of nature, it wasn't a pejorative."

"The English settlers didn't respect the culture of the Native peoples? Were they all the same? Weren't there some people who tried to adapt?" *asked Great Heart.*

"There was a minority of those who came who did try to learn and understand all that they saw. But they were few and far between. Among those who came were men who had only a limited understanding of the land and environment they were entering. They held a firm belief that the land belonged to them since King James I had authorized settlement. They believed the land belonged to England."

"And that God had given them the land," *added Scorching Tail.*

"Yes, God's will," *agreed Gray Ear, adding*:

"Man's interpretation of God's will as interpreted from Biblical passages has a lot to do with how the land is taken by the Puritans."

"Why did James believe that he had the right to authorize settlement of land that wasn't his?" *asked Great Heart.*

Fire Eyes responds:

"Well, James, in his 'Charter of New England' put it this way:

> ... 'And also for that We have been further given certainly to knowe, that within these late Yeares there hath by God's Visitation reigned a wonderfull Plague, together with many horrible Slaugthers, and Murthers, committed amoungst the Sauages and brutish People there, heertofore inhabiting, in a Manner to the utter Destruction, Deuastacion, and Depopulacion of that whole Territorye, so that there is not left for many Leagues together in a Manner, any that doe claime or challenge any Kind of Interests therein, nor any other Superiour Lord or Souveraigne to make Claime "hereunto, whereby We in our Judgment are persuaded and satisfied that the appointed Time is come in which Almighty God in his great Goodness and Bountie towards Us and our People, hath thought fitt and determined, that those large and goodly Territoryes, deserted as it were by their naturall Inhabitants, should be possessed and enjoyed by such of our Subjects and People as

heertofore have and hereafter shall by his Mercie and Favour, and by his Powerfull Arme, be directed and conducted thither. In Contemplacion and serious Consideracion whereof, Wee have thougt it fitt according to our Kingly Duty, soe much as in Us lyeth, to second and followe God's sacred Will, rendering reverend Thanks to his Divine Majestie for his gracious favour in laying open and revealing the same unto us, before any other Christian Prince or State, by which Meanes without Offence, and as We trust to his Glory, Wee may with Boldness goe on to the settling of soe hopefull a Work, which tendeth to the reducing and Conversion of such Sauages as remaine wandering in Desolacion and Distress, to Civil Societie and Christian Religion, to the Inlargement of our own Dominions, and the Aduancement of the Fortunes of such of our good Subjects as shall willingly intresse themselves in the said Imployment, to whom We cannot but give singular Commendations for their soe worthy Intention and Enterprize;
...'

"Kind of makes it clear what he thought!" *expressed Scorching Tail.*

"And the settlers. Remember, European settlers felt these Natives were savages who had no right to the land or claim of ownership to it since they didn't 'subdue the land', as the Puritans believed the Bible told them to do, to own land. It took the bureaucrats and lawyers to make it all clean and legal," *said Matted Fur.*

"Clean?" *remarks Scorching Tail.*

"Point taken," *says Matted Fur, scratching himself.*

Gray Ears added:

"Yes, and don't forget, land claims by countries that legitimized the taking of land started much earlier."

"You mean in terms of the human way to history life," *added Scorching Tail.*

"Yes. This whole land claim issue started back in the late 1490s, after Columbus 'discovered' the Americas in the European year of 1492..."

"Don't get him started!" *warned Matted Fur, referring to Scorching Tail who raised his eyes.*

"Too late!" *quipped Fire Eyes as Scorching Tail readjusted himself.*

"You mean bumped into," *remarked Scorching Tail.*

"He's got a point!" *said Fire Eyes.*

"True. Columbus didn't discover North and South America. He, as Scorching Tail notes, 'bumped into' the Carribean islands," *adds Matted Fur.*

"Right. Bumped into," *continued Fire Eyes.*

"It was John Cabot who discovered North America," *said Matted Fur.*

"You mean rediscovered since the first European to 'discover' North America was Norse," *said Gray Ears.*

"Well, there was nothing to be 'discovered' since the Native peoples knew they were there!" *said Scorching Tail.*

"Moving along," *began Fire Eyes, smiling:*

"King Henry VII granted letters patent to the Cabots to:

"'...discover and occupy isles or countries of the heathen or infidels before unknown to Christians, accounting to the king for a fifth part of the profit upon their return to the port of Bristol.'

"Because of the explorations of John Cabot and his son, Sebastien, in the name of their king, England would later use these discoveries to lay claim to all of what became known as the North American continent. But it was Henry Hudson who claimed the land for England."

"But remember. Columbus didn't feel he had discovered a 'new world.' He felt that he had reached Asia," *said Fire Eyes.*

"Looking for a passage to Cathay and Zipangu [Japan]," *added Gray Ears.*

"Which is how the Native peoples of what would be called the Americas became known as 'Indians.' He thought he'd reached India," *added Scorching Tail.*

"That's right," *agreed Fire Eyes.*

"In point of fact although the land had been unknown to the English, Spanish, Portuguese and others, it wasn't 'discovered.' He discovered nothing. In terms of European people discovering the Americas, the Norsemen did it under Leifr Eiríksson."

"And the Chinese who arrived on the West Coast," *suggested Matted Fur.*

Fire Eyes continued:

"True."

"Don't forget the Irish who escaped Iceland when the Vikings invaded there," *reminded Matted Fur.*

"But what about Henry VII? Didn't he think of sending English to settle the 'New World?'" *asked Great Heart.*

"Henry VII seemed to have been more interested in trade than settlement. He didn't know what lie beyond the shoreline. In fact, like Columbus, he may have believed China was beyond the hills," *said Fire Eyes.*

"Well, as mentioned previously some Englishmen did also kidnap natives and brought them back to England. In their year 1502 three natives were kidnapped and brought to England. A man named Fabyan, wrote in <u>Chronicle</u> in 1502:

"'There were clothed in beastes skinnes, and ate rawes fleshe, and spake such speech that no man coulde understand them, and in their demeanour like to bruite beasts, whom the king kept a time after. Of the which upon two yeeres past after I saw the two apparalled after the manner of Englishmen, in Westminster Pallace, which at that time I coulde not discern from Englishmen, till I learned that they were. But as for speech, I heard none of them utter one worde.'"

"But why did it take so long for the English to settle land that they claimed?" *asked Great Heart.*

"There were many reasons, among them was that Henry VII's son, Henry VIII, had other matters that he was interested in," *said Fire Eyes.*

"Certainly did," *remarked Scorching Tail.*

"Surely it was all government related, economy and such," *suggested Matted Fur.*

The other Bear Council members harrumphed.

"You mean six wives!" *remarked Scorching Tail.*

Scorching Tail's comment was met with laughter that bounced from planet to planet.

"Although Henry VIII's Cardinal Wolsey was interested in exploration of land, not women..." *added Gray Ears.*

"You mean exploitation of wealth..."

"Well, he was interested more in money than anything else," *said Matted Fur, scratching his fur then smacking himself.*

"Got it?" *asked Scorching Tail, amused at perennially unkempt Matted Fur's attempt at cleanliness.*

Fire Eyes rolled his eyes and continued:

"True, but the renewal of interest began anew under Henry VIII's son, Edward VI. In fact, under his reign, the Privy Council brought Sebastien Cabot back from Spain and gave him an annuity," *said Fire Eyes.*

"So exploration and possible settlement began again?" *asked Great Heart.*

"No. Edward VI died suddenly. The next English monarch, Queen Mary, was married to King Philip II of Spain. Since Spain was already establishing themselves in Mexico, Peru and 'exploring' all over the Americas not claimed by Portugal there was no need for England to explore and settle lands that the Spanish claimed for themselves," *answered Fire Eyes.*

"That's right. Interest didn't restart until Elizabeth I's reign," *agreed Scorching Tail, pulling a seed out of his claw.*

"And you think Matted Fur is messy!" *joked Gray Ears. The universe echoed in laughter.*

"The difference between us is that he'd eat the seed and I would not!" *exclaimed Scorching Tail as he flung it at Matted Fur.*

"Therefore, to him I'll fling it for his snack!"

Laughter resounded as Matted Fur, without missing a beat, plucked the seed from his fur and swallowed the tiny seed. Instead of ingesting it, however, the seed merely clung to his lip. Scorching Tail fell backward in laughter causing the others to laugh so loud their voices sounded like exploding stars. Fire Eyes eventually regained composure and continued:

"Yes. Then Richard Hakluyt called for an empire to protect England against Spain because that country was now against England."

"I see," *said Great Heart.*

"The English first attempted settlement in 1585 and 1586 under Queen Elizabeth I in what would become North Carolina. The settlement was called Roanoke Island. The settlement failed and the colonists disappeared. It wasn't until 1607 that a viable English colony actually took hold in North America. The colony was named Jamestown, after King James, and was located in Virginia. It survived thanks in no small part to Pocahontas, daughter of Wahunsenacawh, who the English called Powhatan."

Gray Ears noted:

"In fact it was to Virginia that the Pilgrims were headed before they settled for Patuxet."

"Slightly off course. Lucky for the Penagok," *snarked Scorching Tail.*

"Of course, the English weren't the first to establish a viable colony in what would become known as 'North America,'" *noted Matted Fur.*

"That's right. The French had made a colony at Fort Caroline in 1564 but the Spanish expelled them and established San Agustín (St. Augustine) in 1565. San Agustín and other forts were established by the Spanish to protect their treasure ships from pirates that prowled the Carribean. As I said before, the French had attempted settlement at Sable Island, Tadoussac near Quebec in 1600, St. Croix Island in 1604 and Port Royal at Acadia in 1605-07. Now, in terms of England, King Charles I, James I's son, granted a patent, the First Charter of Massachusetts on March 4, 1629, which stated, in part:

> "'Given and granted vnto the Councell established at Plymouth, in the County of Devon, for the planting, ruling, ordering, and governing of Newe England in America, and to their Successors and Assignes for ever all that Parte of America, lyeing and being in Bredth, from Forty Degrees of Northerly Latitude from the Equinocticall Lyne, to Forty Eight Degrees...'"

John Smith's Map of New England c. 16th century

"We get it," *remarked Scorching Tail.*

Fire Eyes stopped and said:

"You get the picture. The land was, in the settlers' minds, English by royal sanction. Anyway, Great Heart, you can see the mindset of those who eventually came to settle. They felt they had the right to the land," *said Gray Ears.*

"Yes, right of discovery; right that England's King Henry VII first made claim to the land; rights accorded by the Patents of King James I and King Charles I, and, in accordance with Genesis 1:28, just for good measure, the Natives did not 'subdue the land,'" *added Fire Eyes.*

"Because they didn't feel the need to do so," *said Scorching Tail.*

"Right" *agreed Fire Eyes.*

"In the 1622 publication 'A Relation or Journall of the Beginning and Proceedings of the English Plantation Setled at Plimoth in New England' a man with the initials R.C. promoted the lawfulness of removing out of England and into the parts of America. He wrote, in part:

> *"'It [the land] being then, first, a vast and empty chaos; secondly, acknowledged the right of our sovereign king; thirdly, by a peaceable composition in part possessed of divers of his loving subjects, I see not who can doubt or call in question the lawfulness of inhabiting or dwelling there, but that it may be as lawful for such as are not tried upon some Special occasion here, to live there as well as here. Yea, and as the enterprise is weighty and difficult, so the honor is more worthy, to plant a rude wilderness, to enlarge the honor and fame of our dread sovereign, but chiefly to display the efficacy and power of the Gospel, both in zealous preaching, professing, and wise walking under it, before the faces of these poor blind infidels.'"*

Fire Eyes continued:

"Those who came from England during the Puritan Great Migration of the 1630s and then their children and other arrivals, steadily pushed against their colony's northern frontier, thrusting into Penagok territory without requesting permission from the native populations whose lands they took over."

"Right, because they didn't feel the need to do so," *agreed Gray Ears.*

"In terms of the people who come and settle, these settlers, as Fire Eyes mentioned, were by and large people who did not understand the world they were entering. And they didn't feel the need to," *added Scorching Tail.*

Fire Eyes added:

"Most of the settlers were people who fervently followed the Bible and believed it word for word. Therefore, they thought they understood what they saw, but more often that not interpreted what they saw as wild and savage and Godless without trying to understand that it was a different way of life from their own. In short, to say the least, they were culturally insensitive."

"To say the least," *snarked Scorching Tail.*

"Agreed," *said Fire Eyes, who continued:*

"In reality what they saw was not wild and savage but because of their limited understanding of non-European cultures, was considered by them to be 'heathen' and 'uncivilized.' Some settlers, in their solitude away from their own people released themselves from their own culture's restrictions, themselves becoming that which they accused the native populations of being, 'savage,' unprincipled and unscrupulous. Still other settlers learned their true selves, but didn't realize how different it was from their own people or from the people whose lands they entered. There were others who stayed in the 'civilized' side of the frontier out of fear, clinging to their beliefs and customs, some superstitions and fears, as a way to protect themselves in the world they considered barbarous and evil. The majority of the Puritans, though, felt that they were the elect of God and believed that only they as the elect of God were following God's Divine Plan, fulfilling God's purpose. They and their children believed that as long as they followed God's word, as interpreted by them and their ministers, they would go to Heaven. Reverend John Wheelwright and later Major Walderne were just such men. Men of the Bible who profited from the Bible, using holy words to justify their unholy actions."

"That were also backed up by charters," *remarked Scorching Tail.*

Gray Ear added:

"Almost as soon as the Pilgrims and Puritans arrived they looked for leaders who represented the native populations so that they could negotiate to buy land. When they found that person or persons whom they considered kings or princes but were in reality simply sachems or sagamô with no power to act on their own, they made those 'leaders' sign treaties. In cases where treaties were signed, the treaties were highly technical and legalistic, and were largely if even barely understood by the natives who affixed their mark on the documents. It didn't mean those leaders had any right to sign such documents, either, since the land wasn't theirs. The right of usage to that land was for the clan who used it. In native belief, land couldn't be owned. No one could own grandmother land. From the Native people's perspective, the rights, if they did confer them to settlers, were again to allow joint usage of the land, meaning that along with the natives who used the land the settlers could also use the land. Unfortunately, the natives had no idea that the settlers would then build a permanent settlement on that land and fence it in so that no native could come on to the land as they had since the beginning time."

Scorching Tail interjected:

"Imagine saying:

"'Okay, you can use the land with us. We accept your gifts as tokens of respect and of the deal to use the land with us.'

"Then, the shock when you come back to your hunting ground and find a settlement on the land your ancestors had entrusted to your care to leave for the next seven generations! I'd be upset, too! Then, of course, there were documents that no native ever saw or if they had, never read, such as the Wheelwright Deed."

Fire Eyes nodded his muzzle in agreement:

"It's true. The land had been handed to you from the seven previous generations; you, as clan leader, were to hold it for the next seven generations. You could let others use it, but, like you, no one could own it. Your clan had primary user-ship of that land."

The universe grew silent. The Bear Council Members readjusted themselves and looked toward the human plane where Passaconaway can be seen.

(c)

With the passage of the moons and seasons, my people's ways changed. We didn't change because we wanted change; we changed because we had no choice but to change. Change was forced upon us by outside forces: forces over which we had no control.

The first change to my people's way of life came with the Great Dying Time when more than 90% of our people died a lingering, horrible death. Next came the great battle with the Mohawk. Yet, the greatest change of all arrived as we tried to adjust to the deaths: the English settlers. After the arrival of the English our ways could no longer be the ways of our grandparents, great grandparents and the seven generations before us. The English were a people whose minds were unlike ours. The ways of the English settlers made no sense to us and seemed out of balance with nature and the way of the Great Spirit. The English stayed in one place from season to season and insisted that only they had the right to the land that was everyone's. The English then built palisades and stone walls to keep in the strange animals that they brought with them from far across the sea. Most alarming to us, however, was that the walls seem to have been built to keep us out. The English held the animals more precious to them than they considered us to be. We were less than their animals to them.

"Absolutely," *said Scorching Tail.*

We Penagok, Wampanoag, Massachusett (Masajosek) and others would also make an agreement to share land with English settlers in the belief that we both understood the verbal agreement in the same way. Our understanding was that we would share the land for compensation. But we soon learned that the understanding of the English regarding the agreement was very different. Later we'd learn that the English would take our words and put them onto talking leaves, which changed our words so that the land was no longer our land and we could not use the land in any way or "trespass" upon it. For this reason, we came to distrust their "talking leaves" and didn't want to use them.

"It's also why many traditional Native stories from the ancient times became lost. The Native peoples didn't trust the white man's ways. They also didn't trust writing the stories down as the spirits of the stories would get lost or destroyed by the English," *said Fire Eyes.*

In later years some of our people who learned how to read and write on these talking leaves thought to write down some of our traditions, but our elders warned them that to do so would become like the whites. The elders said:

"You could start with the truth and once on the talking leaves the truth will become a lie."

"That is so. Talking leaves have taken our land. Now the white men want our spirits."

"I do not trust talking leaves. It is white men's magic," said others.

"Using white men's talking leaves will be like pointing an arrow against ourselves!" said yet others.

Through such trickery I learned the English were like raccoons who stole from you right under your nose. Even I, who was a great magician and shapeshifter who could turn ice into water during a Northeaster, and water into ice during the middle of summer and who could tame rattlesnakes so that they curled up and slept in my palms, had no sorcery to match that of the English settlers. The English were even greater sorcerers than me. As the winter moons passed I learned to trust very few of the English settlers.

The English who came to our lands were not like the French who lived along the Gchigok (St. Lawrence River) among our Algonkian brothers, the Montagnais, Algonkin, and Huron as well as the Mi'kmaq. From my contacts with those peoples I learned that the French carried on peaceful trade with them. The French lived alongside the Algonkian peoples and did not treat the Native peoples as invaders in their own nations. The French even helped the Algonkian (Huron) to fight our enemy, the Mohawk who were trying to hone in on the Algonkian fur trade with the French. I had originally hoped that the English would assist us like the French did. For that reason I encouraged Yellow Feather (Massasoit) to help the English at Patuxet and reminded him of the Great Spirit's message to allow them to remain in peace and not molest them."

"Did the Penagok people really understand what was happening in Canada at that time?" *asked Great Heart.*

"There was such a large distance and in later times the English thought of it as 'wilderness' but the Native peoples did maintain contact with each other," *answered Matted Fur who was also busy scratching himself.*

"Yes. There was much cultural exchange between the Native nations. There was even trade between the Mohawk and Penagok, even though they fought with each other. As the fur trade increased the French had unwittingly exacerbated the rivalry between the Algonkian and the Iroquois peoples of which the Mohawk were leading members. The Penagok, like other nations, had long established elaborate networks of family and trade that extended all over what one day would be Canada and the United States of America. The trade went back thousands of years to a time before the 'time of the snows' as the Penagok referred to the last ice age," *said Fire Eyes.*

"Remember, Passaconaway's own wife was from the St. Francis River (called Alsogôntegok in Abenaki) near the St. Lawrence," *added Scorching Tail.*

"That's right and she kept in contact with her family who remained there," *agreed Fire Eyes.*

"So, you see, although it would later be thought by the descendants of settlers that there wasn't much interaction amongst the Native peoples, there was much interaction. Usually it was through family members, friends and trading partners. But it was also through messengers who brought news from all over the northeast and beyond," *said Scorching Tail.*

"That's right. In that way, the Native peoples had a very strong communication system throughout the land," *commented Fire Eyes.*

Passaconaway continued:

I was kept informed by messengers of the activities of the settlers at Patuxet and later those who came to settle and build permanent villages along the seacoast at Naumkeag and Shawmut. The English settlers started small but later swarmed like ants around spilled maple molasses. I soon realized the prophecies were true: there was no stopping the invasion and takeover of our lands. There would soon be problems around land, land use, and the most evil of all trade items that the settlers brought to our lands - skwedainebis (fire water – rum). We had never had any experience with such problems and found it difficult to deal with them. Later would come the settler's war on the Pequot.

First and last, though, our problems with the settlers began and ended with land. The problems around land and who had the right to control land, gave rise to many fantastic stories about the land hungry English settlers. We had heard from messengers who lived along the St. Lawrence River where some French had settled that the English lived on an island, while the French came from a vast land. The French boasted to the Native peoples there that:

"Our great chief is powerful and great. The English great chief is weak and only controls an island. Our great chief wants to make friends with all Native peoples and to trade with them. We do not need land."

A messenger explained to me:

"That is why the English come. They want your land. With your land the English will gain power among their people."

Another messenger had also been told by some of the French:

"The English love land because their land is small and they need more in order to survive. They also like to push other countries around, like the Mohawk do to the Penagok and other Algonkian brothers. The English have too big a population and their great chief cannot find any more land. The French will not allow them to come onto their vast land nor will any other white men's country. Some of the English who come to your lands are mad in the head about their God and their king wants these people to leave his island so they will no longer bother him. Among the settlers who come are many who, as I've said, are mad in the head about their God and they believe their God is more powerful than any of your spirits. They believe that their God can easily destroy your spirits. They also believe their persons-of-medicine are more powerful than any of your persons-of-medicine and plan to destroy your places of power. You will see; all I say will come true."

Still other messengers warned me:

"Keep your eye on the coast and on the rivers. Soon the English plan to move onto more of your people's land. The French have told me so and I believe it to be true."

I was also informed that the French wanted to make friends with all the Native peoples and to sign documents that would assure their eternal friendship with us. But I was always wary of such talking leaves and also did not want to antagonize the English and didn't know enough about the French. Also, the Great Spirit had told me to leave the English alone which I took to mean, "don't antagonize or molest them." I did not want to go against the Great Spirit's admonition to us. But, as one winter passed into another, my people brought up the subject again and again:

"A friendship with the French will keep the English away as they are afraid of the French," said another messenger.

But the majority of my people were not so sure:

"All white men are the same," some Penagok said.

"Land crazy. The French say they aren't but why else are they here? Don't they also bring their black robes (Jesuit priests) with them to convert people?"

"They are all God crazy," agreed others.

Others said:

"The white men all love to brag about how powerful and smart they are. But they have come here because they weren't smart enough to grow their own food and to take care of their own land and ancestors."

I had also heard that the French were having problems of their own with the Mohawk and that they were not as powerful as they wanted to appear. When I mentioned to my council about the possibility of an alliance with the French we all came to the same conclusion. Better to keep the enemy you know, then one you don't, or as stated by Gray Moose:

"It's better to maintain a respectful relationship toward a bear whose territory you lived on and know what to expect, than to invite an unknown powerful bear onto your land and learn to regret it later."

It was hard to disagree with such logic.

Great Heart inquired:

"But didn't the French eventually get involved?"

Fire Eyes responded:

"Yes. Some were even involved at the beginning. The English and French circled each other like they were in a wrestling match. It would eventually lead to war."

The words that the messengers spoke to me about land and the English coming from an island made sense, especially in the context of what I had seen and what I experienced. As I said, we would agree to let settlers use land, but the agreement was that we continue to use it as well. That was not their idea. It was our hunting and fishing grounds. There was plenty for all of us, even for the settlers. So I saw no problems making treaties with the settlers, especially if we could use the settlers as a buffer against the Mi'kmaq and the Mohawk. These settlers; however, without permission, took over the land, claiming we had given it to them. There was nothing further from the truth.

2

NAUMKEAG

Pride

Leads prejudice

Hand in hand

As lies and deceit

Subdue justice

Across the land

And fear and ignorance of truth

Assume command.

(a)

"Didn't it ever cross settlers' minds that it wasn't their land and instead that it belonged to the Native peoples?" *asked Great Heart.*

"No. If it had occurred to the settlers, they would have felt that after they'd settled the land and subdued it that the king would have had no choice but to protect the interests of the settlers. After all, the land belonged to the king," *responded Fire Eyes, stirring the fire to bring coals to life.*

"Don't forget if the Native peoples didn't accept the fact that the settlers subdued the land and as such it was now the property of the settlers, it would have been the pretext for war to show the Natives 'who's the boss,'" *added Scorching Tail.*

"But again, the Native peoples did not understand the concept of 'property.' They understood only 'stewardship' of the land, meaning the Native people took care of the land from one generation to the next," *said Matted Fur.*

"It was not only problems of land ownership that plagued Passaconaway, but also maintaining his peace," *noted Fire Eyes as the Bear People council members refocus their eyes on Passaconaway.*

Maintaining the peace was not easy. There were many times when my people wanted to give up the path of peace and walk the path of war with the settlers.

"We must fight!" said some.

"It's intolerable," said others.

Each time I spoke to my people at council, urging restraint and forbearance.

"They do not know our ways' I'd say to my people. We must be patient. These people are not like us. They need to learn our ways."

"They refuse to listen. They think us stupid," said one to the agreement of others.

I hoped beyond hope that the settlers would learn our ways. But they were stubborn. The settlers wanted us to learn their ways and adapt to their beliefs, not the other way around. There were some settlers who did try to learn our ways, but they were few and far between. Others could have cared less about our ways or us. Disagreements between us and the English over the land were the main cause for the tensions that grew and grew. I soon learned that some of the English came with two faces. One face was shown to us when they wanted land; the other was shown to us after they got it. Among those who had two faces was John Wheelwright of whom I'll speak more on later.

Swirling eyes peer into the year 1625.

Fire Eyes begins:

"Christopher Levitt is visiting David Thompson. Thompson, along with other settlers commissioned by the Laconia (Lygonia) Company, came to Pannaway (Little Harbor) in 1623 to trade and fish. On Flake Hill at Pannaway, later to be known as Odiorne's Point, the settlers constructed a plantation consisting of a fort, a manor house, and buildings to process and store fish and trade goods. The plantation, known as Pannaway Plantation, became New Hampshire's first English settlement. It was during his 1625 visit to Pannaway that Levitt met the man he called 'Conway' who was in fact, 'Passaconaway.' Passaconaway often travelled the length and breadth of Penagok Federation lands from Namaskik and Penagok to the seashore as well as to Pawtucket, but this time, instead of visiting friends and sagamores, he wanted to see for himself the settlement that had seeded itself into the soil at Pannaway. He'd received many complaints about it and the behavior of those settlers there."

The bear council members focus their attention on Passaconaway.

I was not pleased to learn the English had come onto Penagok Federation lands. I had hoped that they would confine themselves to Patuxet, but soon came to learn that they had other plans. One of the first Englishmen I had met was David Thompson. It was at Pannaway, where he had started a village and was making fields and drying fish that I met Christopher Levitt sometime during the third or fourth snow after the settlers arrived at Patuxet. The English settlement at Pannaway was unlike anything I had seen before. When I was at Patuxet five winters previous I had spied dwellings similar to our wigwôk. At Pannaway the settlement had large buildings made of logs, and were shaped similar to long houses. Trees had been cut all around the settlement. There were some ships off shore, dried fish on racks and other things. I had heard through messengers that Levitt had started a settlement near Casco Bay (Portland, Maine). The settlement at Casco Bay was also causing angst among the Native people who lived there.

"Yes, and that failed," *said Scorching Tail.*

"The settlement, called Popham Colony, failed and Levitt, like a bear bit by wasps, then high-tailed it to England. He never returned to Maine."

"True, but Levitt returned in time to welcome John Winthrop's Puritan group when they landed in Massachusetts in 1630," *added Matted Fur.*

"Who is Levitt?" *asked Great Heart.*

"Christopher Levitt was an explorer and an associate of Sir Ferdinando Gorges. He was also a member of the Council for New England," *answered Fire Eyes.*

"Actually the whole name was 'Plymouth Council for New England.' The council was granted a royal charter by King James to found colonies in North America," *explained Scorching Tail.*

"Wasn't it they who started the Popham Colony that failed in Maine?" *inquired Great Heart.*

"That was them. In 1620 King James I gave the company settlement rights for lands in New England. In fact, the settlement at Patuxet was on land 'owned' by the Plymouth Council. Seeing that Patuxet had become successful, more grants were given. One of these grants was the Massachusetts Bay Colony in 1628; the other was the Province of Maine to Sir Ferdinando Gorges and John Mason in 1622. This set the stage for the Wheelwright Deed, the first written treaty between the Native peoples and the English."

"What did the Great Chief and Levitt think of each other?" *asked Great Heart, more interested in personalities and feelings than cold hard facts.*

"Let's listen in as Passaconaway relates his encounter with him."

"One thing was clear. Levitt couldn't pronounce 'Babiwseso-Ogawinno' and so, exasperated, Levitt proclaimed Passaconaway as 'Conway,'" *Scorching Tail said.*

The bear council members refocused their attention on Passaconaway.

Levitt had many questions and was a man who didn't mince words. I also felt he was barely able to keep his contempt for my people from expressing itself on his face. He was impatient and didn't look me in the eyes when he spoke, and was always fidgeting, like a bear with black flies circling his maple molasses coated muzzle.

Scorching Tail motioned Fire Eyes, Gray Ears and Great Heart to take notice of Matted Fur who was at that moment pawing a fly circling his honey soaked muzzle.

"We're familiar with the analogy," *said Scorching Tail.*

Matted Fur smirked wryly.

"What are those mountains?" he asked me, referring to the hills he saw from the sea. At first I was unsure of what he meant. Then he mentioned the white color of the hills that was visible to him from far off at sea. Of course, we spoke through a translator who wasn't of my people and whose accented Abenaki was hard to follow. Anyway, I eventually came to understand that he meant Wôwôbadenak – the White Mountains when I realized that the mountains could be seen off the coast as I had seen them once as a boy while in a canoe coming down the coast from Pemaquid. I realized he meant the White Mountains and mighty Agiocochook, home of the thunder spirit.

"Wôwôbadenak," I said. Levitt attempted to pronounce the word several times. "Ow-wohn-ow-wohn-ba-den-ak," I offered, slowly.

"Waumbek," Levitt proclaimed proudly.

The other chiefs looked at me, and I at them. We let "Wôwôbadenak" become "Waumbek" for Levitt. It was easier than repeating the correct pronunciation over and over. Also, in Abenaki tradition, it is not our way to argue with people over such trivial matters. Harmony in all things was what we most sought.

Levitt asked many questions about the mountains and the land near the sea. I didn't have many thoughts about Levitt, except that he seemed interested in the lands to the north east of the Penagok Federation. I suggested he speak with the clans who lived there. I later learned his real intent was further settlement.

Rev. John Wheelwright

(b)

As I mentioned, I also met with John Wheelwright.

"He is a man who talks with the Great Spirit. You can trust him" the translator said to me when I first met John Wheelwright. Trust I did; until I learned that my trust was misplaced.

"You mentioned his name before. Who is John Wheelwright?" *Great Heart asked Fire Eyes.*

"Reverend John Wheelwright was a preacher and a brother to Anne Hutchinson. Both would be banished from the Massachusetts Bay Colony for non-orthodox religious views," *responded Fire Eyes.*

"Antinomianism," *said Scorching Tail.*

"What is antinomianism?" *asked Great Heart.*

"It means that moral law is of no use since faith was all that was necessary to reach salvation," *responded Fire Eyes.*

"Which was a problem because the Puritans held the view that only a certain select few were granted a place in paradise and all had to follow moral law," *said Scorching Tail.*

Fire Eyes continued:

"John Wheelwright was a man who'll go down in the early history of New Hampshire as claiming to have secured an extensive grant of land from the Penagok," *added Scorching Tail.*

"In fact, the treaty was a sham. Smoke and Mirrors to disguise real intention. Like beads and baubles for land."

"I don't understand. Did he actually secure a grant of land from the Penagok?" *replied Great Heart.*

"Wheelwright, like all who came to settle in 'New England' believed the King of England owned the land, so it was a matter of getting the native peoples to accede to that 'fact,'" *said Fire Eyes.*

"That's right," *said Gray Ears who continued:*

"As mentioned previously, for all practical purposes, the land was already believed by the English to be English land."

"That's right. King James had already authorized settlement of the 'English' land by the Puritans. It was just a matter of each settler getting 'official' permission from the grant owner who had secured the grant from the king and then staking out his own plot of land. One way of doing it was to get the Indians off from it so it could be worked. It was easier to do it through a sham treaty than to fight them off or move them off forcefully later. Once a plantation was set up no one else could dispute it."

"Well, it didn't matter if they acceded or not. It was so that one settler could claim rights over another settler. It didn't really matter if the native peoples agreed to anything. The land, to English thinking, belonged to the king," *added Scorching Tail.*

"True. But for his part, Wheelwright goes down in later written history as a reserved, spiritual and exacting man and he probably convinced himself that he had agreement with the native peoples to own a grant of land that allowed him and his people to enclose the land and have primary rights, but he certainly did not secure a grant of land in the minds of the Penagok. The Penagok, who knew nothing of the King's proclamation that all the land belonged to the King of England, who could divvy it up as he chose, allowed him equal usage to the land as long as the Penagok could continue to use it as they had since the beginning time" *said Scorching Tail.*

"To give you a better understanding, the 1629 Wheelwright Deed stated:

Indian Sagamores to Wheelwright and Company

Whereas wee the Saganores of Penacook, Pentucket, Squamsquot and Nuchawanick, are Inclined to have ye English inhabit amongst us, as they are amongst our countrymen in the Massachusetts bay, by such means wee hope in time to be strengthened against our enemyes, the Tarratens, who yearly doth us damage, likewise being perswaided yt itt will bee for the good of us and our posterity &c. To that end have att a general meeting (att Squamsquot on Piscataqua river), we the aforesaid Sagamores with a universal consent of our subjects doe covenant and agree with the English as followeth: Now know all men by these presents that wee Passaconaway Sagamore of Penacook Runawitt Sagamore of Pentucket Wahangnoawitt Sagamore of Squamscot and Towls Sagamore of Newchawanick for a competent valluation in goods already received in coats, shurts and victuals and alsoe for ye Considerations aforesaid doe (according to ye limits and bounds hereafter granted), give, grant, bargaine, sell, Release, Rattafie and Confirme unto John Wheelwright of ye Massachusetts baye Late of England, A minister of ye Gospel, Augustin Story, Thom. Wite, Wm. Wentworth and Thom. Levitt, all of ye Massachusetts bay, in New England to them, their heirs and Asignes forever, all that part of the Maine Land bounded by the River of Piscataqua and the River of Merrimack, that is to say to begin att Newchewanack ffalls in Piscataqua River aforesaid and soe downe said River to the sea and soe alongst the sea shore to Merrimack River, and soe up along said River to the falls at Pentucett aforesaid and from said Pentucket ffalls upon a Northwest line twenty English miles into the woods, and from thence to run upon a Streight Line North East and South West till meete with the Main Rivers that Runs down to Pentucet falls and Newchewanack ffalls and ye said Rivers to be the bounds of the said Lands from the thwart Line or head Line to ye aforesaid ffalls and ye maine Channell of such River from Pentucet and Newchewanack ffals to the maine sea to bee the side bounds and the maine Sea betweene Piscataqua River and Merrimack River to be the lower bounds and the thwart or head Line that runs from the River to river to be ye upper bound, Togeather with all the lands within said bounds, as alsoe the Iles of Sholes soe called by the English, together with all Proffitts, Advantages and Appurtenances whatsoever, to the said tract of Land, belonging or in any wayes appertaining. Reserving to our Selves, Liberty of making use of our old Planting Land, as alsoe ffree Liberty of Hunting, fishing and fowling, and itt is Likewise with these Provisions following, viz;

First, that ye said John Wheelwright shall within ten years after the date hereof sott Down with a Company of English and begin a plantation att Squamscott ffalls In Piscataqua River aforesaid.

Secondly, that what other Inhabitants shall come and live on said tract of Land Amongst them from time to time and att all times shall have and enjoy the same benefits as the said Wheelwright aforesaid.

Thirdly, that if att any time there be a number of people amongst them that have a mind to begin a new plantation, that they be encouraged soo to doo, and that no Plantation Exceede in Lands above ten English miles Squaire, or such a Proportion as amounts to ten miles squaire.

Fourthly, that ye aforesaid granted Lands are to be Divided into Towneshipps, as People Increase and appear to Inhabitt them, and that no Lands shall be granted to any particular person, but what shall be for a Township and what lands within a Township is granted to any particular person to be by vote of ye major part of ye Inhabitants, Legally and orderly settled in said Township.

'Fifthly, for managing and Regulating and to avoide Contentions amongst them, they are to be under the Government of the Collony of the Massachuseetts (their neighbors), and to observe their laws and orders until they have a settled Government Amongst themselves.

Sixthly, wee the aforesaid Sagamores and our subjects are to have free liberty (within the aforesaid granted tract of land) of ffishing, fowlng, hunting, and planting, &c.

Seventhly, and lastly, every Township within the arforesaid Limits or Tract of Land that hereafter shall be settled, shall Paye to Passaconaway, our chief sagamore, that is now and to his successors forever if lawfully demanded, one coate of trucking cloath a year and every year for an acknowledgement and alsoe shall paye to Mr. John Wheelwright aforesaid, his heirs and successors forever, if lawfully demanded, two bushel of Indian Corne a year, for and in Consideration of the said Wheelwrights great paines and Care as alsoe for ye Charges he have been at all to obtain this our Grant, for himselfe and those afore mentioned, and the Inhabitants that shall hereafter settle in Townships on Ye aforesaid granted premise. And we the aforesaid Sagamores, Passaconaway-Sagamore of the Pennacook; Rnawitt, Sagamore of Pentucet; Wahangnonawitt, Sagamore of Squamscott; and Rowls, Sagamore of Newchewanack, doe by these Presentes, Rattafie and Confirme all Ye aforesaid (excepting and Reserving as afor Excepted and Rserved, and the Proviseos aforesaid fulfilled.) With all the meadow and marsh grounds therein, Together with all the woods, timber and Timber Trees, Ponds, Rivers, Lakes, runs of water or Water Courses thereunto belonging, with all the freedoms of ffishinge, ffowlinge and Hunting, as ourselves with all benefits, Proffitts, Priviledges and Apputeneances whatsoever thereunto, of all and any Part of the said Tract of Land, belonging or in any wayes Appertaining unto him, the said John Whelewright, Augustin Storer, Thomas Wite, William Wentworth and Thomas Levitt and their heirs forever as aforesaid. To have and to hold Ye same As their owne Proper Right and Interest without the least Disturbance, molestation and Troble of us, our heirs, Executors and Administrators, to and with the said John Whelewright, Augustin Storer, Thomas Wite, William Wentworth and Thomas Levitt, their heirs, Executors, Administrators and assignes, forever shall warrant, maintaine and Defend. In witness whereof, we have hereunto sett our hands and seals the Seventeenth day of May, 1629. And in the fifth year of King Charles, his Reigne over England, &c.

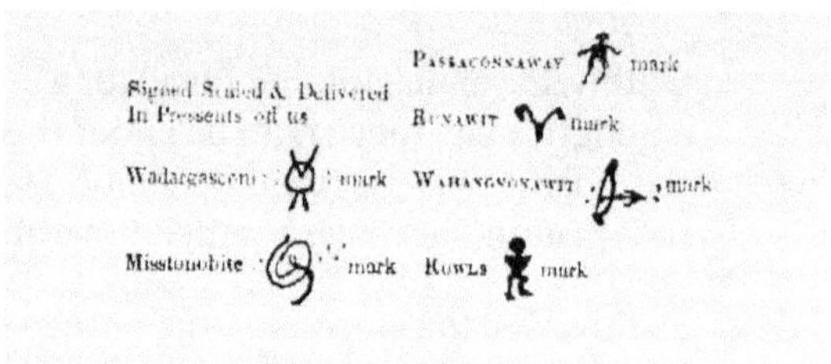

Fire Eyes shook his head, adding:

"Again, to the Penagok way of thinking, the Wheelwright Deed allowed Wheelwright to use the land, but not to 'own' or use it exclusively."

"The deed does say that they had that right. It says:

"'Sixthly, wee the aforesaid Sagamores and our subjects are to have free liberty (within the aforesaid granted tract of land) of ffishing, fowlng, hunting, and planting, &c.'"

Scorching Tail interjected:

"However, it was a set up for failure. The deed indicates 'you can do as you've always done' but Wheelwright knew that the settlers wouldn't allow free passage to the Indians as settlers planned to use the land for their own needs. Wheelwright knew the settlers would use all the land, woods, fish, fowl and animals that they could get. He knew the native ways were not English ways and that the native peoples would soon be outnumbered and the land would be taken over. The English settlers wouldn't share. What use would 'free liberty' be to the Indians? As I have said, the Wheelwright Deed was a sham. A farce," *noted Scorching Tail.*

"The first of a long line of such shams," *noted Gray Ears.*

"Because the native peoples had no concept of land ownership, right?" *asked Great Heart.*

"Yes. As we've said, Native peoples, like the Penagok, viewed themselves as stewards of the land from one generation to the next," *answered Fire Eyes.*

"If the Penagok had understood the word 'own' and Wheelwright's thinking, they would never have let Wheelwright even cross onto the land. The Penagok never gave up their rights to use the land or their right to primary land use of their ancestral lands. However, the settlers didn't seem to care about the rights of the Penagok," *added Scorching Tail.*

Passaconaway continued:

I met with Wheelwright at Cocheco sometime after the eighth winter that the settlers had come to Patuxet. He was there with members of his company. Among the members was Abraham Drake.

"A man whose ancestors had once been ale tasters in England," *noted Gray Ears.*

"Yes, and two of the ancestors during the 13th and 14th centuries would be fined for not doing their jobs," *added Scorching Tail.*

"How do you mean?" *asked Great Heart.*

"To do the job right as an ale taster, you didn't necessarily taste it. You sat in the ale. Your job was to sit in a pool of ale that had been poured onto a wooden bench. You sat in leather britches, which, if there was too much sugar, stuck to the bench. You didn't want that. Of course, this was done in drafty castles in all types of weather so sometimes the ale tasters became derelict in their duty and didn't want to sit atop cold ale in a freezing castle," *answered Scorching Tail.*

Fire Eyes, after listening patiently, said:

"Back to the story. This man of whose ancestors Scorching Tail just mentioned will settle along with his descendants on the land 'deeded' to Wheelwright."

Wheelwright was insistent about land and about needing a place for his people to get away from people who had settled near Naumkeag. His people and those who were settled at Naumkeag had a different opinion of spiritual views that made no sense to me. Why argue about such nonsense? This was new to me and was very difficult to understand. I would later learn that this was a common source of problems for the English.

"The Narragansett have different ceremonies for the spirits," I told him.

"So do the Mohawk, and the Huron. But we all worship the same Creator. Why should living with people who have different beliefs and practices be a problem?"

"We do not agree with them and we want to be at liberty," was his abrupt answer.

During my meeting with Wheelwright he asked me, as representative and Gchi Zôgamô of the Penagok Federation, about usage of land. He wanted to reduce our words and agreement to talking leaves.

"Will these talking leaves say to all that you will have permission to occupy, hunt and fish the same as we do?"

"Yes, yes," he answered me.

I clarified for him because I'd heard stories about confusion over land useage with the Penobscot peoples.

"These are not my lands. They are held by the Pesgatakwa peoples. They do not agree to let you use the lands but I will meet with them and encourage them to allow you use of the land.

I then travelled to Squamsquot on the Pesgatakwa River and met with the Sagamôak of Pentucket, Squamsquot and Nuchawanick to discuss Wheelwright's request for land.

"If their presence will mean that the Mi'kmaq will be less inclined to terrorize our people, then my people will agree to allow these English on our land," said Wahangnoawitt, the Sagamô of Squamscot.

What do you think about an agreement with the English, I asked Runawitt Sagamô of Pentucket:

"Are these Inglizmônak strong enough to keep the Mi'kmaq from attacking us?" he asked.

I told him:

"The Great Spirit told me that I must not destroy the Inglizmônak. If I do so we will be destroyed. If we do not harm them, the Great Spirit will be pleased. If the Great Spirit has said this then it stands to reason that these Inglizmônak are strong enough to stand with us against our enemies. I think they will also help us against the Magua if we ask."

The Sagamô Towls of Newchawanick assented to the English using our lands. Together we then spoke with our people at council:

"We have met with the English. They have requested our permission to use our lands. The chiefs of Pentucket, Newchawanick, Squamscot and I have agreed to let them use our land."

The council, after I explained the reasoning I had given to Chief Runawitt, assented to the English use of our lands. After the meeting I met with Wheelwright and told him:

"They have agreed to allow you to use the land, but in order to use the lands you must give them furs, coats and other such articles in goods for each village you make for as long as the treaty between us is in effect."

He agreed and said he would put such an agreement in the talking leaves as it was English custom to do so.

Fire Eyes notes:

"On Fast Day in 1636 at Boston Rev. Wheelwright preached a sermon that rankled the Boston authorities. He was banished. He eventually made his way to Exeter where he continued to live."

(c)

"By the 1630s the Dutch and English increased their migration into not only the Connecticut Valley but Pequot territory, as well," *explained Fire Eyes.*

"It would continue like a tsumani through 1650."

"That's right. There was a large flow of English into New England," *added Scorching Tail.*

"Why?" *asked Great Heart.*

"During the reign of England's King Charles I, life as a Puritan became increasingly difficult, especially in 1630-1640, the period of Charles I's personal rule. As a consequence of it, the Great Migration occurred. In 1630, Bradford and 1,000 Puritans landed at Massachusetts. In the 'New World' the Puritans were free from authority to make their Bible Commonwealth wherein a few lorded over the many. Because he had more than enough problems with the Parliament, King Charles I paid little mind to the goings-on in New England. The crown's role was merely legal," *said Fire Eyes.*

"What does that mean?" *asked Great Heart.*

"Its role was basically to issue charters giving rights to people to settle land," *responded Fire Eyes.*

Scorching Tail interjected:

"But the charters bound only the English; not the French, Dutch or Spanish and certainly not the Native peoples."

Passaconaway continued:

Within a short time after the Wheelwright Deed, English settlers began to arrive on the lands southwest of Zobagw. Suddenly they came in droves from the sea as well as north from the land of the Massachusetts. My people began to complain to me:

"They will not allow us to cross the land that is ours."

Another complained:

"The Inglizmônak will not let me fish in our pond."

While another:

"The Inglizmônak threaten our lives if we hunt on the lands they have begun to circle with stones."

The Inglizmônak behavior reminded me of something my father once told me about. He'd seen a mockingbird attacking a squirrel. My father told me that while walking along a trail one day, he noticed a squirrel whose home had always been in a pine tree, was attacked by a mockingbird. Now it hadn't made sense because neither a squirrel nor a mockingbird wanted a white pine tree as their home. They had other ideas usually about what they wanted as a lodge. Squirrels had a variety of places where they'd make a drey. Mockingbirds don't like pine trees and prefer maples and other leafy trees. But this squirrel had chosen the place and was determined to live there as it was safe and he could share with other animals.

My father who liked to fish early in the morning went out early along the trail toward the river that day. As he came near the pine tree where this one particular squirrel lived, he watched the squirrel who had a drey of dry leaves and twigs in a fork of the tree, headed back up the trunk of his tree only to be accosted by a mockingbird who now claimed his tree. Now, as I said, mockingbirds don't like pine trees and prefer maples and other leafy trees. But this mockingbird decided to lay claim to the pine tree and in particular, the highest branches of the pine where the squirrel had his drey.

Not unlike crows, mockingbirds can also distinguish one human from another as well as a particular squirrel from another. The squirrel, intelligent and cunning though he was, knew he'd be unable to withstand the onslaught of the mockingbird that'd chosen his tree. Mockingbirds will attack anyone and anything they consider a threat. I've seen them even attack snakes and hawks as well as humans. Still, hoarder of nuts as he was, gray squirrel didn't want to give up his cache of acorns and walnuts that had been stored away, so he continued darting for the tree.

The mockingbird, stretching out his wings to show the white underside, hopped up and down and aggressively defended his new nest, chasing squirrel around the tree and bushes nearby. Gray squirrel was bound and determined that the persistent adversary would not win. After calling to his fellow mockingbirds to join in and attack the gray squirrel, gray squirrel gave up his tree.

We knew, as did squirrel, that our land, once taken by the English settlers, would be defended by them as their territory, just as mockingbird had done to gray squirrel. Mockingbirds like the English settlers, were unafraid and we knew even though we were larger and knew the land better than they, were unafraid to attack us.

The land of my birth was a land of woods, hills, forested mountains, rivers, lakes, streams and the sea. The winters were harsh and bitter in the mountains where the thunderers lived, yet they were milder and less severe along the lakes and along the Morôdemak. In the south, near the land of the Massachusett, the winters were even milder. The summers were generally mild with plentiful rain and thunderstorms that started after the snows left and before the snows returned. Hurricanes could be severe, causing much flooding.

Just as the land was beautiful and could be peaceful, grandmother land could also be dangerous. For many seasons of the year the land was hostile and harsh with snows that stretched on for many months. Some years it seemed that the snows would never end. The land was also filled with nwaskwomak. Spirits were everywhere. Some were good; others bad. This made some people superstitious and there were many, many stories that could make your hair stand on end. Stories about the mountains, the Ghost Fire Jibayskweda, the Ice-Hearted wizards called Meeteekolenol and many others.

For all its trials and tribulations, grandmother land provided for us. Whenever we needed new planting grounds or the woods became too thick and animals too difficult to find to hunt, we'd burn the woods. At such times our forests burned brightly against the horizon at night, appearing like the northern lights. When we saw the fire against the horizon it brought to mind the northern lights that burn when our ancestors burn their own fields and forests in the sky.

Before the English arrived on our lands we had shared the land with the animal people. The land thrived with grouse, geese, ducks, turkeys, deer, porcupine, wild pigeons, moose and black bear as well as hunters such as wolves, fisher cats, catamounts and bobcats.

At first the English who came to settle on our lands were interested in fishing and furs.

"And furs are what led to the first problems between the Europeans and Native peoples," *commented Scorching Tail.*

"True," *agreed Fire Eyes.*

"The hostilities between the Mi'kmaq and Penobscot grew worse as they began competing to provide fur to the French traders."

"Which led to the Tarratine War and the death of Bashaba in 1615. The Mi'kmaq then swept down along the coast bringing disease and death."

Swirling bear eyes continued watching Passaconaway.

It didn't take long for animal people who wore fur that was of interest to the English to begin disappearing. The English were especially interested in the furs of the fishers, wolves, bobcats, minks, otters, beavers, martens and even black bears. By and large, they only wanted the fur; not the meat.

Among the most senseless things the settlers did when they began arriving and settling along the Pesgatakwa and later along senojizobagwa was to kill animals for no purpose other than to rid the land of them.

"Porcupine noses!" *commented Scorching Tail.*

"Ah yes, a bounty on porcupine noses," *commented Fire Eyes.*

"There was a bounty on many animals at some time or another."

The English began almost as soon as they settled to eliminate the animal people that they considered "pests" and "vermin." These were bittôlo – or "much tail" and you know as "cougar;" bezo – or "wild cat" which you call "bobcat;" and ogawinno – "he-who-likes-to-sleep-so-much" which you know as black bear. We also respected the timber rattlesnakes. At Penagok timber rattlesnakes lived atop a hill of granite opposite the palisade. Many of my people feared rattlesnakes but I did not.

Although there was an attempt to understand the settlers' ways regarding animals, they didn't try to understand our ways. What made us most sad and confused was they killed black bears for no reason. Ogawinno is shy and will not fight unless he has no choice. Most of the time bear is in the deep woods and only comes out if he is hungry. He isn't particular about what he eats and will settle for anything. But this made the settlers mad. They seemed to treat the killing of bears as though it was lacrosse. It seemed to us the settlers liked killing like it was a game. They took some of the meat sometimes, but other times they let it rot. They left behind the skins, teeth, everything. To us it was natural to kill an animal if you were going to use everything. However we took no delight in the kill, especially if it was brother bear. No matter what animal is killed, you must first ask for its forgiveness.

"Forgive me. I must take your life in order that I and my people may survive," was one of our requests for forgiveness.

To ask forgiveness of the animal people was our way. To respect animal people was our way. The settlers; however, did not ask permission because they felt it was their right to kill. Animals were there for them. They did not view themselves as brothers and sisters to the animal people.

Before long, many of the animal people who had lived along the Pesgatakwa and senojizobagwa were disappearing. Along with their disappearance went meat. It was harder to hunt and we had to go further away. To us the behavior of the settlers was as foolish as a man starting a fire under a branch loaded with snow.

We also knew that we must not overuse the land, so we would rotate our stay on the land. But when the English arrived, more and more came and they didn't rotate their stay on the land. They built to stay, all taking land away from my people as well as the animal people. The English brought their own animals; cows, horses, pigs that ravaged our planting grounds and destroyed our crops. Then they began to take the trees; the trees that had been with us since the beginning: goa, the white pine.

White pine trees were esteemed by my people. It therefore came as a shock when the English began chopping down all of the oldest and tallest of the grandfather pines and then hauling them away to the sea. We believed the grandfathers, like corn, were a special gift to the people from Gchi Nwaskw, the Great Spirit. They protected us in the winter by providing us with shelter from the heavy snows. The needles, when fresh and green, were used to make a tea that gave us energy. The branches provided us with firewood and the bark was used to cover and bury our dead. The inner bark of the tree was made into flour, which provided us with food when we were hungry. The trunk was also used for dugout canoes. To see vast areas of our land stripped of grandfather filled our hearts with deep sadness.

(d)

"Now, to truly understand the settlers' way of thinking, let's listen in on a conversation about the 'savages,'" *said Fire Eyes.*

"These savages are a bad influence," *said Samuel.*

"They are immoral. They are always happy. It is a sin! There is no happiness outside the Word of God."

"Well, it is because these savages have no boundaries. They are like children who must be taught the Word of God, but because of their savage nature, they must never be trusted."

"Yes. They can become Christian, but never English. They can never inherit the Kingdom of God," *agreed Jonathon.*

"Nor can they be a Saint," *agreed Edward.*

"They are savages, ignorant of God's Word, live like wild men and therefore have no right to the land. Genesis 1:28 is clear:

'And God blessed them: and God said unto them, be fruitful, and multiply, and replenish the earth, and subdue it; and have dominion over the fish of the sea, and over the birds of the heavens, and over every living thing that moveth upon the earth.'

"It is clear that the savages are not fruitful, have not replenished the land or subdued it; they act as brothers to the fish, birds and creatures. Therefore, they have no right to the land," *said Jonathon.*

"I hear that Reverend Wheelwright has secured a land grant from the Indians," *said Edward.*

"Yes, but we would have gone there anyway, with or without their permission. Their numbers are so reduced due to plague and war, how would they push us off once we took the land that is ours by right of God?" *scoffed Jonathon.*

"True, but we must do things proper, mustn't we? Reverend Wheelwright had his lawyers draw up the agreement and the chiefs have affixed their marks on it."

"Do they know what it says?" *asked Edward.*

"I highly doubt it since they can barely speak a word of English. Which of them would be able to understand the King's English much less legal documents?" *commented Jonathon.*

"Well put. I mean, after all, these savages can't be allowed 'free liberty' as the deed states. It's already less than a fortnight and trouble is already brewing. Mark my word, the settlers, when they arrive, will not stand for unwashed savages traipsing across their fields and moving on their newly acquired lands."

"Possession is three quarters of the law," *agreed Jonathon.*

(e)

After the Wheelwright Deed that led to much misunderstanding and distrust, I knew even friendship with the English wouldn't ensure that the English wouldn't try to take over more land. It was better that they owe us, not us them. It was better to remain friendly. It was better to stay away from them. Therefore, an event that greatly disturbed me was the murder of Reginald Jenkins, an Englishman who was living at a place the English called Cape Porpus. I had warned my people that whenever one of our people hurt an Englishman that we must turn that person over to the English. To not do so would be cause for the English to attack us. Messengers said that the man who killed Jenkins was Mohawk. I suspected if he was a Mohawk that the Long House Confederation knew of the incident and may have instigated it to ensure the English would want to fight us. It was the same retaliation methods used by Native peoples. I suspected the same would be true for the English.

As I said I heard about the murder of Jenkins by a messenger. Indeed it had been a Mohawk who attacked and killed him and I continued to suspect, to implicate the Penagok. After meeting with council, I ordered that the Mohawk be apprehended and given to the English.

"John Winthrop in 1631-32 recorded the event in his <u>Journal</u>" *said Fire Eyes.*

> One [Reginald] Jenkins, late an inhabitant of Dorchester, an now removed to Cape Porpoise [Maine], went with an Indian up into [the] country with store of goods to truck, and, being asleep in a wigwam of one of Passaconaway's men, was killed in the night by an Indian, dwelling near the Mohawk's country, who fled away with his goods, but was fetched back by Passaconaway. There was much suspicion that the Indians had some plot against the English, both for that many Narragansett men, etc., gathered together, who, with those of these parts, pretended to make war upon the Neipnett men, and divers insolent speeches were used by some of them, and they did not frequent our houses as they were wont; and one of their powwows told us that there was a conspiracy to cut us off to get our victuals and other substance.

"The years 1632-33 were difficult years for the English. It was also difficult for the Native peoples. In September 1632 it was rumored among the English that the Indians were about to attack. It was false. In November 1633 another epidemic struck out among the Native peoples, this time affecting mostly those in southern New England. The

Narragansett, who had escaped the Great Dying of 1616-1619 that had dealt a heavy blow to the Penagok, Massachusett and Wampanoag, were hit the hardest this time. Chickatobot, the chief of the Naponsett died as did many of his people. The disease was smallpox," *added Fire Eyes.*

"Ah yes, but let us not forget the clarion call from the pulpit," *began Scorching Tail:*

"'God is displeased with the heathen,'" cried ministers from their pulpits. The ministers viewed every death and natural disaster, including the terrible hurricane of 1635, as punishment of the Indians for their non-conformity to English ways."

(f)

Fire Eyes says:

"During these years, an event at Penagok amazed the English. It was a conflict between father and son-in-law, Passaconaway and Montowampate. It was resolved by Passaconaway's wife.

Through all the trials and tribulations that followed events it was my wife who gave me strength. Her spirit never wavered when mine did.

"Passaconaway's wife, Kicking Bear, was also named 'Newissit' though to her people she was 'Gchi Zôgemôskw, or 'Wife of the Great Chief," *explained Fire Eyes.*

Kicking Bear was a good cook. Very few women at Penagok could match her skill at making stews. She knew the right herbs to add and just the right amount of ingredients to add to ensure you savored her food. My wife was also very wise and many sought her counsel even in things that others might consider men's affairs. It was to her that I owed the return of my daughter to her husband.

"Is that true?" *asked Great Heart.*

"Oh yes. Indeed," *replied Fire Eyes.*

Scorching Tail interjected:

"If it had been up to Passaconaway, the husband would still be waiting for his wife to return to him from Penagok!"

"It's the 'bear' in him!" *said Gray Ears to which the assembled bear people council let loose hearty laughter that shook the tail of a comet.*

"No doubt," *agreed Fire Eyes.*

(g)

The bear council members were correct about Passaconaway. There is another side to Passaconaway's personality that hasn't been mentioned. Although the Great Chief was a man of great courage, wisdom and compassion, he was also stubborn as a bear with a temper to match when riled.

In the <u>New England Canaan</u>, which was written in 1632, Thomas Morton relates:

The Sachem, or Sagamore of Sagus, made choise, (when hee came to man's estate,) of a Lady of noble discent, Daughter to Papasiquineo, the Sachem or Sagamore of the territories neare Merrimack River – a man of the best note and estimation in all those parts, (and as my Countryman, Mr. Wood, declares, in his prospect,) a great Nigromancer. This Lady the younge Sachem, with the consent and good liking of her father, marries, and takes for his wife. Great Entertainment hee and his received in those parts at her father's hands, where they weare fested in the best manner that might be expected, according to the Custome of their nation, with reveling, and such other solemnities as is usuall amongst them. The solemnity being ended, Papasiquineo causes a selected number of his men to waite upon his Daughter home; in thos parts that did properly belong to her Lord and husband – where the attendants had entertainment by the Sachem of Sagus and his Countrymen. The solemnity being ended, the attendants were gratified. Not long after, the new married Lady had a great desire to see her father, and her native country from whence shee came. Her Lord, willing to pleasure her, and not deny her request, (amongst them) thought to be reasonable, commanded a selected number of his owne men to conduct his Lady to her Father, where, with great respect, they brought her; and having feasted there a while, and, in the end, desired to returne to her Lord againe. Her father, the old Papasiquineo, having notice of her intent, sent some of his men on ambassage to the younge Sachem, his sonne-in-law, to let him understand that his daughter was not willing to absent her selfe from his company any longer; and, therefore (as the messengers had in charge,) desired the younge Lord to send a convoy for her; but hee, sanding upon tearmes of honor, and the maintaining of his reputation, returned to his father-in-law this answere: that when she departed from him, hee caused his men to waite upon her to her father's territories, as it did become him; but, now shee had intent to returne, it did become her father to send her back with a convoy of his own people; and that it stood not with his reputation to make himself or his men so servile to fetch her againe.

The old Sachem, Papasiqueineo, having this message returned, was inraged, to think that his young son-in-law did not esteeme him at a higher rate than to capitulate with him about the matter, and returne him this sharpe reply; that his daughter's bloud and birth deserved no more respect than to be so slighted, and, therefore, if he would have her company, hee were best to send or come for her.

The younge Sachem, not willing to under value him selfe, and being a man of a stout spirit, did not stick to say that he should either send her, by his owne Convey, or keepe her, for hee was not determined to stoope so lowe.

So much these two Sachems stood upon tearmes of reputation with each other, the one would not send her, and the other would not send for her, lest it should be any diminishing of honor on his part, that should seeme to comply, that the Lady (when I came out of the Country) remained still with her father; which is a thing worth the noting, that Salvage people should seeke to maintain their reputation so much as they doe.

"Let's listen to Kicking Bear speak with her daughter, Wanunchus, about the situation," *says Fire Eyes.*

Swirling bear eyes focus on the land of the Penagok as Kicking Bear and Wanunchus prepare a quillwork basket.

"I'm getting too old for this. Both of them are as stubborn as crows!" *sighed Kicking Bear.*

"My husband will not relent," *said Wanunchus, flattening a quill with her teeth.*

"It is because Montowampate is proud. Just like his father-in-law," *replied her mother.*

"I think some of this stubbornness is because Montowampate believes father could have done more to save his father against the Mi'kmaq," *said Wanunchus.*

"Why does he think that?" *asked Kicking Bear, positioning a quill into a hole in the basket's outer bark.*

"When the Mi'kmaq attacked the lower Morôdemak, Montowampate's father, Nanapashemet, was sagamô of Pawtucket. He was killed at Winnisemet (Malden). Montowampate and his mother both believe father could have stopped Nanapashemet's murder," *responded Wanunchus.*

"How?"

"By sending warriors to protect Pawtucket."

"You and I both know that would have been impossible. We had our own problems at Penagok with the Mohawk and the deaths due to the Great Dying Time," *said Kicking Bear.*

"Yes, you and I know that, but Nanapashemet and Skw Sachem's ears are closed to reason. Remember, although Montowampate is sachem at Saugus, his brother Winnepurkit is sagamô of Naumkeag and mother is Skw Sachem is chief at Pawtucket, father is the leader throughout Pawtucket, Agawam and the Pesgatakwa. They say for that reason alone he should have protected Pawtucket."

Kicking Bear pondered.

"Unreasonable. Each of these areas retains their own local zôgemôak. We can only stop things we know about. We did not know about the Mi'kmaq attack."

"I know."

Kicking Bear sighed and said:

"Your husband has to give in, daughter. You know your father. He will not give in. Once he sets his mind on something, there is no way of changing him. He's worse than a crow who never forgets, or a she-bear protecting her cubs."

Wanunchas, smiling weakly, shook her head slowly in agreement. Her mother, smoothing out a piece of wet birch bark, continued:

"I tell you, how a man with so much wisdom and medicine can act so much like a small boy fighting over a toy is beyond me. Men never grow up! And now I, like a she-bear, have to protect my daughter from her father's and husband's ferocious stubbornness. Men! It's always us women who have to find ways to get the men out of a jam that they got themselves into because of their egos. They are like a quill work basket: beautiful to look at but difficult and painful in shaping their minds."

As Kicking Bear said this she shook her head in disgust, and exhaled loudly, her white hair shimmering in the firelight.

"Hehhh... I'm too old for these shenanigans. We Penagok have enough to worry about with the Mi'kmaq and Mohawk, and now these men from across the great water. These people have come to settle on your husband and his brother's lands. Soon all of us will have more problems than we can imagine. Your father was shown this by the Great Spirit."

"Yes, mother, but what are we to do?" asked Wanunchus in resignation.

Kicking Bear thought for a long while and then looked up, smiling.

"Leave it to me! This has gone on long enough. We've more important things to do than posture about who is snubbing whom."

"Thank you mother," *Wanunchus smiled.*

"In time you will also have to deal with a headstrong husband and son-in-law. You will see. It's the lot of women," *she said as she looked over her basket, pleased with the results.*

Wanunchus looked over at her mother.

"How will you do it, mother?"

Kicking Bear put the basket down on a mat and gazed toward the river.

"I will ask Gray Moose to help us. Your father always listens to him even when I can't get through his stone head. Gray Moose is respected by both your father and husband. It was he who arranged the marriage for you and your husband. I will see what he thinks about trying to make a waterfall flow back up hill."

They both laugh. A while later Gray Moose arrives.

"You wanted to see me," *asked Gray Moose, sitting on the matting in front of the fire.*

"Yes. Thank you for coming. Have you eaten yet?" *Kicking Bear asked Gray Moose, motioning toward a clay pot suspended above the fire.*

"Deer meat stew," *she added.*

"Thank you," *responded Gray Moose, placing a gourd spoon full into a burl bowl.*

"I've asked you to come here because I need your help."

"What sort of help?" *asked Gray Moose.*

"The sort that only you can help sort out," *answered Kicking Bear.*

"Let me guess. It must involve the Great Chief, his son-in-law and your daughter who has stayed too long at the wigwô."

"You pierce to the heart of the matter."

"How can I help you?" *asked Gray Moose.*

"We both know the Great Chief will never give in. I have an idea to resolve it."

"Which is?"

"I want you to go to Pawtucket. See if you can help Montowampate to understand that as Passaconaway is the Great Zôgemô of the Penagok Confederation and is also the greatest Medôlinôwinno that it would not be beneath Montowampate's dignity to send a convoy for his wife. It would, in fact, be well appropriate and would fill the Great Chief's heart with happiness to know that his daughter is valued so highly by his son-in-law, whom he esteems."

Gray Moose considered and replied:

"It might work. It is very politic. If I didn't know any better I would think you are the master diplomat, not the wife of the Great Chief."

"A wife has to do what she can to help when she sees her husband has made a mess that he won't clean up for himself," *responded Kicking Bear.*

"And his best friend sometimes has to help without his knowing."

"The message had the desired effect. Wanunchus returned to her husband shortly after Gray Moose returned from Pawtucket with an entourage. The next year (1633) Montowampate had died of the plague. It would be another fifty winters before Wanunchus would die near Naumkeag," *said Fire Eyes.*

Bear eyes return their focus to the celestial council fire.

"Montowampate was nicknamed 'Sagamore James' by the English," *explains Fire Eyes.*

"The English had a way of affixing names to Native peoples. Names that the Native peoples didn't chose for themselves," *said Scorching Tail.*

"Right. Montowampate was the son of Nanapashemet and Skw Sachem. He was also the brother of Winnepurkit, who was also known as 'George Nobhow,' and 'Wonohaquahan.'"

Scorching Tail interjected:

"Winnepurkit was sold into slavery after King Philip's War, but would return to Salem in 1684. Winnepurkit's son, Manataqua…"

"Whom the English nicknamed 'Black William' *interjected Matted Fur.*

"Yes, Black William," *agreed Fire Eyes*

"Black Williwam who was later hung by English sailors near the mouth of the Saco River."

Fire Eyes continues:

"Our story takes place after the marriage in 1629. Mind you, the Great Chief Passaconaway, in the poem written by John Greenleaf Whittier, isn't held in a good light.

"True," *agrees scorching Tail.*

Fire Eyes shakes his muzzle in agreement, takes a deep breath, and relates the facts.

"Now, Montowampate was twenty when he married Passaconaway's daughter, Wanunchus, in 1629. He, as well as his brother Wonohaquahan, were both wounded in 1631 at Agawam by the Mi'kmaq. On August 8, 1632, Wanunchus was taken prisoner by the Mi'kmaq and ransomed two months later and returned to Saugus," *Fire Eyes added.*

"It's interesting to note that the English said Montowampate never caused trouble for them" *commented Gray Ear.*

"True, however, they also said that they believed his disposition to be worse than that of his brother Wonohaquahan," *responded Fire Eyes.*

"Well, that was only because Montowampate wouldn't become Christian," *snarked Scorching Tail.*

"In any event, even the settlers at Lynn testified that Montowampate allowed them to settle on his people's land.

"So, how did Wenuchus return to her husband?" *asked Great Heart.*

"You can imagine that Kicking Bear was anxious to settle the matter, but she knew her husband. She knew Passaconaway, partly because of pride, partly to maintain his position as regional leader, as well as the fact that he was a powerful Medôlinnôwinno, would not relent," *explained Fire Eyes.*

"It was also wrong for the sachem of Naumkeag to show such disrespect to not only an elder, but also to his father-in-law, as well as the fact that Passaconaway was the great Medôlinnôwinno," *added Scorching Tail.*

"You are correct," *agreed Fire Eyes.*

"The fact that he was a great Medôlinnôwinno alone should have made Montowampate (Sagamore James to the English) relent. Eventually it was Kicking Bear who settled the matter. Kicking Bear sent a messenger to Montowampate who conveyed to the sachem that as Passaconaway was the Great Chief of the Penagok Confederation and as Passaconaway was also one of the greatest Medôlinnôwinno that it would not be beneath Montowampate's dignity to send a convoy for his wife. In fact, it would be appropriate and would fill Passaconaway's heart with joy to know his daughter was valued so highly by his son-in-law, whom he esteemed," *said Fire Eyes.*

"How did Passaconaway respond to this?"

"Let's listen."

My wife, as was always the case with her, settled the matter for once and for all. You see, when my wife looked at me it was as if she was a bear, she would not back down and would stare to see who gave in first. Of course, I gave in first. I always back down from her.

"Enough is enough!" she said to me.

"Your son-in-law will send for our daughter. You will forget the incident and will be a good father-in-law."

That was all there was to be said. I hoped.

(h)

"In 1635 Richard Walderne (Waldron) began trading with the Penagok. It would be the beginning of a relationship that would be fraught with a multitude of problems and misery for the Penagok and profits and land for the English. It could be said that the arrival of Wheelwright, his land deed and then the arrival of Walderne was the beginning of the end for Penagok sovereignty," *said Fire Eyes.*

"Walderne, from the settler's point of view, was honest, trustworthy, and God-fearing. To the Penagok he was like a timber rattlesnake. He was the son of William Walderne, Sr. and Catherine Ravine. Richard's older brother, William Jr., drowned in 1646. It was the mother-in-law of his daughter Abigail Walderne, named Elizabeth (Hull) Heard, who would be spared by a Penagok in 1689 when Richard was killed for his transgressions against the Penagok."

"Yes, and Elizabeth was the aunt of Peter Coffin and Thomas Paine who were at the truck house near Passaconaway's island at Penagok when the rum incident occurred. This island and land would later be called Sewall's Island and Sewall's Falls after the Judge Samuel Sewell who married and received them as part of his wife's dowry, who was also a 'Hull,' daughter of Massachusetts Bay Colony's master mint maker."

For many winters after I joined the English and met with Walderne my people lived in peace. Occasionally a trader would make his way north from Boston to trade with us. For my people, the beads, iron pots, kettles, knives, cloth and other items were highly valued. In return for the English goods we traded furs. Our women loved the iron kettles to cook in, especially because it cut down their cooking time and also kept sand out of the broths. Our traditional way was to add heated stones to the clay pot or birch bark container to cook broths. The men valued the same metal that was used in kettles for their arrowheads, tomahawks, etc. Prior to this we used bone, quartz, quartzite, flint or other workable stones to make arrowheads and tomahawks. The change that came to my people with these new English goods was tremendous. Naturally some, like Walking Bird, complained:

"Why should we use English kettles and arrows? We have everything we need. It was good enough for our ancestors; it's good enough for us."

The traders also brought blankets and cloth, which we used more and more in place of furs. Our diet also began to change. We began to use flour, butter, milk, chicken, eggs, etc. I began to let my guard down and believe in the peace.

3

WIWINIJOANEK

To truly know peace

You must know war

But to know war

You can never again know peace

For where war has gone

Fear remains

And no one who has been to war

Is ever the same

(a)

Fire Eyes continues the story of the Shapeshifted Peace:

"For almost a decade after the English settled at Patuxet, which became known as Plimoth Plantaion, the English settlers and Native peoples traded peacefully with each other. Although Walderne began to establish trade on a relatively large scale with the Penagok in 1635 other English had begun trading with the Penagok within a few years after the Pilgrims landed at Patuxet. There were also English who settled at the Isles of Shoals and off Pesgatakwa. In the land of the Wampanoag, the Pilgrims and Wampanoag lived as neighbors, trading, eating together and living near each other. Of course, there were misunderstandings and irritations, but each got along with the other in their own way.

Plimoth Plantation (Patuxet)

"In the autumn of 1621 the Wampanoag and English celebrated the first celebration of the harvest together.

Scorching Tail notes:

"For Native people annual harvest festivals were the norm."

Fire Eyes continues:

The English, in <u>Mourts' Relations</u>, described the feast:

> 'Our Corne did proue well, & God be praysed, we had a good increase of Indian-Corne, and our Barly indifferent good, but our Pease not worth the gathering, for we feared they were too late sowne, they came up very well, and blossomed, but the sun parched them in the blossome; our harvest being gotten in, our Governor sent foure men on fowling, that so we might after a more speciall manner reioyce together, after we had gathered the fruit of our labours; they foure in one day killed as much fowle as with a little helpe beside, served the Company almost a week, at which time amongst other Recreations, we exercised our Armes, many of the Indians coming amongst vs, and amongst the rest their greatest King Massasoyt, with some ninetie men, whom for three days we entertained and feasted, and they went out and killed five Deere, which they brought to the Plantation and bestowed on our Governour, and vpon the Captaine, and others.'

When I returned to Pawtucket I was told of the harvest feast that the settlers and Massasoit shared together.

"We came to the village and learned the white men were feasting to celebrate the harvest. Massasoit brought nearly one hundred men"

I was not surprised. Massasoit always liked a good show, especially to let the English know he was a respected chief.

Gray Ear notes:

"If Passaconaway had attended, he would have brought as many warriors."

"Probably more," *suggested Scorching Tail.*

The messenger continued:

"As you know, the white men only succeeded in getting a harvest because the Wampanoag instructed them on how to plant corn."

"Yes, I am aware of that," I responded.

"We were invited to join the English along with Chief Massasoit.

Altogether there were some three hundred settlers and Wampanoag, or more, who feasted together for three days. As the English had mostly fowl some of our people went out and killed five deer which we gave to the English chief."

"What food did you eat?" I asked

"We ate corn, turkey, deer, squash, fish and a variety of English foods that I had never seen."

"How did the English treat you?" I inquired.

"Well, for the most part."

"What do you mean?"

"Some of the English have a haughty manner and are quite reserved, especially their women who keep themselves removed from the men."

This was some news to me since Penagok women are always part of festivals.

"The English don't laugh much and go on and on about their God."

"Their God is the same as Nawawas," I replied.

"The English say 'no' that Nawawas is not the same," the messenger replied.

"How can this be?" I asked.

"Nawawas is the maker of all," I added.

"They are adamant that their God is different."

I was intrigued. I decided to learn more about their thoughts regarding the Great Creator later.

The messenger continued:

"The English also do not eat on the ground or on a mat. They eat at something they call a table which they usually have in their lodges but during the festival placed outdoors."

"Tables?"

Fire Eyes notes:

"Our chief is always curious and likes details about others' customs. It's part of what makes him intrigued by the English. It's probably what saved the English, as well. His curiosity and belief that although their minds appeared twisted, the English, Penagok, Wampanoag, even the Mohawk, were the same. All people made by the Creator after the stone people had been destroyed."

Passaconaway continued:

"Tables are hard to describe. The white men said that most people across the big waters eat their food atop such things. The tables are made of wood and are long, flat and are set atop wooden legs. They look similar to our sleeping platforms, only higher. The white men also sit atop 'stools' which are smaller and lower versions of a table. The food is set atop the table which is covered by a something they call a carpet which is woven from animal hair."

"Carpet?"

"A cover made of some animal hair that is very thick. The white men say it comes from very far away and is very expensive."

Entrance to Plimoth Plantation (Patuxet)

"And they eat on it?"

"Yes."

I thought it good that the English and Wampanoag ate together. It was a way to improve understanding. It is a tradition among my peoples to share of their harvest and add to it. During the spring run of salmon at Namaskik we often have such feasts that last for days. The same it was with my daughter's wedding. We ate turkey, deer, fish, clams, roast goose, eels, corn bread, wild plums, dried berries and we danced. But to me, to know the settlers and Massasoit's peoples had feasted together was good. I knew if it hadn't been for the Wampanoag people's help at teaching the English how to sow corn, fish and live with the land, that none of the English would have survived. I believed that now the English would treat us kindly as friends. They did, but as they increased, they began to feast on the fat of our lands.

Although issues arose from time to time regarding land usage and problems with settlers impinging on native rights, it wasn't that way at first. Passaconaway's peace held. Even when the Puritans came almost a decade later, the peace held. However, there were suspicions founded on misunderstandings that with time grew into major issues. The real problems didn't begin to arise until after the great hurricane of 1635," *remarked Fire Eyes.*

(b)

For the Penagok and other native peoples, "the weather during the summer of 1635 was an omen of what was to come. A great hurricane was coming and destruction would follow in its wake. Within two years time, in 1637 the English would massacre the Pequot people. The massacre was a sign for the native peoples throughout what had become known as New-England of what would happen to them if they didn't submit themselves to the English settlers' sovereignty."

Fire Eyes continued:

"As I said, the weather was ominous. On August 25 and 26 (Gregorian; Aug 14 and 15 Julian), 1635 a great hurricane churned up the east coast of North America, making landfall at Narragansett Bay then heading northeast up the coast. Plimouth Plantation suffered greatly with houses blown down. Governor William Bradford noted:

> "This year, ye 14 or 15 of August (being Saturday) was such a mighty storme of wind & raine, as none living in these parts, either English or Indeans, ever saw. Being like (for ye time it continued) to those Hauricanes and Tuffons that writers make mention of in ye Indeas. It began in ye morning, a litle before day, and grue not by degrees, but came with violence in ye begining, to ye great amasment of many. It blew downe sundry [211] houses, & uncovered others; diverce vessels were lost at sea, and many more in extreme danger. It caused ye sea to swell (to ye southward of this place) above 20 foote, right up & downe, and made any of the Indeans to clime into trees for their saftie, it took of ye borded roofe of a house which belonged to the plantation at Manamet, and floted it to another place, its post still standing in ye ground; and if it had continued long without ye shifting of ye wind, it is like it would have drouned some part of ye cuntrie. It blew downe many hundered thousands of trees, turning up the stronger by the roots, and breaking the higher pine trees of in the middle, and ye tall yonge oaks & walnut trees of good biggnes were wound like a withe, very strang & fearfull to behould. It begane in ye southeast, and parted toward ye south & east, and vered sundry ways; but ye greatest force of it here was from ye former quarters. It continued not (in ye extremitie) above 5 or 6 houres, but ye violence begane to abate. The signes and marks of it will remaine this 100 years in these parts wher it was sorest. The moone suffered a great eclips the 2 night after it."

Governor Wm. Bradford in Of Plimoth Plantation

"It was a category 4 storm. The storm had originally visited Jamestown in Virginia and then followed up the east coast. The hurricane's eye led a path of destruction between Boston and Plymouth, but the destruction was felt between Rhode Island and the Piscataqua River. At Penagok, the Morôdemak flooded, leaving behind death and destruction. The Kwenitegw also flooded and killed many people, sweeping away others. Planting grounds were also destroyed. The people sought their great chief's intercession on their behalf."

Passaconaway begins to speak while the Bear Council members fade into the stars.

Fifteen winters after the settlers arrived at Patuxet, a great wind and flood came on our lands. Many of my people were drowned and wigwôak were flattened, planting fields were devastated. We were used to flash floods and could sense their coming. This storm, however, was very different. There was no warning. I'd heard of worse hurricanes that had happened during the time of my father's grandfather. But this one, we felt, was a sign of what was to come. The storm came without wanring. The sky was hot and heavy and then clouds appeared from the south. The clouds revolved and moved fast across the sky. Some of my people who had gone to Zobagw were pulled out to sea by a huge surge of water that flooded everything.

A few days later the sky grew dark and the sun died. It wasn't long after the devastation along the Kwenitegw that the English settlers began to move up the Kwenitegw. Messengers of the Pocumtuck came to tell me:

"The English are coming onto our lands."

"Governor Bradford relates this as well in his <u>Of Plimoth Plantation</u>:

"Some of their neighbours in ye Bay, hereing of ye same of Conightecute River, had a hankering mind after it, (as was before noted), and now understanding that ye Indeans were swepte away with ye late great mortalitie, the fear of whom was an obstacle unto them before, which being now taken away, they begane now to prosecute it with great egernes. The greatest differances fell between those of Dorchester plantation and them hear; for they set their minde on that place..."

Throughout the winters that followed the arrival of the English at Patuxet and later on the lands of the Massachusett and Pocumtuck, I spent my time between my lodges at Penagok during the planting season, Namaskik during the salmon run and Pawtucket and Naticook during harvest. I sometimes remained at Penagok during winter after the English arrived, but found the winter snows and wind at Penagok were too chilling on my old bones, and so came to spend them more at Pawtucket.

"Of course, the real reason that he wouldn't admit was that his favorite child, Wanunchus, lived at Saugus, very near Pawtucket," *said Scorching Tail.*

As I have said, to the west of us lived the people of the Long House, amongst whom were the Mohawk. To the northeast of them were the Wyondot (Huron), to the north were the Iroquois and Algonkin, and to the east were the Penobscot and further east the Maliseet, Passamaquoddy and Mi'kmaq. To the south were the Massachuset, Wampanoag, Niantic, Narragansett, Pequot, Nipmuc, and Nauset and the southeast the Mahicans, Pocumtuck and Wappinger.

During those winters I often thought about the words spoken to me at the Great Stone Face and of the actions taken by the English against my people afterward. I often wondered if I'd chosen the right path by making peace. Whenever I voiced such thoughts my wife would tell me that it was too late to change my path and that I was on it and to change it would show indecision. She reminded me that the path had not been my choice anyway, but the decision of the Great Spirit.

The Great Stone Face (late 19th century photo)

Still, I longed to return to the peace of the mountains where a medôlinôwinno is made stronger by the good medicine there, but as the days passed, the affairs of my people began to occupy me more and more. War loomed on the horizon and would become almost as constant in later years as Day Traveler. It was almost as if the English who'd settled at Patuxet which the English named Plimouth Plantation were anxious to pick a fight. It reminded me of young men who wanted to prove themselves as warriors so that they could feel that they'd become men. I warned my people, no matter what happened, we Penagok must remain neutral.

(c)

As the moons rose and fell and one winter gave what to another, I received reports from messengers. The interaction between the English and the Penagok, Massachusett, Wampanoag, Narragansett and Pequot became more and more strained. Later we learned the Narragansett had also attacked Chief Massasoit of the Wampanoag.

"The shape of your peace is shifting," Walking Bird mocked me at council.

I did not respond to him.

"We should aid our ally," Walking Bird muttered.

"We should strike at the Narragansett on the side of the Wampanoag. Unless we fear the Narragansett!" he added.

"We Penagok fear no one, not even the Magua!" said Tall-Bear, standing up to face the old man.

"Let the English protect the Wampanoag," said Gray Moose.

"Chief Massasoit has not asked for our help. We should not intervene," added another.

"Then we are cowards against these interlopers! We should not be scared to fight them!" scoffed Walking Bird. "Unless we are now led by a toothless bear, we should assault the English from the north, while the Pequot and Wampanoag fight from the south!"

"Who's to say the Wampanoag will take the side of the Pequot?!" asked Gray Moose.

"The Pequot have not made many friends."

"Cowards!" yelled Walking Bird.

"Cowards!" agreed Slow Turtle.

Some of the warriors jumped to their feet to strike Walking Bird for his lack of respect at council.

"Enough! Enough," I urged, waving my hand, motioning them to be seated.

"We should not aid the Wampanoag or the Pequot. It is not our concern. The English have left us unmolested. If we get in the middle of this feud, the English will attack us. The Great Spirit has said so."

I looked at Walking Bird, focusing on his beedy eyes and reed-like body. He cowered and skulked into the shadows. Walking Bird was up to his old tricks. He and Fast Turtle, who was slow witted and hung on the words of Walking Bird, had been trying to find a way to aggravate the peace I'd made with the English. To strike at the Narragansett would involve my people who were just now able to regain their strength.

"Yes. It is not wise to intervene. If you meet a bear sleeping, do not say 'good morning' to him," I concluded.

Walking Bird grumbled, but relented. So we left the problems of the Wampanoag and Narragansetts to be worked out amongst them. We didn't realize at the time that trouble was coming to all of us.

The Narragansett began to join the English against the Pequot and eventually led to war. The war was one that the land had never seen. My people were shocked when they learned of it.

"They are cruel," said one counselor.

"The English, Narragansett and Mohegans are brutal," mentioned another.

"It is not the Narragansett and Mohegan who are brutal. It is the English," said Gray Moose.

He was right. The Narragansett and Mohegan wanted to settle the score with the Pequot who had been haughty and heavy handed in their domination of the Narragansett and Mohegan. But the manner of the Pequot's destruction was unconscionable to them.

"We should have fought the English and this would not have happened," opined Walking Bird.

I again had to advise my people against involvement and to remain silent in the face of the inhuman war. The brutality of the settlers, the Narragansett and Mohegans toward the Pequot is unconscionable.

I did not witness the battle myself but the reports back to me were shocking. After the Pequot massacre, nations all around the English seemed to be of the same mind:

"Imagine if we fight them," I told my people. "The English would destroy us in the same way. They don't want to just kill. They want to annihilate all who stand in their way."

But I always kept in my mind and heart the Great Spirit's admonition to leave the English in peace. I knew if I was to have struck, the Mi'kmaq would have attacked us from the east, and the Mohawk would have come at Penagok from the west. No. It was a hard lesson for us all to learn that we could not trust the English and that they were cruel, but we did the right thing. We maintained the peace when peace was the most needed.

The bear council members look toward the human plane and watch as the mists evaporate and they are back in 1637. Fire Eyes begins the story of the massacre of the Pequot by the English and the Narragansett.

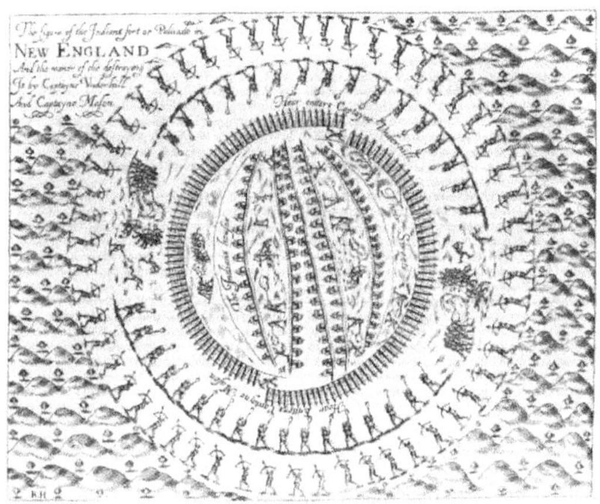

17th century engraving of Pequot massacre

"The massacre was horrendous. The Pequot, many of who followed Chief Sassacus, who had become sachem after Totobem was killed in 1632 and others Chief Mononotto, fought bravely against the English, the Mohegan led by Chief Uncas, and the Narragansett led by Miantinomo. I relate in part what Governor Bradford wrote to illustrate what happened:

> "From Connightecute (who were most sencible of ye hurt sustained, & ye present danger), they sett out a partie of men, and an other partie mett them from ye Bay, at ye Narigansets, who were to joyne with them. Ye Narigansets were ernest to be gone before ye English were well rested and refreshte, espetially some of them which came last. It should seeme their desire was to come upon ye enemie suddenly, & undiscovered. Ther was a barke of this place, newly put in ther, which was come from Conightecutte, who did incourage them to lay hold of ye Indeans forwardness, and to show as great forwardnes as they, for it would incorage them, and expedition might prove to their great advantage. So they went on, and so ordered their march, as the Indeans brought them to a forte of ye enimies (in which most of their cheefe men were) before day. They approached ye same with great silence, and surrounded in both by English and Indeans, that they might not breake out; and so assaulted them with great courage, shooting

amongst them, and entered ye forte with all speed; and those ye first entered found sharp resistance from the enimie, who both shott at & grappled with them; others rane into their howses, & brought out fire, and sett them on fire, which soone tooke in their matts, &, standing close together, with ye wind, all was quickly on a flame, and therby more were burnet to death then was otherwise slain; it burnte their bowstrings, and made them unservisable. Those that scaped ye fire were slaine with ye sword; some hewed to pieces, others run throw with their rapiers, so as they were quickly dispatchte, and very few escaped. It was conceived they thus destroyed about 400 at this time. It was a fearfull sight to see them thus frying in ye fyer, and ye streams of blood quenching ye same, and horrible was ye stinck & sente ther of; but ye victory seemed a sweete sacrifice, and they the prays thereof to God, who had wrought so wonderfuly for them, thus to inclose their enimise in the hands, and give them so speedy a victory over so proud & insulting an enimie. The Nariganset Indeans, all this while, stood round aboute, but aloofe from all danger, and left ye whole [224] execution to ye English, except it were ye stoping of any that broke away, insulting over their enimies in this their ruine & miserie, when they saw them dancing in ye flames, calling them by a word in their owne language, signifying, O brave Pequents! Which they used familiarly among them selves in their own prayes, in songs of triumph after their victories."

Scorching Tail shakes his muzzle.

"Victory at any price. Their price for peace," *comments Scorching Tail.*

Fire Eyes continues:

"The English then returned to their ships. As they did so the Pequot grew in a group to accost them and taunt them for massacring their people. As they saw the English would fight back, the Pequot retreated. After refreshing and repairing themselves, the English were determined to 'pursue their victory, and follow ye war against ye rest,' but the Narragansett forsook them leaving only a few as guide. Even these the English found cold and 'backward in ye business.'"

"The rest of the war was just as terrible. The Pequot were devastated. Sassacus wanted his men to continue fighting, but they chose instead to flee. They killed all the relatives of Uncas, chief of the Mohegan, and burnt their fort. The English followed the Pequot, determined to destroy them as a nation forever. The English learned from the Narragansett that the Pequot were hidden in a swamp in what would later become Fairfield, Connecticut. The English surrounded the swamp. Eventually local

Indians, Pequot women, children and old men came out. The Pequot warriors did not. Those Pequot that tried to escape, about sixty men, were tracked down and murdered. About 180 became prisoners. The Pequot Sachem Sassacus was not amongst them. Chief Sassacus attempted to find sanctuary with his former enemies, the Mohawk. The Mohawk would have none of it. The Mohawk beheaded all of them, except the Sagamore Mononotto who escaped. The Mohawk then sent Sassacus' scalp to the English as a symbol of their friendship to the Connecticut Colony. The Pequot who survived were forced into slavery. Uncas and Miantinomo met with the Englsih at Hartford where they divided their Pequot captives. The Mohegans got 100 of them, the Narragansett and Nehantics another 100. Many of those who went to the Narragansett, Nehantics and the Mohegans were tortured and killed. Revenge. The remaining Pequot were divided between Massachusetts and Connecticut; most being shipped to be slaves in the West Indies. There were Pequot warriors who survived and went to Uncas. Miantinomo complained of this to the English for which Uncas came to despise Miantinomo. As Bradford wrote:

> "'The rest of ye Pequents were wholly driven from their place, and some of them submitted them selves to ye Narigansets, & lived under them; others of them betooke them selves to ye Monhiggs, under Uncass, their sachem with the approbation of ye English of Conightecutt, under whose protection Uncass lived, and he and his men had been faithful to them in this war, & done them very good service. But this did so vexe the Narrigansetts, that they had not ye whole sweay over them, as they have never ceased plotting and contriving how to bring them under, and because they cannot attaine their ends, because of ye English who have protected them, they have sought to raise a generall conspiracie against ye English, as will appear in another place.'"

The mists fade and Passaconaway appears.

I had seen war. I knew its taste. Before the Great Dying Time the Penobscot and Mi'kmaq had been at war. The war started, I was informed, by the raid of a Mi'kmaq village by the Penobscot. The Mi'kmaq took revenge by killing Bashaba. But the Mi'kmaq did not stop and they went on to kill all who were allied to Bashaba. When the Great Sachem of Massachusetts, Nanepashemat, sent a war party, he too was killed and his confederation destroyed. It was after this, and knowing that the Magua would try to take advantage, that I created the Pine Tree Federation (Goanegok). Among those who allied with me was the Sachem who was also allied to the Narragansetts.

But the Pequot War was a warning to us all. War would never be the same again. The English way of war meant destruction worse than that inflicted by the Mi'kmaq. The English meant to decimate the people so that no one survived. After the war, the English settlers became haughtier, demanding, suspecting treachery everywhere.

One of the great lessons of my life I learned late in my life. Patience. Patience was difficult for me, especially as I watched everything around me change. Thousands upon thousands of English settlers arrived to live on our lands. They spread out, pushing everywhere beyond the land of the Wampanoag, Massachusetts, Naragansett, Pequot, and others, into Penagok lands. We were slowly becoming a minority in our on land, marginalized and colonized. Our sacred places of nwaskwmak rocks, rock walls, marshes or trees became known to the English as Devil's rock, Devil's pond or Devil's tree and were then, as the French told us the English would do, desecrated. I spoke with Reverend Eliot about my concerns, but his response was that such places were the houses of the Devil and his demons and thus evil and had to be destroyed.

As the winters wore on, people began to forget the old ways, the stories, the heart of our culture, all in a desire to adhere to English customs so that we'd be accepted. Some became Praying Indians, thinking that in that way they'd be accepted, have enough food to eat, a future. Native people turned on Native people. But, time after time, English turned against Native people, preying on Praying Indians. It didn't matter – we were thought of by the English as only "Indians" and "Savages."

My people complained to me:

"Even our language is considered 'heathen' and if we don't speak English we are looked down upon and made fun of. But when we speak their language, they laugh and make even more fun of our English, calling us stupid and ignorant savages!"

My people began to learn shame. It was not something with which we were familiar.

Fire Eyes notes:

"They were also experiencing cultural genocide, but didn't know it."

Among our peoples, we believed in mercy. We also believed in hospitality. If there was not enough food, we would forgo eating to ensure a guest had food. We also, unlike the English, very seldom killed a prisoner. We would either hold them for a ransom, setting them free once a ransom was paid, or we'd adopt them into the clan to take the place of one of ours who had been killed. The English did not believe in this way of thinking. When they massacred the Pequot, a word we'd never used before, the English killed indiscriminately. They killed warriors, old men, women and children. To them, human lives have no value. Only our land had value to them.

4

MORÔDEMAK

Discovery

Of the unknown

Can awaken the mind to life's beauty

And expand the heart's depths

Beyond ignorant cruelty;

Foremost be wary of pride's tenacious sway

For defeat will be the end

Of those who lack respect of nature's way

1634 Map by Wood

(a)

Fire Eyes begins:

"The General Court of the Massachusetts Bay Colony in July 1638, ordered Goodman Woodman and a Mr. John Stretton with an Indian and two others, appointed by the magistrates of Ipswich, to:

"Lay out the line three miles northward of the most northernmost part of Merrimack for which they were to have 5 shillings a day apiece."

The survey took place in the early autumn.

We Penagok not only valued man and animal life, but we also valued the life of grandmother land. We never took life for granted. For us, Wôbanaki, the "Land of the Dawn," was "nwaskw" or "spirit."

Wôbanaki is a land of water; it is also a land of nwaskwak. Rivers, lakes, ponds, brooks... any body of water can be nwaskw. The great lake Wiwninebesaki, beyond which rises the White Mountains, is nwaskw. The same is true for the Morôdemak. The Morôdemak, in particular, had a mind of its own: a mind that was respected by my people. The Morôdemak was one river but we knew her by many names. The name depended upon where along the river you were. The river was known as Gabasak (Cabassauk – Place of the Sturgeon); Kaskaashadi (Place of the Broken Water) and Menahanek (Moniack – Place of Islands).

During the planting season, growing time and time of harvest the Morôdemak could be placid, its skin shiny and smooth as mica, especially after mud season had passed. But just after winter, when the water was heavy and rapids and currents grew, the river could be dangerous and was not navigable. Because of the river's fierce nature, we often lived high above the flood plain at Penagok. When the river receded to its normal shore in the midst of the summer, when Day Traveler was especially cruel, we'd move to the islands. My family had planting grounds at the falls above Penagok; another at Natigok.

The river provided us with many things. Besides water, there were salmon, alewives, eels, river snakes, shad, freshwater clams and freshwater mussels, which, though not as good eating as those at the ocean, were nonetheless, edible. We often boiled them first and ate them in stews. In addition to rivers, freshwater mussels were also found in lakes and streams. Likewise, freshwater clams were found in lakes, ponds, rivers and brooks. The freshwater clams liked sandy places; freshwater mussels liked mud. The river was also home to suckers, which we planted under corn as fertilizer. Along the banks of the Morôdemak grew red raspberries, black berries, blueberries, strawberries, chokecherries as well as other plants that we ate. The banks also had an abundant source of clay that was used to make pots, bowls and pipes. In the heat of summer, lumps of clay, some from many generations ago, could be found up and down the riverside. The clay was nearly as hard as a rock. In the bigger lakes, especially where the water was colder, there were lake trout, crayfish and razor clams.

I learned to swim while young. All along the Morôdemak at Penagok and north, as well as at the ponds, there were sandy beaches, and during the growing time, the river would lower and sand bars would rise out of the river.

"You plunge in like a bear going after a salmon!" my grandfather said.

"Try to be more like the salmon, and dive like you're going up a waterfall."

As I said, just as the water was nwaskw, so was the land. In the year of the 18th winter after the English came to settle at Patuxet, grandmother land shook. Both events filled us with fear and dread.

"It's the year 1638," *begins Fire Eyes.*

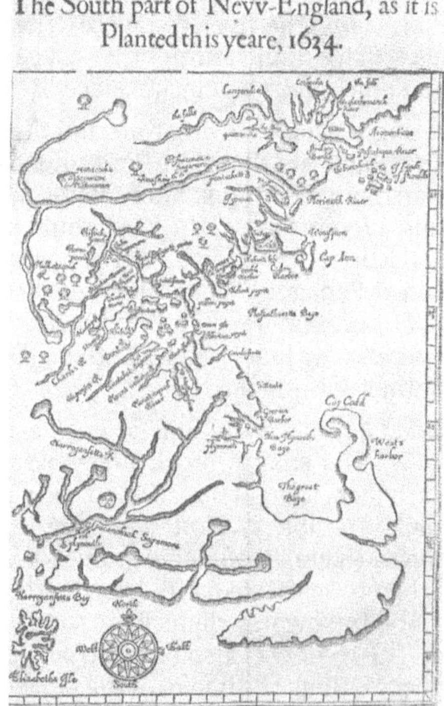

Close-up of previous map showing "Merimakk River" as shown in 1634

"It's been almost ten years since the Puritan settlers have arrived at the hilly peninsula settlement known to the Massachusetts people as 'Shawmut.' The English name their settlement 'Boston' after a town of the same name in Norfolk, England. During this year the Massachusetts Bay Colony's Governor, Winthrop, also sends an official expedition by boat up the Morôdemak River to discover the river's source."

"The survey expedition was also to stake out the Massachusetts Bay Colony's territory since Boston had laid claim in 1628:

> 'to all that part of New England lying between three miles to the northward of the Merrimack River, to the source of the same, and three miles to the southward of Charles River; and in length, within the described breadth from the Atlantic Ocean to the South Sea.'

Mind you, by this time the headwaters of the Morôdemak was also claimed by New Hampshire," *snarked Scorching Tail.*

"Of which we'll speak more later," *said Fire Eyes.*

"Almost as soon as Puritans arrived at Shawmut and nearby Naumkeag they had heard tales about a fortified village situated atop a high bluff that overlooked the Morôdemak River which twisted and turned through the fertile intervale below. It was here at Penagok, the Place of the Falling Bank, it was said, that the Penagok peoples stayed during the summer months until their crops were harvested."

"Penagok was also their favorite planting ground," *added Scorching Tail.*

"Yes," *agreed Fire Eyes.*

"Puritan traders did travel to Penagok and wove wondrous tales of the rich planting land that they found here."

"'The ground is fat and corn grows along both sides of the river here' those who saw Penagok said," *Scorching Tail added.*

"Yes, and I'm sure land greed meant they'd eventually want to take it," *opined Matted Fur.*

As the discussion between the Bear Council fades, the members focus their attention on a small party of English traders and their native guides. One of the members of the party is Richard Walderne who had arrived at Cocheco, part of the Penagok Confederacy, in 1635 to see the country. He stayed a few years during which time he had traveled around the Penagok confederation lands, even going to Penagok itself. He then traveled to England where he married. Prior to sailing for England he acquired a large tract of land at Cocheco where he later constructed a sawmill at the lower falls of the Cocheco River. After returning from England, Walderne journeyed to Penagok on a trading expedition.

"Ah, ahead of us is the Penagok palisade," *Walderne notes as the pointed tops of an immense palisade comes into view.*

A few minutes later, as the party continues moving northeasterly through Pine Barrens toward the fort, Walderne motions to where the land suddenly drops off.

"Beyond the bluffs is the finest land, to my way of thinking, in the entire country," *says Walderne as he motions to the land below the Penagok palisade.*

Over one hundred feet below the party, beyond the bluff, cornfields stretch for miles along both sides of the Morôdemak. Ever since the first time he saw Penagok, Richard Walderne had desired to someday set up a truck house here. He knew business would be brisk since Penagok was the focal point of neighboring tribes as well as the capitol of the Penagok confederation. Upon his return from England, Richard Walderne grew to become a major player in the ensuing drama between the Penagok and Boston authorities.

Walderne, who is 23, comes from an old family and has eight brothers and two sisters. He is rugged and muscular; his appearance not unlike that of a youthful King Henry VIII prior to the latter's late-life corpulence. Walderne, in other words, wasn't unpleasant to look at and had a ready smile that helped him to make deals. What Walderne lacks in portliness; however, he makes up in his appetite for power and money, both of which he will exert with increasing authority in the years to come.

Richard Walderne is a staunch Puritan who feels nothing but contempt for the Natives who he views as wild and heathen and believes them to be inferior to Englishmen. As with other Puritans he feels Indians must be tolerated, certainly not viewed as friends and that they must be driven from their land.

Paine, one of the expedition members, views the land with appreciation.

"Aye," agrees Paine, whose son one day will join Walderne in establishing a truck house further upriver.

"A year ago this land was conferred to John Mason. But now there is a dispute between Mr. Mason and the Massachusetts Bay Colony about who owns this land. Boston intends to send an expedition to survey the land and secure it for itself," *adds Walderne.*

As the party reaches the palisade, their native guides announce their arrival to the guards. Walderne and his companions are led inside and brought to the Confederation longhouse where the Penagok chief, Mettacomon welcomes them.

Lowering his head to enter the long house, Walderne sees an elderly man seated atop bear furs in front of a fire. Walderne makes a slight bow to the seated figure.

"I come with greetings to the Penagok peoples from their friends at Boston," *explains Walderne.*

Mettacomon nods his head in acknowledgment and motions with his hand for the party to be seated. As the party is served refreshments, Mettacomon extends a pipe to Walderne.

"The Great Chief Passaconaway would have met you himself, but he is attending affairs upriver at his summer lodge near the rapids," *explains Mettacomon.*

Walderne merely gives a wry smile.

"I have brought items to trade," *Walderne explains, and offers first a bottle of rum to the chief.*

Neither Chief Mettacomon nor Passaconaway consume alcohol. The chiefs view rum as evil. Alcohol, which was unknown prior to the arrival of the English and French, is referred to in Abenaki as "skwedainepis" or "Fire Water" since it builds a fire inside men whose brains become consumed by the water. The chiefs also know that rum always accompanies any English trading expedition as a way of lubricating the deal. Although the authorities at Boston had made laws that forbade the selling of rum and other liquor and firearms to Indians, Walderne and others were not above using it to assist in deals or to sell outright for a profit.

Mettacomon nods at Walderne in appreciation of the offer and then hands the bottle to the man nearest him who takes a swig.

"I have also brought news that my chief at Boston asked me to convey to you. Boston will send an expedition here after the snows to locate the source of the Morôdemak. Governor Winthrop requests that you render any assistance you can offer to the expedition," *Walderne explains.*

Mettacomon nods. It is the Penagok way to offer assistance to friends and visitors; however, he is, as is Passaconaway, aware that there is more than meets the eye with the Puritans. Mettacomon measures his words before offering them.

"What is the purpose of locating the source of the Morôdemak," *he asks.*

Walderne realizes the chief is aware that there is an ulterior motive to the expedition. Thinking quickly he answers:

"We are looking to open up even more trading opportunities with peoples who live further north."

Mettacomon nods his understanding.

After hours of negotiations, Walderne leaves the long house and discusses the meeting with Paine.

"I rather think that went well," *says Walderne*

"Do you think they suspect the real intention for the survey?"

"Passaconaway appears a rather politic and astute man, but he's old and can't last much longer. I rather doubt they'll give it much thought. Show them pretty beads and they'll be happy," *he adds.*

After a night at Penagok Walderne leaves to return to Oyster River the next day. From Oyster River he'll travel to Boston with his report. A few days after Walderne's departure for Oyster River, Passaconaway returns to the palisade.

"So, it has begun," *Passaconaway responds upon hearing the news of Walderne's visit and the upcoming expedition.*

Passaconaway says to Mettacomon at council:

"They come not to trade but to set their boundary stones. I have heard through my son-in-law that Boston and Portsmouth are in disagreement regarding which of them owns the Morôdemak. I am also aware that this man Walderne is more interested in land than trade."

"Who owns the Morôdemak?" *inquires Mettacomon.*

Passaconaway explains:

"Who controls it. The white men believe a human can own grandmother land. We know that the land is held in trust from one generation to the next. But, these people are land hungry. Land is never enough for them. It is just like what happened with the man Wheelwright and Cocheco and other of our hunting grounds. We agreed to use land with them, but they ended up taking it over and putting up boundaries to keep us away; however, we need to keep them in balance. Remember, the Mi'kmaq and Mohawk must be kept off balance with the English. Diplomacy is the only answer we have to the question of our people's survival."

"But we cannot let them take Penagok," *insists Mettacomon.*

"Of course we cannot and will not," *responds Passaconaway.*

That evening Passaconaway speaks with his wife, his son Waolinasad and Gray Moose about the English.

"They think us stupid," *says Waolinasad.*

Gray Moose shook his head in agreement.

"Whatever they may think, they intend to settle here at some point," *Gray Moose said ominously.*

"They had said that they were exploring but I believe they feel all the land is theirs," *says Kicking Bear.*

"Remember the words of the Great Spirit," *she reminded her husband.*

"It seems clear that the English will come and that we cannot fight them for to do so will mean our destruction," *she added.*

Passaconaway merely listened. His heart ached. In the distance Gôwizawajo's brow shimmers under the darkening sky. In reality, it was already too late. The English had already taken the land; the Penagok just didn't know it.

On May 22, 1639, Goodman Woodward was:

"Ordered to have 3 pounds for his journey to discover the running up of Merrimack."

Ten shillings more were added by order of the Governor and deputies:

"and they which went with them, Thos. Houlet, Sargent Jacobs, Thos. Clark & John Manning to have 50 shillings apiece."

A pine tree at the convergence of the three rivers at what would become Franklin, was marked to indicate the extreme limit of the colonial charter, and was known for many years as "Endicott's Tree."

(b)

"It begins,"*Fire Eyes continued:*

"Winthrop, as with other Puritans, would like to have settled this fertile plain, and indeed, the official expedition is sent up the river with the purpose of establishing the colony's claim to the Morôdemak's headwaters which, after moving past Penagok and coming to the confluence of the Bemijijoasek and Wiwninibesaki they determine to be at the site that will be known later as Franklin. As Scorching Tail predicted, Penagok would be part of the Massachusetts Bay Colony land claim; however, at this time Penagok itself is the headquarters of the Great Chief Passaconaway's Pine Tree Confederation and not even Winthrop would claim that land."

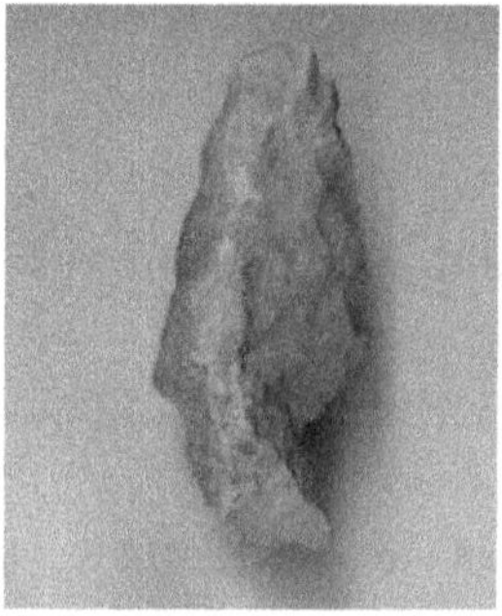

"For now," *Scorching Tail adds.*

"Right," *agrees Fire Eyes.*

Fire Eyes continues:

"After portaging around the falls at what would one day become known as Garvin's Falls at Bow, the survey expedition continues onward, eventually passing through the wide fertile plain where the river twists past the sand bluffs that rise over 100 feet above the right bank of the river. As they pass the bluff, their Algonkian guides relate the story of how the Penagok fought their deadly enemies, the Mohawk, on the plains, along the banks, at the ancient palisade and the pine barren itself. When all seemed lost the Penagok woke up to find the Mohawk gone."

"Did the Penagok abandon Penagok after the battle with the Mohawk?" *asked Great Heart.*

"No. The Penagok also did not give in to the Mohawk invaders. The Mohawk did not give up to the Penagok. The Mohawk; however, were wary of Passaconaway and his powers as a medicine man," *said Fire Eyes.*

"In other words, they didn't want to incur his wrath. The Mohawk attack on the Penagok happened before the confederation of the Penagok and before Passaconaway became the Penagok leader. After their attack, Passaconaway was chosen head of the confederation that he helped to found. It was also well known throughout the Iroquois Long House Confederacy of which the Mohawk were a member, that Passaconaway was a very powerful medicine man. He had control over the elements and communicated with the Great Spirit," *added Gray Ears.*

Fire Eyes continues:

"After the battle the Penagok return to Penagok, but now the Penagok live on constant guard against any further Mohawk incursion onto their lands," *added Gray Ears.*

Fire Eyes continued:

"Indeed, although some Penagok watched as the expedition passed by, and corn ripened all along the banks, the intervale seemed quiet to the expedition."

"Well, in their minds they conveniently believed the land was abandoned since not many people could be seen. Many had gone to sea, others were at the falls north and south of Penagok," *said Scorching Tail.*

"The land, however, was not widowed. All of its inhabitants would return at harvest."

"Was Passaconaway at Penagok when the expedition passed Penagok," *asked Great Heart.*

"The Great Chief was at Pawtucket. He came to Penagok from time to time and stayed at his island that would later be known as Sewell's Island, but most of the time he now lives at his lodge overlooking the great falls at Namaskik and at Pawtucket Falls. Since Passaconaway was the Great Chief of the Pine Tree Confederation (also known by the English as the Penagok Confederation) his duties as chief of the territory at Penagok were assumed by chief Mettacomon."

"Did the English take Penagok as theirs during this expedition?" *asked Great Heart.*

"No. But by conducting the survey they made it clear that the land was the property of the Massachusetts Bay Colony and not the territory of New Hampshire now claimed by John Mason," *Fire Eyes explained.*

"The fact that it was Penagok land didn't matter to the settlers who considered it their land anyway," *reminded Scorching Tail.*

"Mason? I heard Walderne mention him. Who is he?" *inquired Great Heart.*

"John Mason. In 1622 Mason and Sir Ferdinando Gorges were given a patent from the Council for New England to all the land between the Morôdemak and Kennebec Rivers, extending 60 miles inland. Seven years later, in 1629, Gorges and Mason divided the grant of land. Mason named his share between the Morôdemak and Pesgatakwa Rivers "New-Hampshire. Three years later, in 1635, the land was confirmed to Mason when the Council for New England surrendered its charter," *said Fire Eyes.*

"In effect both Massachusetts Bay Colony and New Hampshire claimed the same land," *added Scorching Tail.*

"Talk about confusing things!"

"Yes. The patent of 1629 stated that the grant was:

> 'from the middle part of Merrimac river, and from thence, northward, along the sea coast, to Piscataqua river, and up the same to the farthest head thereof; and from thence, north-westward, until sixty miles from the first entrance of Piscataqua river; and also thorough Merrimac river to the farthest head thereof; and so forward up into the land westward, until sixty miles were finished, and from thence, to cross over land to the end of the sixty miles accounted from Piscataqua river, together with all islands and islets within five leagues distance of the premises.'"

"Did the English travel officially to Penagok again?"

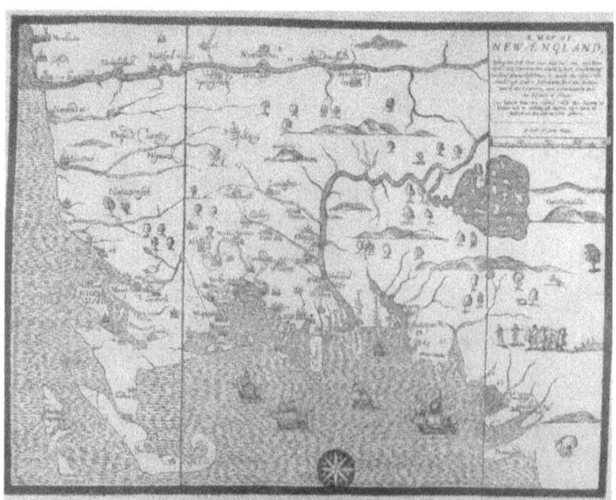

1677 map by Hubbard

"Yes. In August of 1652 the colony sent another team up the Morôdemak to decide the head source of the river."

"And to make a stronger land claim on the land," *commented Scorching Tail.*

"Yes, well, from 1641-1680, New Hampshire towns agreed that to better defend their land that they should be placed under the jurisdiction of Massachusetts Bay Colony."

"In 1657 a survey was conducted at Sewell's Falls by the Massachusetts Bay Colony's surveyor, Jonathon Danforth," *said Fire Eyes.*

"And, during March 1658 Governor Endicot conveyed Sewell's Falls for 50 pounds to John Hull, the mint master for the colony. The Penagok; however, at this time had not given up this land at Penagok," *added Scorching Tail.*

Fire Eyes nodded his muzzle in agreement.

"True. In 1659 Passaconaway, while at Penagok, sends for Richard Walderne to attend him at Penagok. During that same year Walderne was among those Dover men who petitioned for land at Penagok to make a plantation. Land was becoming a hot commodity. During that same year, Waolinasad sells his home in order to free his brother who was in debt. But that's a story for a later time."

(c)

"The same year, 1638, and within a short time of each other, an earthquake shook New England," *says Fire Eyes.*

"Bradford recounts it here in <u>Plimoth Plantation</u>:

> This year, aboute ye 1 or 2 of time, was a great and fearfull earthquake; it was in this place heard before it was felte. It came with a rumbling noyse, or low murmure, like unto a remoate thunder; it came from ye norward, & passed southward. As ye noyse aproched nerer, the earth begane to shake and came at length with that violence as caused platters, dishes & such like things as stood upon shelves, to clatter & fall downe; yea, persons were afraid of ye houses them selves.

Fire Eyes continued:

"Another earthquake happened a half hour later, but was less severe. The reaction to it was fear and awe. Bradford, again, writes:

> It was not only upon ye seacoast, but ye Indeans felt it within land; and some ships that were upon ye coast were shaken by it. So powerful is ye mighty hand of ye Lord, as to make both the earth & sea to shake,

and the mountains to tremble before him, when he pleases; and who can stay his hand? Much Indean corne came not to maturitie.

The bear council members listen as Passaconaway recounts the incident.

After the earthquakes, the summer for many years afterward was less hot and crops suffered due to cold and early frosts. We were greatly concerned that not only did the English come to Penagok and went northward, but grandmother land shook. We viewed both events as one. We Penagok made offerings to nwaskwmak and asked for answers. It was long after; however, that we got our answer. The moon was swallowed.

"The lunar eclipse happened on June 25, 1638. It was deemed a great omen by native peoples and English alike."

(d)

"Wilderness. Utter wilderness. The lands are so closed in by big trees, with white pines six feet around the trunk and two hundred feet high that they block out the sun. The land is spongy and you sink to your knees in mud. All is dismal shade. But along the Morôdemak at Penagok the land is bountiful. It is in only the rivers, ponds and intervals that the Indians are numerous for they fear the mountains. This is the opinon of the English traders who came into the Penagok heartland. The one other place, besides the rich planting grounds of the Native peoples that piqued the interest of the English settlers was the White Mountains. Especially Agiocochook. The English believed Agiocochook contained gemstones," explained Fire Eyes, who adds, "Agiocochook is the home of the Great Spirit. It is a place where no one treads."

Agiocochook is the home of the Great Spirit. It is a place where no one treads.

Fire Eyes explains:

"It has been said that the mountain is the home of the Great Storm Spirit. It has also been called 'the Hidden One' – Gôdag Wajo. Some people believed that the mountain was the home of the Great Storm Spirit; others that it was the home of the bad spirit – Maji Nwaskw; others that the mountain is the home of Bemola; while others said Bemola lives atop another mountain, Gitaden (the Great Mountain). Even the meaning of the name 'Agiocochook' had been lost in later generations. The name came to be interpreted to mean 'Place of the Great Storm Spirit,' but may be from the word 'Ôgakwajok' meaning 'a Shady Mountain' or 'Hidden' or 'Out-of-Sight Mountain,'" Passaconaway relates.

None of my people had climbed the mountain. There are many stories told about the mountain's origins. The tale I heard was told to me by my grandfather. He said:

"After the ash tree people came to be and the grandfathers, the stone people had been destroyed by the Great Creator that a hunter was wandering lost one night in the midst of a great Nor'easter. The snow blinded the hunter and the gale force wind blew against him like a hurricane in the winter. After trudging for days and nights with no food or water, the exhausted hunter lies down to die on the snow. As he slept the Great Spirit appeared to him in a dream. In his dream the Great Spirit revealed to the hunter a beautiful valley filled with animal people. There were deer, elk, bear, turkeys, pheasants and countless others. In this valley was gushing stream that poured into a beautiful lake. In the lake were trout, bass, clams, mussels, salmon and many other fish."

"'I will guide you here' the Great Spirit said to the hunter.'"

"The next morning the hunter arose and the Great Spirit guided him to the valley. As the hunter entered the valley the Great Spirit gave him a spear and a piece of dry coal."

"'You can use the coal to make a fire,' said the Great Spirit."

"That day the hunter fished all day in the lake. That night he placed the piece of coal on the ground. As soon as the coal touched the ground, flames shot out from the coal as well as smoke rose to the sky. The hunter's eyes smarted but as they adjusted the hunter heard a thunderous crash and boom. As the smoke cleared he noticed in the distance a tremendous pile of rocks rising up above the clouds. The top of the rocks was coated with snow. From the snowy summit came a booming voice:

"'Here the Great Spirit will dwell and watch over his favorite children.'"

My grandfather, who often went to the White Mountains, also told it to me that there was a giant deep red stone in the mountains. It hangs high on the side of one of the mountains and overlooks a large magic pond. There were chiefs who had seen this stone for themselves and were so amazed and dazzled by it that they wanted it for themselves; however, they knew they could not possess it because it belonged to the Great Spirit. All those who know of the red stone's exact location, keep it secret. When the white men came it was said:

"If a white man comes to steal the Great Gem, a mist from the magic pond would hide the gem from him."

As another being casts aside their earth-bound body and enters the above land, their spirit adds brightness to the Milky Way. Fire Eyes stirs the flames of the council fire. He then continues with his tale of the English in the land of the Penagok.

"In addition to trying to discover the source of the Morôdemak, another settler residing at Pesgatakwa, set off to explore the White Mountains."

Scorching Tail explains:

"In centuries that will follow, Darby Field will be celebrated as the first man to climb what will be called 'Mt. Washington.' In fact, Darby climbed Agiocochook with two Cocheco Indians, one who reached the summit with Darby."

"Yes, as you said. In 1642 Governor John Winthrop of Massachusetts Bay Colony recorded in his <u>Journal</u> about this settler named Darby Field. He writes, 'an Irishman, living about Piscat, being accompanied with two Indians, went to the top of White Hill.' As Scorching Tail indicated, from that simple statement, followed a few lines later with '...and his two Indians took courage by his example and went with him' it is clear that Darby Field wasn't, as many claim, the first person to climb Mt. Washington. Field was accompanied by two Cocheco Native Americans."

"Did the Great Chief Passaconaway know about Darby Field's climb?" *inquired Great Heart.*

"He learned about it after the fact."

"How did he feel about the ascent?"

"He was not happy. He felt that the climb disturbed the Maji Nwaskw who dwelt atop Agiocochook. What distressed him more was that it was a Cocheco Indian, who was part of the Penagok Confederacy, who reached the summit with Darby."

Fire Eyes continued:

"In terms of the climb what is significant about it being two Native Americans is that these two men climbed what was considered by their people to be sacred ground, a place, according to Winthrop's Journal, that:

'no Indian ever dared to go higher, and the he would die if he went.'

"Abenaki children were told by their elders about Agiocochook and about the mysterious power that lived atop its peak. But, who's to say that other Native Americans hadn't climbed it even earlier than the recorded event?"

"Indeed," *murmurs Matted Fur.*

Fire Eyes makes a motion with his paw to clear away the veil that separates realities. Passaconaway begins:

I was very disturbed that the English had intruded upon one of our most sacred places, Agiocochook. A Bigwaki who lived in the shadow of Agiocochook told me how it happened.

"Two men from Cocheco brought this Englishman named Field to the Bigwaki village. The Bigwaki people have many stories about Agiocochook and the strange happenings that occur there. They told Field not to climb the mountain," the messenger related.

I knew the Bigwaki above all people know the true power and majesty of the mountain. Their stories warned of death to anyone who climbed the mountain. Not even a person of medicine could withstand the powers there.

The messenger continued:

"The Bigwaki objected to Field and told him about the Maji Nwaskw (Bad Spirit) who lived atop Agiocochook. Field scoffed at them. At the Zawkwtegok River several Bigwaki, who decided to go with them at the urging of the elders, joined the Cocheco men and Field. The elders were suspicious of the Englishman coming onto their lands and wanted to know what he was doing. They had heard about the trouble the white people were causing in the land of the Penagok and further south in the land of the Wampanoag and Narragansett. They had heard that they possessed powers. Powers like fire and thunder that they controlled in their hands. But now others had that power which they had traded furs to get. Now even some Bigwaki had guns. We were told that the white man Field was looking for shining rocks."

I had my own suspicions. This latest incursion confirmed those suspicions. The English were showing too much interest in our lands.

Scorching Tail commented:

"After the Wheelwright Deed, the Second Great Dying, the Hurricane, the Pequot Massacre, the expedition up the Morôdemak, the earthquake, the eclipse, and then the climbing of the sacred mountain, it was clear balance was being upset. It was also clear the English settlers were scoping out their 'new' land. At the time, Passaconaway didn't even realize just how much the English, wittingly or not, were planting the seeds for spreading out like weeds across the whole of Wôbanaki."

I noted to the messenger:

"Shining rocks? There are plenty of the grandfathers everywhere. Why did they want shining rocks?"

Fire Eyes:

"Indeed it did sound stupid. But, he didn't know Darby Field was looking for diamonds or silver, or that English valued such things. Those things were valuable in Europe and worth climbing a mountain for, even if you warn them about bad spirits living on top."

"Where was the Bigwaki village," *asked Great Heart.*

"The Bigwaki village was located near the 'Zawkwtegok' known now as the 'Saco' River and was not far, as a hawk flies, from the foot of Agiocochook. But on most late spring and summer days Agiocochook could barely be seen at the village. And it was late spring when Field chose to slog up the peak, just past raspberry picking time. The mountain usually covered itself with too much haze and clouds. It was during the winter moons that it showed itself as it really was, standing out as a boney hulk against the icy sky."

Passaconaway continues:

Mountains, as well as rivers, balanced boulders, great lakes, some people with special powers, and the ancestors were Nwaskwomak. Nwaskwomak were spirits, like that of the Morôdemak. Nwaskwomak could be good or they could be bad. The spirit atop Agiocochook was known to be bad. The evidence was the angry storms that showed its power. Other mountains had power, too. Atop them lived the thunder birds, the badogiak. But the badôgiak were, by and large, easier to get along with than the Maji Nwaskw. Badôgiak could be satiated with respect and offerings. The Maji Nwaskw couldn't.

The messenger related the story to me from one of the Cocheco named Lone Wolf who went up with Field.

As Passaconaway begins, time fades, and Lone Wolf relates his tale to Passaconaway's messenger:

"'Why indeed go up?' I thought now that I was shivering and wet through to the bear skin slimed against my back due to sweat, causing bear musk to float to my nose with each blast of wind that was thrown at me from Maji Nwaskw. My joints ached each and every time I thrust a leg up another rock. Ascending the mountain hadn't been easy. I was used to walking trails that twisted, turned, were muddy in late autumn and early spring, and up and around boulder strewn paths to get to the best hunting sites along mountain ridges, but this was beyond anything I'd experienced before. It was like I'd entered a new land. Yet I saw in front of me that the climb was nearly over. Something was there. Something I cannot explain."

"I was afraid, but I was determined to go to the summit, as was the other man from Cocheco, Fighting Bear. We'd left the last of the spruce and had passed over what looked like open land covered here and there with moss and plants the likes of which I'd never seen before. We'd also passed two deep valleys in which snow glimmered at us from far below. In looking through the clouds at the land below them we noticed something that looked like a giant snake. Field had said it was a river. It could be a great snake – Gchi skog. Who knew? At that point a howling wind pushed down at us and the group that had set out from Bigwaki would go no further, leaving just me and Fighting Bear and Field to continue the journey."

"'You will be killed,' one of the Bigwaki said to us."

"'This man is possessed by Maji Nwaskw. Don't go with him' they urged. 'Leave him to his fate!'"

"But I'd dreamed the night before the climb and the dream wasn't a warning. My dream would tell me what to do. The dream had been a good dream. Fighting Bear said that his dream had been good, too. When I thought about it I realized that the dreams for the last several moons had been the same. In it I'd seen a beautiful woman. I'd also seen children. I thought of Mist-on-the-Hill and knew it had to be her that I'd dreamed about. It warmed me to think of her. No, I knew you could trust what the dreams told me. I knew that after I returned I'd ask her to set up a wigwam together with me. Dreams like that don't prophesize that something bad will happen to you."

"In determination upward we went. Most of the way after we left the Bigwaki men behind was spent walking in and out of clouds and mist. Field kept looking at the ground for his shining rocks, inspecting some every once in a while, placing some in a bag he carried. Below them, through a hole in the mists, we had also glimpsed a great lake that he and Fighting Bear thought must be Wiwninebesaki. From time to time, Field had to rest so we did; too, sitting on wet rocks, trying the best we could to keep warm.

"'Maji Nwaskw is not happy with us,' Fighting Bear commented, his eyes constantly darting back and forth to scan the sky, wondering when the bad spirit would swoop down and gather them up."

"'Are you scared?' I teased him. 'I thought you were brave!' I knew that questioning Fighting Bear's courage was what my friend needed to give him strength to finish."

"But as I listened to Fighting Bear, I still didn't know why I did it. I knew the Great Chief would not be happy. Perhaps I climbed for the adventure of it. Perhaps because Fighting Bear was my best friend and I always did what I thought Fighting Bear wanted to do. Fighting Bear was always the troublemaker. Anyway, I'd always been curious to see

Agiocochook up close, but I knew the danger. Not that danger stopped any real man. Didn't I scout around a Mohawk camp intent on raiding? And they were known as Maneaters. Still, Agiocochook was the home of Maji Nwaskw – the Bad Spirit. It was never climbed. Well, it had been – not to see what was on top or for the purpose of looking for shining rocks that you could find anywhere, though. It had been climbed, according to my grandfather, by persons of medicine who did it shortly after a fiery arrow shot across the sky and the sky had turned dark during mid day."

19th century engraving of Mt. Washington

The bear council members watch as Passaconaway comments to the messenger:

"Is that so? Do you know of someone who had climbed Agiocochook?"

He didn't know for certain.

Passaconaway appeared reflective, and amused. They both knew the truth. Fire Eyes interjected:

"The Great Chief Babiwseso-Ogawinno had climbed Agiocochook, but when he was young. It was one of the reasons why he was esteemed, because few would have ever attempted the feat. But he did it as a person of medicine."

"I thought no one had ever climbed Agiocochook," *commented Great Heart.*

Fire Eyes responded:

"Other persons of medicine had headed out for the summit, but they'd never returned. One man did return, but he'd gone mad. But generally speaking no Bigwaki, Wiwninibesaki, Penagok, or any other people climbed above the tree lines. Not even a Mohawk would do it. To do so would anger the thunder beings who lived atop the peaks. Still the two Cocheco men had set out to climb it. Maybe they wanted to prove their manhood. Darby Field was 32 years old. He spoke the language of the Massachusetts that was mostly understandable to the Abenaki speakers. But he never was really able to explain his reasons enough for them to understand. No, they never did figure out why he wanted to climb. He had said something about shiny stones and silver. But he couldn't translate exactly what it was he was hoping to find. Field had carried something that looked to the Cocheco men like birch bark paper and used a small stick to draw on it symbols of which they had no idea the meaning. Field was a strange sort of fellow, as were all white men to the Penagok who did things without much meaning. They'd learned that more and more of the English had come to the flat land in the south. There were also the Français to the north. The outsiders were becoming more and more like ants crawling across the land looking for food. Field, they knew, lived near a white settlement near Zobagw – the ocean. They didn't know much else."

The council watches as Lone Wolf continued:

"Eventually we passed two ponds among the rocks, one of black water, the other red like blood. The sight gave them chills.

"'Maybe this is the lake created when Gluskab shot an arrow into the sky,' Fighting Bear said to me. I agreed it must be. Long ago, in contest with Mekomwiso, Gluskab had shot his arrow at Agiocochook and it made a hole in grandfather sky. At night you could see this hole as the evening star. This hole was the lake.'"

"The higher our small group climbed, the more our chests pounded like drums in our ears and our hearts raced as if in anticipation of something awesome. The mists grew darker and denser, but we continued onward, ever upward."

"'We've entered the land of dreams?' Fighting Bear said to me.

"'This gray is like in dreams. Maybe we are in a nightmare?'"

"It was unnerving. It was then that Fighting Bear decided he would go no further."

"'You go with him alone. I have had enough,' said Fighting Bear."

"Field and I clamored upward. I stubbed my toes against quartz boulders, jamming them in between cracks and crevices, and sliding on the slimy gravel. Sometimes we nearly tripped and fell, but we quickly righted ourselves. I was worried we'd fall off the mountainside, or, that the bad spirit would snatch us away if we showed fear. I wouldn't give into fear. I knew then that even if the Maji Nwaskw tried to terrorize me, I could live up to that challenge. My spirit protector, wolf, was a powerful spirit protector."

"Without warning the gray cleared and Day Traveler appeared above us. Soon we reached the top not realizing we had done it. The clouds that had concealed the summit all day gradually lifted and in front of us we saw a flat gravel area with nothing higher in front except boulders strewn about everywhere. We walked forward a bit further then stood and looked all around us. The land spread out beneath them. The Bad Spirit was nowhere to be seen. I thought maybe he'd taken off. Catching a whiff of Field's smell told me that maybe the smell of the white man was too strong for his nose."

"I remained on full alert. In a valley below us I noticed the sun no longer shone, and darkness had crept in. Perhaps Maji Nwaskw was down there in the valley where Day Traveler no longer walked. If Maji Nwaskw wasn't atop the mountain, he probably was in a valley, perhaps the one that was now covered in darkness. Whatever the case, I was unable to relax until Field headed back down the mountain. Before heading down the mountain Field picked up a few quartz crystals and put them in his pack. I looked at him."

"'You should not just take the grandfathers. You must make an offering of tobacco to them if you take them and ask them to come with you.'"

"Field ignored me."

"'Maji Nwaskw will punish you,' I warned him."

"'He will go crazy,' I thought to myself."

"I placed a bit of tobacco atop the stone covered ground and asked forgiveness of the stone people. Although I worried the offering might be rejected, I also placed a tobacco offering to Maji Nwaskw, begging his forgiveness for our trespass. If he accepted the offering we would be alive tomorrow. If he accepted it we would not go insane. Field laughed at me and told me it was the white man's God who protected us not a tobacco offering. It was never wise to laugh at spirits, even if they weren't at home. The journey back to the Bigwaki village was uneventful. Before leaving the village Field asked the Cocheco and Bigwaki me to accompany him as well as back up Agiocochook during the next moon."

Fire Eyes says:

"Since nothing bad had happened to them the first time, all except one agreed. During the next moon one returned again, emboldened by Lone Wolf's ascent, to climb to the summit of Agiocochook. Three other men went with them to pick quartz crystals. Again Field and the three other white men made no offering to the stones."

Passaconaway comments:

I knew that Field would go crazy. You could not mock the nwaskwmak. The English settlers would learn this, too. Someday. Maybe they didn't fear war, but nwaskwmak, they would come to fear.

Seven winters would pass but, as Passaconaway predicted, Darby Field, went insane and died. Maji Nwaskw has had his revenge.

5

BIGWAKI

Fear

Is life's one constant companion

Without it

Evil will flourish

And goodness perish.

Fear to do evil

So that only good

Will ever prevail.

(a)

A war was coming again.

"A pattern was developing," *noted Matted Fur.*

"Developing?!" *responded Scorching Tail.*

"It had already been developed."

The Bear Council members nodded in agreement with Scorching Tail.

"As the numbers of settlers increased, so did the occurrences of conflict," *Scorching Tail added.*

The Bear Council members refocused their attention and eyes on Passaconaway:

The war this time was with the Narragansett. I began to fear for my people, that we would soon become a target. Fear was not unknown to me, but as a Penagok we were trained from birth to fear nothing, to never show much less know fear. To harden us, as babies our parents placed us in the snow to know cold. But the Great Maker made me a human and as such, we cannot escape certain realities. Fear is part of life. Even a bear knows fear; his response to it is to run away from it, if he can. If he can't run away from fear, he has to face it. For humans, we also sometimes must face it. It's how you handle it that determines who you are.

"The English will come to make war with us, as well," *I said to Kicking Bear.*

"Has the Great Spirit told you this?"

"No. It is a gut feeling that I have. It is my instinct that tells me that they will come. They will try to create problems for us," *I responded.*

"Then you must be even more clever and you must be on your guard at all times. You must not show any fear toward these settlers. You must always remember the Great Spirit's admonition to you and you must also train Waolinasad to ensure he knows what to do if something should happen to you."

I had begun training Waolinasad from an early age. He was, in many ways, like me: fearless and dedicated to peace, but he was not a person-of-medicine. The Great Spirit did not speak to him. Also, unlike me, Waolinasad had never had to fight.

"Son, you must show no fear. You must stand strong like bear," I would say to him.

"Bear is our totem. He is our protector. Show courage and no fear like the bear."

For the first time in my life, after the Pequot war, I knew fear – or at least, admitted to myself. I was afraid for my people. I knew now that no matter what I did, it would never be enough for the English to leave us in peace. I had risked my life many, many times with no fear at all or thought whatsoever about it. When the Mi'kmaq attacked: no fear. When the Mohawk attacked: no fear. When the Great Dying Time killed most of the Penagok up and down the Morôdemak: no fear. When the English settled at Patuxet: no fear. But now. Now I am afraid. Maybe it's because I am an old man, older than almost anyone left alive. All I know and am surrounded by is fear. Fear for my people. Fear for the land. Fear that the English will take everything.

"But fear can turn you into a coward or it can sharpen your wits. It can bring out the hero in you," *said Fire Eyes.*

"In a lesser human it could make that person a coward," *agreed Matted Fur.*

"This fear will make Passaconaway stronger and wiser," *said Fire Eyes.*

"And given that he is nearly one hundred human years old, that would be an amazing change in a person, but remember, our Passaconaway has always been strong and wise."

"Yes, but it's the addition of 'fear' that will be the essential element. He had not known it before. It is what will hone him as a human," *said Gray Ears.*

"It's that fear that would keep his people alive," *added Scorching Tail.*

As bear eyes star the night sky, Fire Eyes addressed the bear council members:

"The relationship with the English settlers weighed heavily on Passaconaway's mind. Just when he felt that he could relax and let down his guard, more problems came. He found the whole relationship with them perplexing. Additionally, the Great Chief continued to be haunted by death. Death from the Great Dying Time; death from the Mohawk and Mi'kmaq attacks; the death at Wessagusset where the Pilgrims and, to the dismay of Passaconaway, Massasoit, slaughtered other Indians; the Pequot War of 1637, where 400 Pequot men, women and children were slaughtered and the murder of the Narragansett Chief Miantonomi by the Mohegan Chief Uncas. The English betrayed Miantonomi, who had been ally to the English and who had made war on the Mohegan at Connecticut's agreement, after the Mohegan defeated him. The English turned Miantonomi over to the Mohegans so that the bloodied hands of the English would appear clean. The men who turned him over to the Mohegans were a committee of five clergymen. That fact confirmed Passaconaway's suspicion."

Fire Eyes looked around him. Planets blinked back. He continued:

"To Passaconaway's mind, the clergy were the real power holders in this New England. It was to the Puritan 'men of medicine,' Passaconaway realized, he needed to ally his people to survive. The Puritan clergy were the real power brokers behind everything in this new land. He also realized, though, that in allying himself with the Puritan clergy he'd have to be more astute than Miantonomi. He'd have to use all his wits and be more politic than he had been in bringing together the diverse clans into the Penagok Confederation."

Scorching Tail interjected:

"As he said:

"'The Pequot War also haunted Passaconaway. He saw what happened to them and Miantonomi as harbinger of what could happen to the Penagok. Passaconaway was, like the Narragansetts, shocked at the wanton slaughter of the Pequot. As the Narragansetts, who had joined the English against the Pequot said at the time:

"'It is too furious and slays too many men.'

"Passaconaway and others felt the same.

"'We Penagok fight for our honor and bravery and to protect our people. The English fight to destroy.'"

Fire Eyes agreed:

"The Pilgrims, as represented by Bradford, saw the destruction of the Pequot as the work of God."

"Kind of says it all. The Narragansett complaint was probably what doomed Miantonomi and the Narragansett," *opined Scorching Tail.*

Fire Eyes shook his muzzle in agreement and added:

"It also distressed Passaconaway greatly that native peoples were allying with the English against each other instead of helping one another to survive. Around 1635 the Mohegan chief Uncas became friends with Englishmen in Connecticut. He made important connections, so much so that Jonathan Brewster remarked that Uncas was 'faithful to the English.'"

"Then, during the Pequot War, Uncas allied his tribe with the English against the Pequots, both the Mohegans and English attacking the Pequot at Saybrook and the palisade on the Mystic River. As the Great Chief Passaconaway felt: 'They slaughtered their brothers in order to take their land just as the English have done.'"

"The Mohegan, under Uncas, proclaimed allegiance then to the Connecticut River Colony. This made the Mohegan a power with which to be reckoned. It also planted a seed in Passaconaway's mind about how he should handle the relationship with the English. Later, after events proved the true intentions of the English, which was to play native groups against each other and to betray alliances in order to then take land, Passaconaway determined that Uncas' way was the best way to survive. In 1644 he therefore decided to join the English under the Massachusetts Bay Colony."

Fire Eyes continued:

"I get ahead of myself. By 1638 the Penagok had received their furs and guns from traders. The English suspected the Dutch who were at Nieuw Amsterdam (later New York City) had given the Penagok guns, but it was actually Boston traders who'd been forbidden to do so by the Massachusetts Bay Colony. Of course, the traders never admitted to it. Several years later, in 1642 the English received word from Connecticut that the Indians were about to massacre all whites. Colonists were thrown into frenzy. It was pure bunk, but the English, perhaps fearing retaliation for the Pequot, Wheelwright Deed, Wessagusset and other injustices, determined to take prompt measures to: 'strike a terror into the Indians.'"

"It was also a perfect pretext to take land," *added Scorching Tail.*

Governor John Winthrop

"Yes," *agreed Fire Eyes who continued:*

"The English sent men to Cutshamekin at Braintree. The order was to take him and his guns, bows etc. Cutshamekin went willingly with the English. Since it was night, when they arrived at Boston, the English threw Cutshamekin into prison. The next day, after he and his men were questioned, it was found that there were no grounds to hold him since Cutshamekin, it was clear to the examiners, was not a participant in the conspiracy against the English and indeed he could be useful in the future. A warrant was then sent out to Ipswich, Rowley and Newbury. The warrant was to disarm Passaconaway 'who lived by Merrimack.'"

Governor Winthrop, in his <u>Journal</u> wrote:

> "Upon the warrant which went to Ipswich, Rowley, and Newbury, to disarm Passaconamy, who lived by Merrimack, they sent 40 men armed the next day, being the Lord's day. But it rained all the day, as it had done divers days before, and also after, so as they could not go to his wigwam, but they came to his son's and took him, which they had warrarnt for, and a squaw and her child, which they had no warrant for, and therefor order was given so soon as we heard of it, to send them home again. Upon the intelligence of these unwarranted proceedings, and considering that Passaconamy would look at it as a manifest injury, we sent Cutshamekin to him to let him know that what was done to his son and squaw was without order, and to show him the occasion whereupon we had sent to disarm all the Indians. He returned answer that he knew not what was to become of his son and his squaw (for one of them was run tio the woods and came not again for ten days after, and the other was still in custody), if he had them safe again, then he would come to us."

Scorching Tail continues:

"As Winthrop stated, the next day forty armed men were sent to find Passaconaway. The men were hindered, however, by rainy weather from finding him at his wigwam 'but they came to his son's and took him.' The son was Waolinasad. Fearing Waolinasad would escape they 'led him in a line, but he taking an opportunity, slipped his line and escaped from them, but one very indiscreetly made a shot at him, and missed him narrowly.'"

Scorching Tail interjected:

"The English believed that the Great Chief was gathering a mighty army to cast the settlers into the sea. Of course, it wasn't true, as the English soon learned. They English then feared they'd made a fatal mistake by going after Passaconaway. But Passaconaway remained friendly."

Fire Eyes reflected:

"True. Although Passaconaway was angry about his son's capture and treatment when he was fired at like a dog while trying to escape his noose, Passaconaway continued in his friendship to the English. The Penagok people, though, began to grow more and more wary of the English."

Wigwô

As Fire Eyes finishes his sentence, time evaporates and the bear men watch as Wonalansit is taken by force from his wigwam along with his wife and children. Passaconaway explains:

The English, without regard to the truth, placed a rope around my son's neck like they did with their dogs. When he escaped from them, the English shot at him. He was wounded. Brutally, the English recaptured him. This action made my blood boil. I did not find out about their actions until Cutshamekin came to me to tell me what had occurred. I didn't trust him, as I believed it was he who told the English that I was gathering an army and that they should capture me. The English invited me to Boston to talk with the authorities. They wanted to explain why they had come to disarm me and why they took my son and his family. I would not meet with them. I told them:

"Tell the English when they restore my son and his skw (wife) then I will come and talk with them."

I felt their behavior was uncivilized and that they had breached all protocol and behavior expected of civilized people. A short time later my son was set free. My blood calmed but I never forgot how the English betrayed my trust. It was just one more example of their cunning.

Fire Eyes interjects:

"Passaconaway, always mindful of Gchi Nwaskw's admonition to remain at peace with the English, eventually let the resentment against the English for their transgressions against him out of his heart and remained friendly to the English. About a fortnight after, Passaconaway sent his son and delivered up his guns to the authorities at Boston."

(b)

The winter after my son was taken captive (1642), my spirit became a captive. That was when my wife died. Up until that time I had walked the trail of life through much pain, sadness and death. I had been in the battle with the Mohawks; I had watched many of my people die of disease; had seen the arrival of the English; had encouraged cooperation and peace with people who only wanted our land at every turn; and then my son had become a prisoner. I had survived through all of the many trials and tribulations that faced my people. I had survived for many reasons, one of which was the strength of my wife. All through that time my wife was there to reassure me and urge me forward. But then one day a sudden illness came into the land. The death came like the hand of death. It reached along the coast of Shawmut and Naumkeag and traveled up the river where it poisoned people along the shore, killing many in its wake as it travelled northward. At the time I was at Penagok. I soon learned the true meaning of loneliness and heartbreak.

My wife had been healthy one day and the next she lay in a fever. That night, as she moved in and out of consciousness, I heard the haunting call of the whippoorwill.

"Pa-po-les. Pa-po-les. Pa-po-les." It called.

Because of its call "pa-po-les: we refer to the whippoorwill as "papoles." Some of my people believed that the whippoorwill is a harbinger of death. The bird it is said, can tell when someone is about to die. If you are not vigilant and make the person who is dying focus on life, the whippoorwill can capture the dying person's spirit. But papoles didn't capture my wife's spirit that day. He captured mine. With my wife's physical death, my spirit also died.

19th century engraving of Miantonomo's death

My attitude and disposition became affected. I soured against the English and wanted to keep my distance from them.

That winter more trouble came. The Mohegans and Narragansetts continued to argue. The reason was disagreement over who would control the remaining Pequot. Miantonomo attempted to get all other tribes to unite against the English. That was not a wise choice. Even though I had every reason to want to join I refused to join in what I knew would anger the English. I also knew that if I had joined Gchi Nwaskw would destroy my people. That winter Miantonomo invaded Mohegan lands. He was defeated and taken prisoner by Chief Uncas. Uncas then turned Miantonomo over to the English at Hartford. Miantonomo trusted the English too much. Something I know never to do. Never underestimate a rattlesnake. The English had created the war, but now they turned against their ally, Miantonomo. The English turned Miantonomo over to Uncas. The brother of Uncas, Wawequa, then murdered Miantonomo.

"Of course, the English had decided the outcome as they were shaking hands and making an alliance with Miantonomo," *commented Scorching Tail.*

"Remember, it also planted a seed in Passaconaway's mind about how he should handle the relationship with the English," *advises Fire Eyes.*

"Later, after events proved the true intentions of the English, which was to play native groups against each other and to betray alliances, he decided that Uncas' way was the best way to survive. Even the weather again was a sign to the Penagok and Native peoples. On Jul 15, 1643, Governor John Winthrop described a small tornado at Newbury, Massachusetts:

"'Through God's mercy, it did no hurt, but only killed one Indian.'"

"Only one Indian!" *remarked Great Heart.*

Scorching Tail noted:

"No hurt but only killed one Indian. Imagine if it had killed an Englishmen would it then have caused hurt?"

Scorching Tail shook his head.

Great Heart noted:

"The English do appear insensitive sometimes."

"Us against them," *said Scorching Tail.*

"That's the unfortunate mentality."

Fire Eyes continued:

"In 1644 Passaconaway therefore decided to join the English under the Massachusetts Bay Colony."

"Of course," *replied Scorching Tail.*

"The world was turned upside down," *commented Great Heart.*

Sewall's Island on left side of Merrimack River, Concord, NH

Beneath the pines and ancient palisade at Penagok

The time has arrived the three sisters to sow;

Beneath the corn maiden plant the squash to nourish the soil

And entwine sister bean around the stalk

So she on her skyward journey can walk.

Sogalikas, the Sugar Maker Moon, the time when maple molasses is made, has passed and with it, grandmother earth once again warms. It is Kikas, the Field Planting Moon. Mud season; black fly season. Many clans have already returned to their fields, the women planting the three sisters; the men tobacco. So, too, have the Penakok and Passaconaway returned to Penakok. Passaconaway, his wife Kicking Bear and his sons, Nanamocomuck and Waolanisad are seated beneath the white pines on the Great Chief's island at Sewall's Falls. Above them the sky is clear, filled with the slow, soothing "fee-bee" of the Eastern phoebe and the "chick-a-dee-dee-dee" of the black chested chickadees, accented from time to time with the shrill "caw, caw" of the crow.

"Father. What will we do about the English?" Nanamocomuck asked me.

"It is a weighty question. It is a question that I have asked myself almost every night since the English first arrived in our lands," I responded.

"'How should we respond to their request that we join Boston? No matter what we say or do, the English twist our words against us. I believe they only want us to join them so that they can justify taking our land. They are worse than the Magua!" said Nanamocomuck.

"I have asked Gchi Nwaskw for help. I did so: 'Help us against the English who cheat our people at every turn. They make agreements with us and then use talking leaves to change our words.'"

I asked for help but Gchi Nwaskw was silent. Perhaps it was because Gchi Nwaskw had already spoken.

I then spoke to my son:

"My heart, too, is angry that the English took you away from us," *he says to Waolanisad.*

"The English mind is twisted against us. But no matter what wrongs they do, we must follow Gchi Nwaskw's admonition. No matter what harm they do to us, we have to let our anger not rule our hearts. If we do, they will use the Magua against us. It will be the same as with the Mohegan and Narragansett. We cannot win."

"What choices do we have?" *asked Waonolansid.*

Passaconaway answered.

"I think our only choice is clear. We must follow the Mohegan. We must do as Chief Uncas has done with Connecticut. By joining with Connecticut the Mohegan are now powerful."

"Then your decision is to join Massachusetts Bay Colony?" *asked Nanamocomuck.*

"Yes."

(d)

"In 1644 Wintrop writes in his Journal:

> 'Passaconaway and his son desire to come under this government. He and one of his sons subscribe the articles; and he undertook for the other.'

"In 1645 Wintrop writes:

"'Passaconaway, the Merrimack sachem, came in and submitted to our government.'"

Fire Eyes notes:

"Passaconaway believed the agreement with the English would be, as he said, like with other Penagok Conderation members. An alliance of equals; nothing more nothing less.

"The treaty was also signed by the Narragansetts, Niantics, Mohegans and others. What Passaconaway did not know, and could not have known, was that the Governor of Massachusetts Bay Colony visited Albany, New York in person and made an agreement with the Mohawk. The purpose was to use the Mohawks to control the very nations who had just signed a treaty of friendship with the English at Massachusetts Bay. The Mohawks, who had delivered up the head of one of the defeated Pequot chiefs, now earned their reward. The English would maintain a friendship with the Mohawk because they lived far from the lands the English desired to move onto. Also it was a bonus that it would keep the Dutch, who were in New York, at bay. The English also believed it would diminish Dutch assistance to the native peoples and thereby allow more control by the English."

6

NAMASKIK

Life lies

In the heart of being;

To know it

We only have to

Dream

For dreams

Lie at the heart of life.

(a)

The land was changing. The world was changing. The changes that occurred were overwhelming and had not happened in our lands since the Time of the Great Snows when, it is said, snow and ice covered the lands. The change in the land and our world dramatically altered our way of life. The changes were the result of the great storm, earthquake and disease.

Wôwôbadenak from Bear Notch

After the great storm, the shaking of grandmother land and the disease that skulked across the land like a demon looking to suck the life energy out of every living being, animal people began to change their habits. They appeared confused. Their confusion led to our confusion. The animal people who were at the heart of our lives and who helped guide us in dreams were beginning to change their natures. Bears attacked villages as they looked for food that was now scarce due to failure of crops. Birds died from lack of food. Fish began dying, as well.

As my world changed, I had done as my grandfather had advised me, as his grandfather had advised him and his before him: I heeded dreams and I looked to the animals to help me determine the future.

"Grandson, you must always read the signs from the animal people. Whenever you are in doubt, the animal people will guide you," my grandfather had said to me.

"Show special reverence to bear. Bear is our guide and nwaskw."

Awassosak – bears - rarely, if ever, attack humans. We Penagok never killed bears for food, unless we had no other choice. To us, bear was our protector and teacher. He was our totem.

Fire Eyes notes:

"In fact, Penagok people revere bear to the point where they have his image tattooed on their chests. Even our great chief does, as well. Some also have the image of a bear tattooed on their cheeks."

Wôwôbadenak from Bear Notch

The Bear Council members look toward the human plane with smiles of approval.

In fact, in only one story handed down from my grandfather's time did I hear of an attack by a bear on a human.

The story was that it had been a bad year. In that year bears became very hungry due to a lack of their usual food – berries and nuts. The story goes that after Day Traveler had entered the land of dreams, a great disturbance was heard outside the village at Penagok. Men ran out to see what had caused the commotion. Their eyes peered into the darkness. It was then that one of the men felt the hot breath of what turned out to be an immense bear. As the moon made the animal person visible, the men could see it was the largest bear anyone had ever seen. Just then the bear reared himself on his hind legs. The bear was so close to one of the men that the moonlight shimmered like silver on the bear's fangs. The men began to yell and shouted for all they were worth. You see, to have run away would have been the wrong thing to do. The only way to survive a bear attack was to stand up to him and scream and make loud noises. It worked.

The settlers who came to live in our lands, however, always ran from bears. To run from a bear is seen by the bear as weakness. In the end, bear may kill such a man. To this day, we maintain the lesson we learned long, long ago from bear: to not run away from danger. To stand up to danger and shout at it's face. That is why warriors sing their death songs when tortured by the enemy. To not show fear and in that way enter the land of spirits with honor and power.

"The English viewed the native peoples as animals and their respect for bears as proof that the natives were savages," *said Fire Eyes.*

"The English settlers said:

"'They live as savages and are no better than animals.'

"They also viewed the native peoples relationship with animals as evidence that the native peoples were agents of the devil. The forests and swamps were abodes of the devil. The native peoples, Penagok in particular, viewed nature and animals as one," *agreed Scorching Tail.*

It was when all appeared confused, and out of balance, that Reverend Eliot appeared, wanting to preach to my people. He wanted to tell my people that the death, disease and despair all around us were punishment for our sins.

"God is punishing you!" he said to us.

"Repent or burn in hellfire forever!"

Fire Eyes notes:

"Of course all the Native peoples who lived on the land prior to the arrival of the Europeans were doomed to hell, in Puritan thinking, because they did not follow the written word of God."

Scorching Tail rolled his eyes while Great Heart said:

"How could they be held responsible to follow something that they didn't even know existed?"

"It's a dilemma, isn't it?" *replied Fire Eyes.*

Scorching Tail said:

"Well, don't try to analyze it because it didn't even make sense to the Puritans that expressed that thought. When questioned by the Native peoples about the inconsistency..."

Matted Fur jumped in:

"And they were!"

Fire Eyes replied:

"Yes, they were. The Puritans said it wasn't their place to question the Word of God."

"And there you have it. Logic with illogic," *said Scorching Tail.*

Fire Eye continued:

"The winning of hearts and minds was never an English consideration in their dealings with the Penagok and others. The sentiment of the English settlers, as we've discussed, was that only their point of view mattered. All others were irrelevant. Now, although the attitudes of these Puritans was that Natives were no better than savages and that they as Puritans were the elect of God and the Natives were unable to become the elect of God, there were some Puritans who did reach out to the Native peoples. Among these Puritans was Reverend John Eliot. It was actually in him that Passaconaway and later his son, Waolinasad, saw humanity," *commented Fire Eyes.*

"Yes, and Waolinasad would actually convert as a result."

"Was Reverend Eliot different than Reverend Wheelwright?" *asked Great Heart.*

Scorching Tail responded:

"In one important point: Eliot didn't want their land. It should be said here that not all the English who came to settle were bad. Many were good. Eliot was one of those who were good."

Matted Fur added:

"Eliot's work among the Native people can never be over appreciated."

Fire Eyes continued:

"It is true. He even learned the language of the Massachusett people which was an Algonkian language and similar to Abenaki. Eliot learned early on about Passaconaway and the importance of the Great Chief. Eliot had heard that Passaconaway was a great witch and a capable and adept diplomat. He was also deeply concerned with the manner in which the authorities at Boston and many of the recent Puritan immigrants to the Massachusetts Bay Colony were treating the native peoples. As an Englishman and a Christian, he was ashamed of his fellow countrymen's behavior. He believed that it was important to reach out to the Native peoples as he felt they were all children of God. Eliot also knew that in order to secure any type of foothold in the hearts of the Native peoples, he would need the consent, and if at all possible, the conversion of Passaconaway. Eliot had first attempted to meet Passaconaway in 1647 while the missionary preached to Passaconaway's people at Pawtucket. Passaconaway, however, did not attend. Not one to give up, Eliot continued to seek an audience with Passaconaway. The opportunity finally came in 1648 when Passaconaway agreed to meet him at Namaskik."

Reverend Eliot (c. 1659)

As Fire Eyes' voice fades we see Eliot headed on the newly cleared trail for which he had hired a man to make from Nashaway to Namaskik.

For all my grievances against the English settlers, before my wife died, she reminded me of the words of the Great Spirit, and to look for not only the bad in them, but also the good.

"The days we once knew are no longer. They are gone," she said.

"So many have died and we are now too few. You have a duty to our people to get along with these English. As you've said, they are not like the French who willingly trade and who teach us about their ways. We know the English will eventually push northward. The Land of the Dawn is beautiful. They will also want to live here."

I felt this Eliot was an Englishman whom I could trust. But it had not been so in the beginning. I had my experience with Wheelwright foremost in my mind when he first came. The first time he came to my lands, I stayed away from him. After all, he worked with the Massachusetts Bay chief and was a minister. In my mind he was one of those who wanted to take our land. But some of my people convinced me to meet him:

"Meet with him. Eliot is not like the other English or ministers. He believes their 'God' loves us as well as them. You may want to follow him. In doing so, the English will leave us in peace for his words carry much weight among the English."

Eliot's determination to preach to the Native peoples is one of the first civil things that were done to my people by the English. I later decided to meet him, but I was not ready to leave one canoe nearly at the end of my journey across the river of life to enter another. The following season, during the salmon run at Namaskik, I went to listen to the words of Reverend Eliot.

c. 1850 engraving of Eliot preaching to the Indians

Eliot wrote to Captain Willard shortly after the meeting with Passaconaway:

> "Passaconaway did all in his power to keep him [Eliot] at Penacook and offered him any place for a dwelling or anything he wanted if only he would remain and teach them more."

Fire Eyes interjects:

"The Reverend Eliot also recorded his meeting with Passaconaway:

> "'This Spring I did there meet old Passaconaway, who is a great Sagamore, and hath been a great witch in all men's esteem (as I suppose yourself have often heard), and a very politick wise man. The last yeare he and all his sonnes fled when I came, pretending feare that we would kill him. But this yeare, it pleased God to bow his heart to heare the word; I preached out of Malachi I.II.'"

The mists evaporate and Reverend Eliot is standing outside the council long house at Namaskik. Below him, the great falls thunder. Reverend Eliot reads the words in the Massachusett language, which is understood by many present:

"Here me, men of Penagok. Hear the words of Lord God in your hearts and tremble. I read today from Malachi I and II:

"Malachi 1

1 The burden of the word of the Lord to Israel by the ministry of Malachi.

2 I have loved you, saith the Lord: yet ye say, Wherein hast thou loved us? Was not Esau Jacob's brother, saith the Lord? yet I loved Jacob,

3 And I hated Esau, and made his mountains waste, and his heritage a wilderness for dragons.

4 Though Edom say, we are impoverished, but we will return and build the desolate places, yet saith the Lord of hosts, they shall build, but I will destroy it, and they shall call them, The border of wickedness, and the people, with whom the Lord is angry forever.

5 And your eyes shall see it, and ye shall say, The Lord will be magnified upon the border of Israel.

6 A son honoreth his father, and a servant his master. If then I be a father, where is mine honor? and if I be a master, where is my fear,

saith the Lord of hosts unto you, O Priests, that despise my Name? and ye say, Wherein have we despised thy Name?

7 Ye offer unclean bread upon mine altar, and you say, Wherein have we polluted thee? In that ye say the table of the Lord is not to be regarded.

8 And if ye offer the blind for sacrifice, it is not evil: and if ye offer the lame and sick, it is not evil: offer it now unto thy prince: will he be content with thee, or accept thy person, saith the Lord of hosts?

9 And now, I pray you, pray before God, that he may have mercy upon us: this hath been by your means: will he regard your persons, saith the Lord of hosts?

10 Who is there even among you, that would shut the doors? and kindle not fire on mine altar in vain, I have no pleasure in you, saith the Lord of hosts, neither will I accept an offering at your hand.

11 For from the rising of the sun unto the going down of the same, my Name is great among the Gentiles, and in every place incense shall be offered unto my Name, and a pure offering: for my Name is great among the heathen, saith the Lord of hosts.

12 But ye have polluted it, in that ye say, The table of the Lord is polluted and the fruit thereof, even his meat is not to be regarded.

13 Ye said also, Behold, it is a weariness, and ye have snuffed at it, saith the Lord of hosts, and ye offered that which was torn, and the lame and the sick: thus ye offered an offering: should I accept this of your hand, saith the Lord?

14 But cursed be the deceiver, which hath in his flock a male, and voweth, and sacrificeth unto ye Lord a corrupt thing: for I am a great King, saith the Lord of hosts, and my Name is terrible among the heathen."

"Malachi 2

1 And now, O ye Priests, this commandment is for you.

2 If ye will not hear it, nor consider it in your heart, to give glory unto my Name, saith the Lord of hosts, I will even send a curse upon you, and

will curse your blessings: yea, I have cursed them already, because ye do not consider it in your heart.

3 Behold, I will corrupt your seed, and cast dung upon your faces, even the dung of your solemn feasts, and you shall be like unto it.

4 And ye shall know, that I have sent this commandment unto you, that my covenant, which I made with Levi, might stand, saith the Lord of hosts.

5 My covenant was with him of life and peace, and I gave him fear, and he feared me, and was afraid before my Name.

6 The law of truth was in his mouth, and there was no iniquity found in his lips: he walked with me in peace and equity, and did turn many away from iniquity.

7 For the Priest's lips should preserve knowledge, and they should seek the Law at his mouth: for he is the messenger of the Lord of hosts.

8 But ye are gone out of the way: ye have caused many to fall by the Law: ye have broken the covenant of Levi, saith the Lord of hosts.

9 Therefore have I also made you to be despised, and vile before all the people, because ye kept not my ways, but have been partial in the Law.

10 Have we not all one father? hath not one God made us? why do we transgress everyone against his brother, and break the covenant of our fathers?

11 Judah hath transgressed, and an abomination is committed in Israel and in Jerusalem: for Judah hath defiled the holiness of the Lord, which he loved, and hath married the daughter of a strange God.

12 The Lord will cut off the man that doeth this: both the master and the servant out of the Tabernacle of Jacob, and him that offereth an offering unto the Lord of hosts.

13 And this have ye done again, and covered the altar of the Lord with tears, with weeping and with mourning: because the offering is no more regarded, neither received acceptably at your hands.

14 Yet ye say, Wherein? Because the Lord hath been witness between thee and the wife of thy youth, against whom thou hast transgressed: yet is she thy companion, and the wife of thy covenant.

15 And did not he make one? yet had he abundance of spirit: and wherefore one? because he sought a godly seed: therefore keep yourselves in your spirit, and let none trespass against the wife of his youth.

16 If thou hatest her, put her away, saith the Lord God of Israel, yet he covereth the injury under his garment, saith the Lord of hosts: therefore keep yourselves in your spirit, and transgress not.

17 Ye have wearied the Lord with your words: yet ye say, Wherein have we wearied him? When ye say, Everyone that doeth evil, is good in the sight of the Lord, and he delighteth in them. Or where is the God of judgment?"

The words spoken to us by Eliot were good words, although much of it we did not understand. Although we could not understand the words, we knew Eliot to be a good man, one who spoke from his heart.

Fire Eyes noted:

"The Great Chief looked upon Eliot as a man whom he could respect and sent other messengers to ask him to live with them at Penagok. One of the arguments for coming to live amongst the Penagok was that since Eliot only came once a year to teach them, it was of little use since his people easily forgot what they were taught."

"Potter recorded Passaconaway's request to Eliot:

"You do as if one should come and throw a fine thing among us, and we should catch at it earnestly, because it is so beautiful, but cannot look at it to see what is within; there may be in it something or nothing, a stock, as tone or a precious treasure; but if it be opened and we see what is valuable therein, then we think much of it. So you tell us of religion, but (although) we know not what is within, we shall believe it to be as good as you say it is."

Scorching Tail adds:

"Many will later believe that this was proof that Passaconaway was converted. But the Penagok believed in good breeding. It was the height of politeness and good breeding to never doubt the words of another, unless they were given proof that what they were told was a lie. Passaconaway had heard many English lies; this Eliot, it was clear to Passaconaway, believed in what he spoke about, and for that, Passaconaway believed the words as well."

(b)

"In the Land of the Dawn it is the Moon of the Freezing River, M-za-ta-no-skas. November 1650 to the English," *began Fire Eyes.*

"It has already been thirty winters since English settlers arrived at Patuxet. It has also been thirty winters since Passaconaway chose to follow the path of peace and to not fight the English. The Penagok made the peace and the Penagok keep the peace with the English, even when they are shown time and again that the English don't want to live in peace."

"As dawn bleeds across the horizon and the ghosts of stars fade into the light two very old men, Gray Bear and Red Hawk, huddle near their campfire for warmth. The island where Gray Bear and Red Hawk have set up a temporary wigwô is located at Sewall's Island on the Morôdemak River just upstream from Penagok."

"Gray Bear and Red Hawk have just returned from Boston at the request of the Great Chief and council. They had spoken to the Great Chief and council at Pawtucket where Passaconaway and the council spent the winter. They are now en route to their winter hunting grounds just south of the White Mountains."

"The trip was made to once again reinforce Penagok friendship with the English as well as to restate the Penagok position that peace with the English is the overwhelming desire of the Penagok people. The authorities at Boston are increasingly alarmed by perceived threats from their Penagok neighbors who only want to live in peace on the land of their ancestors. The Penagok see more and more settlers arrive at Boston and the surrounding areas. Just a few years past some English had even pushed north of what was now called "Springfield" and were coming up the Kwenitegw. Other English were pushing toward Penagok from the seacoast; others were pushing up the coast of Maine. The Penagok knew that eventually the English will push northward into Penagok territory."

In 1650 the Great Chief Babiwseso-Ogawinno is, according to some estimates, almost 100 years old. He is older than most of the hard wood trees on his island at Penagok.

"Passaconaway was respected by the Penagok for his sagacity and for his abilities as a great chief and great person of medicine, he can't live forever," *said Fire Eyes.*

Red Hawk stirs the dying embers into renewed life.

"It is wrong," *Red Hawk comments to his companion Gray Bear.*

"It is wrong," *Gray Bear agrees.*

"But what can be done? The land is turned upside down."

Red Hawk agrees:

"The land is upside down."

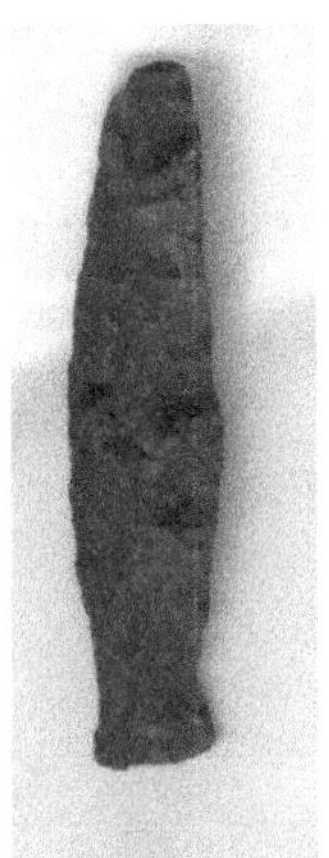

Gray Bear notes:

"What was once considered wrong is now considered right; what was once considered right is now considered wrong. We who were once a powerful people are now fearful while those who were once fearful are now powerful. We should never have let the English grow powerful. It was only because of our desire to stop the Mohawk that we made peace with the English. What has become the result? I will tell you! The result is that now the maneater Mohawks resemble deer while the English greed for our land is like that of a hungry wolf in a forest full of fat game!"

"They have a point," *noted Scorching Tail.*

Fire Eyes nodded his agreement.

"But our chief is wise," *cautions Red Hawk.*

"As he said:

"'If we had engaged the English we would have weakened ourselves. The Mohawk would have attacked and finished us off.'"

"At that time we were weak from disease and from the attack by the Mohawk on our palisade at the Place of the Falling Bank."

"True," *agrees Gray Bear.*

"The peace bought us time. But how do you deal with a person who says one thing to your face and then does the exact opposite? How do you remain at peace with a people who break their agreements? Look at what happened to the Pequot! Look at the English treachery just eight winters ago against our great chief's own son! The Great Chief had refused to break his peace with the English. So what did the English do? You know! The English intended to capture Passaconaway and instead when they couldn't find him the captured his son!"

"Ahô. But they let him go when their chief at Boston realized what had happened," *Red Hawk answers.*

"Yes. Eventually! The English chief said he ordered them free and apologized but one was kept in custody while the other ran for their life once they were free!"

Spruce trees

Gray Bear glared into the flames. For an elder's heart to have the fire of a young warrior was rare. Usually it was the elders who had put out the fires of their young warriors' anger.

Gray Bear continued:

"The English say our Great Chief is under their protection! Since when has the mighty Penagok needed protection from anyone?!" *Gray Bear said loudly.*

"Never," *agreed Red Hawk.*

Gray Bear continues:

"Correct! In the beginning we all believed the English were protected by the Great Creator. Even you."

Red Hawk had to concede that point.

"You are correct."

Gray Bear says:

"Well, remember, we believed, don't forget, that the Great Creator provided the English with fire and thunder in their hands. It wasn't until later that we came to realize that they weren't special people and that we too could have the same abilities since the reason they controlled fire and thunder in their hands was because they had guns. But they won't allow us guns. We now have guns, too. But they don't want us to have them. They are afraid of us!"

Red Hawk exclaims:

"Afraid of us? I don't think so."

"Well, they should be afraid for the shameful way they have treated us!"

"True, but complaining about it won't change anything!"

In the morning stillness the flat-throated squawk of a blue jay momentarily distracts Gray Bear and Red hawk. Glancing toward the line of evergreen trees across the beach from their campsite Gray Bear saw the source of the noise and motions toward it. A blue jay perched on the topmost branch of a lean spruce has just noticed a red tailed hawk circling far above in search of a morning meal.

Red Hawk returns to the conversation:

"All of what you say is true."

"Of course it is true," *Gray Bear asserted.*

Red Hawk continued:

"I fear our warriors will lose patience with peace."

"They will in time," *said Gray Bear.*

"And when that time comes, the white men will pay dearly."

Red Hawk says:

"Well, for the time being they remain respectful of the Great Chief. But even the Great Chief knows he has paid dearly for his peace that has been repaid only with treachery. He is the greatest chief in collective memory and the most powerful medicine man. Yet he feared the English thunder and lightning."

Gray Bear interjects:

"He didn't fear it. He didn't understand it and believed it meant the white men were sorcerers who were protected by their God. He wanted their power."

Red Hawk agrees and continues:

"He did decide to fight them with medicine, to drive them back across the sea, but he failed."

Gray Bear interjects:

"He didn't fail. He knew the Great Spirit's wish was for peace. For that reason nineteen winters ago he gave up one of his own relatives to the English because the kinsman had murdered an Englishman named Jenkins."

Red Hawk interrupts:

"It wasn't his kinsman. The man was Magua."

Gray Bear says:

"I heard he was his kinsman."

"That's what happen when you listen to old lady gossip!"

They both laugh.

Red Hawk continues:

"Instead of the normal procedure where the council agrees to the punishment, our chief felt it more prudent for the English to judge. It was an act of peace. Of course the English sentenced him to death instead of giving him mercy. We were strong and powerful at that time. Now we are reduced to scraping by like our ancestors did during the time of the unending snows."

Scorching Tail says:

"Of course the Puritans would not show mercy. They didn't have any."

Fire Eyes says:

"That's not true. They did have mercy, but they largely reserved it for themselves and their own people."

The bear council members agree and then resume watching Gray Bear and Red Hawk.

"Yes. It is the cost of principle," *responds Gray Bear.*

Red Hawk nodded his head in agreement.

Gray Bear continued:

"Don't forget he also agreed to listen to Eliot preach about their God."

"He listened because he knows the English God is powerful," *said Red Hawk.*

"He also listened because his son, Waolinasad, was interested in what the white men said," said Gray Bear.

Red Hawk added:

"Waolinasad was impressed by the tales from the Holy Bible that seemed similar, in some ways, to Native beliefs."

"True. But it irritated the Great Chief that the English insisted that their God is above the Great Creator," *said Gray Bear.*

"Yes, but the Great Chief made Eliot happy by saying he, the Great Chief of the Penagok, was now a believer in their God. The Great Chief is a very wise diplomat!"

Gray Bear says:

"He didn't say he was a believer."

Red Hawk agrees, saying:

"Right. He simply nodded his head when asked what he thought about the white men's God."

Fire Eyes notes for the Bear Council members:

"In later centuries many will claim that Passaconaway became a Christian. Although he didn't deny it, in his heart he still followed the ways of the ancestors. To leave that canoe to enter another would have been folly."

Gray Ears:

"What he wanted was for Eliot to keep coming."

Red Hawk looks skeptical:

"He didn't really want him to keep coming but knew that if he did then the settlers would be kept at bay."

Gray Bear agrees:

"He knew Eliot was respected at Boston. If Eliot kept coming to the land of the Penagok, Passaconaway believed perhaps the English would leave the Penagok in peace and their God would be happy. If their God was happy, the Great Spirit would be happy."

Scorching Tail appeared to agree.

Great Heart says:

"You seem to agree."

Scorching Tail notes:

"It would have been even more folly for him to say he was not a Christian."

The Bear Council members nod their heads in agreement.

"A very politic man," *Fire Eyes agrees.*

"A very politic man," *says Scorching Tail.*

The Bear Council members refocus on the human plane of existence as Gray Bear continues:

"Yes, he is very wise. The Great Chief is the wisest of all of us. By saying he is a believer the Great Chief makes the English happy."

Red Hawk looks dubious.

"The English never appear happy."

"Okay, but the Great Chief is happy."

Gray Bear says:

"I don't know that happy is the word. Perhaps pleased."

Red Hawk agrees:

"The Great Chief probably figures that "if the English God is happy then maybe the English will leave our land alone!'"

"If that would be true," *said Red Hawk.*

"If it would be true."

Red Hawk continued:

"The problem is that the English don't seem to notice that there is a difference between us and the Mohawk or any of our enemies."

Gray Bear said:

"Of course they don't. All 'Indians' are 'Indians' not 'English.'"

Red Hawk said:

"Agreed."

Gray Bear continued:

"They don't care about anything but themselves and their desire for land. Now I fear for the future. Already our people are anxious to fight the English..."

Red Hawk interjects:

"I'd like to fight them as well but because of our chief's powerful hold on our hearts no one will go against his wishes."

Gray Bear agrees.

"It will be the same with his son," *says Red Hawk, shaking his head slowly.*

Gray Bear says:

"I am afraid that our people will become more like those Massachusett and Wampanoag I have seen who live near the English."

"How do you mean?" *asks Red Hawk.*

Gray Bear responds:

"Those people have taken to imitating English ways, fighting and drinking alcohol. Alcohol turns men into devils."

Red Hawk agrees.

"I have seen it with my own eyes," *says Gray Bear.*

"Some have even become Christians," *Red Hawk notes.*

Gray Bear asks:

"Those who drink alcohol?"

Red Hawk responds:

"No, others."

"Sometimes one is as bad as the other," *observes Scorching Tail.*

Gray Bear says:

"Praying Indians."

Scorching Tail says:

"Notice they aren't called 'Christian' but 'Praying Indians.'"

Red Hawk responds to Gray Bear:

 "What choice have they had? They are surrounded by the English who sell them into slavery, hang them if they break a law or outright murder them. They then teach them to drink alcohol and cheat them of their land and then say all Indians are bad!"

"And don't forget try to get them to become Praying Indians."

"Right."

Both look at each other. One says what the other has been thinking.

"This is the price of maintaining Passaconaway's peace," *says Gray Bear.*

"Both feel the chief was wrong, but neither will acknowledge that feeling. Their chief is their hope. The chief's peace, for good or bad, is their people's future."

7

NATIGOK

All that has happened,

Will happen

And is happening

Is all around you –

You only have to open your eyes

Heart

And mind

To see.

(a)

Fire Eyes begins:

"It's the human year 1659. It has been almost 24 years since the 39-year-old Captain Richard Walderne began trading with the Penagok Indians. Passaconaway is now 109 years old, a venerable age to be sure, but such longevity was not unknown among the Penagok. Captain Richard Walderne, in response to an invitation from the Penagok Confederation Chief Passaconaway, is traveling to Penagok, the capitol of the Penagok Confederation and ancient seat of Penagok power. Walderne believes the invitation was extended to him because he is one of the major trading partners of the Penagok. That is not necessarily the case."

Fire Eyes pauses as another soul crosses the Milky Way. He then continues:

"The real reason is that Passaconaway has learned Walderne has been instrumental in urging Puritan settlement of Penagok. Passaconaway and his counsel are displeased, to say the least, to learn of Walderne's duplicity. The Great Chief has recently been informed by his contacts outside Boston that the English do plan to settle at the Confederation capitol. In fact, a request for settlement has already been submitted to Boston. Among those whose names appear on the petition is Richard Walderne who has long claimed to be the best friend of the Penagok. Other Dover and Newbury residents desiring to settle at Penagok are none other than Peter Coffin and another whose family shall feature prominently in the annals of Penagok and settler relations, Jonathon Heard. The Deputy Governor of Massachusetts Bay Colony, Thomas Danforth, who in 1692 becomes involved with the Salem Witch trials and who, incidentally is also the brother to Jonathon Danforth, the chief surveyor for Massachusetts Bay Colony, judges the settlement request meet.

The petition states:

"'To the Honored Generall Courte, now assembled at Boston.

"'The humble petecyon of us whose names are underwritten, beinge inhabytants of this jurisdiction, and beinge senseable of the need of multeplyinge of towneshippes for the inlargement of the contrey, and accommodateinge of such as want opportunity to improve themselves, have taken into consideration a place which is called Pennecooke, which by reporte is a place fit for such an one – Now the humble request of your petetioners to this honred Courte is, that we may have the grant of a trackte of land their to the quantity of twelve miles square, which being granted, we shall give up ourselves to be at the cost and charge of vewinge of it, and consider fully aboute it, wheather to proceed on for the settlinge of a towne or noe, and for that end shall crave the liberty of three yeares to give in our resolution; and in case that wee due proseed, then our humble request is, that we may have the grant of our freedome from publique charge for the space of seaven yeares after the time of our resolution given in to this Honred Court, for our encorragement to settle a plantation soe furre remote as knowinge that many will be our inconveniences (for a longe time) which we must expeckt to meet with all, which desires of ours beinge answered, your petetioners shall ever pray for the happiness of this Honred Courte, and rest your humble petetioners.'

"The May 18, 1659 response by the committee regarding the request was entered:

"'The Committee do judge meet that the petitioners be granted a plantation of eight miles square, upon condition that at the sessions of the Generall Court to be held in Octo. 1660, they make report to that Court of their resolution to p'secute the same with a competent no. of meet persons that will ingage to carry on the work of the said place in all civill and eclesiasticall respects, and that within two years then next ensuing there be 20 families there settled. Also that they may have imunity from all publique charges (excepting in cases extraordinary) for seven yeares next ensuing the date hereof.'"

Scorching Tail notes:

"The fact that Penagok is already settled by Penagok peoples and that it is the confederation capitol is of no consequence to the Boston officials. None of this information is lost on Passaconaway who, ever the diplomat and strategist, is also not surprised. He is angry and disappointed that the English feel he is so naïve as to not know what is going on."

Fire Eyes agrees:

"In addition to Passaconaway's anger at Walderne's duplicitous behavior for masquerading as a true friend of the Penagok while at the same time submitting a petition to settle at Penagok itself, the Confederation Chief fears if the attempted settlement at the heart and soul of the Penagok homeland by the English does occur, it will break the current peace between the Penagok and English peoples: a peace that he has struggled hard to maintain."

Scorching Tail:

"Only he and the Penagok have struggled to maintain it. The settlers have struggled against it."

"True" *agrees Matted Fur.*

Fire Eyes continues:

"Passaconaway determines to invite Walderne to attend to him at Penagok and to, as he has done so effectively with the English authorities for years now, keep him off balance by finding a way that will make Walderne desire trade more than settlement."

Scorching Tail notes:

"No doubt, given his penchant for making a profit, Walderne will jump at that opportunity."

"And he does," *agrees Fire Eyes.*

Great Heart appears surprised: "He does?"

Fire Eyes:

"He does."

The Bear Council members focus their attention now on Passaconaway and his council who are meeting at Penagok.

"Will Walderne prefer trade more than land?" *asks Gray Bear during council with Passaconaway prior to the arrival of Walderne.*

"Who knows the mind of the English settlers? But I believe it will waylay him for a while, as he likes profit and goods. It should delay him long enough for us to consider other options," *responds Passaconaway.*

The other council members reflect on Passaconaway's words. After a few minutes, Standing Moose speaks.

"Walderne is greedy and wants power to control other people. He would trade his own mother if he could profit from it."

The Penagok council members shake their heads in agreement.

"And therein lies my concern," *says Gray Bear.*

Other council members nod their agreement.

"And mine," *Passaconaway concurs as he gazes ahead of him, past the smoldering coals in front of him, past the children playing outside, past the palisade trunks to where the land drops to the river one hundred feet below.*

Passaconaway adds:

"And it is a concern that has long been with me."

A council member asks:

"How do you mean Great Chief?"

Passaconaway answers:

"I have watched this Walderne for a long time. I have learned many things from watching him. Many things about greed."

Fire Eyes notes:

"Greed was not a big issue for the Penagok prior to contact. If a person was greedy, they would go hungry because other members would not tolerate greed especially in time of want. Everyone had to pull their own weight."

Passaconaway continued:

"I see a dark end for this man. A dark end that ends in blood."

Except for the sudden sharp shouts of chastising crows, all is silent.

Fire Eyes notes:

"Passaconaway sorely missed the wise counsel of two who once helped him to become the sagacious chief that he was – his wife who'd died a few winters before and then Gray Moose who had died shortly afterward. His wife and friend had reminded Passaconaway to follow the path of peace and to look for it when he wanted to fight. As he lay dying, Gray Moose had urged his old friend."

"'Be as a bear. Fight only when you've no choice. Use wisdom to overcome these enemies.'"

Scorching Tail agrees with Fire Eyes' assessment and adds:

"Indeed, Passaconaway missed his wife and friend, Gray Moose. The Great Chief longed to see them once again and looked forward to the day he would, too, walk the path of the ancestors and again meet his wife and Gray Moose."

Fire Eyes nods his agreement with Scorching Tail's words. The Bear Council members refocus their attention on Passaconaway.

"Walderne is arriving," *says Passaconaway.*

"How can you tell?" *asked Gray Bear.*

Passaconaway smiles:

"It's in the air," *he responds and sniffs the air.*

Walderne arrives at Penagok during mid-summer, just after the Strawberry Festival and the beginning of the season of blueberries. The passage of seasons is captured not by the terms spring, summer, autumn and winter but by the "time when corn is planted, when strawberries, blueberries and raspberries are harvested, and so on." Bending through fields of ripening corn, squash and beans, the Morôdemak is calm with not even a dimple creasing the mica like surface of the wide river. Although the land and water were tranquil, the same could not be said for the cacophony that had come from the sky. The sky had been alive since sunrise with the excited songs of eastern phoebes, chickadees and low flying robins. Suddenly, without warning, the air was stilled by the screech of a red tail hawk circling beyond the eye's reach. Eastern phoebes, chickadees and robins scattered for the cover of low branch hemlocks, leaving only the crows behind. Crows were the gifter of corn to the Penagok; the messenger of the Great Spirit; and, were, above all else, wise. Crows aren't easily duped by mimickery of blue jays impersonating hawks so as to steal the seeds of smaller birds. No. Blue jays are as nothing compared to the sacred and wise crow.

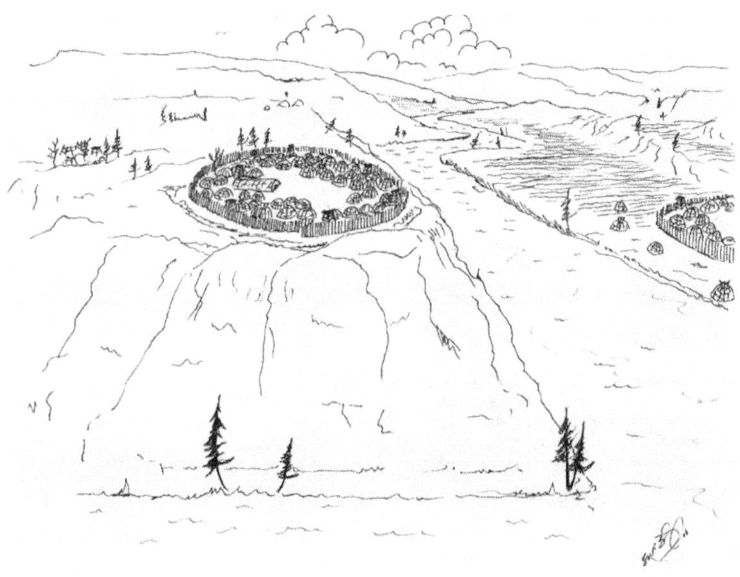

The Penagok palisade at Sugar Ball Bluff and Fort Eddy Plain circa 1659

At a wigwô just outside the palisade, an old woman, is busy flattening a porcupine quill with her teeth and then fits it into the designated holes she has made on a birch bark container. Her grand daughter kneels nearby, using a stone scraper to clean a deerskin stretched on a wooden frame.

"Listen! Do you hear the angry voice of the crow person?" *asked the Grandmother, smiling at her granddaughter.*

Her granddaughter cocks her head and strains to listen.

"Yes."

The grandmother smiles:

"Always show respect to the crow people. Like bear, the crow people have a long memory and recall every human face they see. When the crow person recognizes someone who has treated them wrong, they alert all crow people in the area know that the human who wronged a crow person is near. The word is carried far and wide so that eventually even though the crow person who had met the malefactor is no where around, others who have recognized the human's face will carry on the warning every time the human is seen."

Her granddaughter again cocks her ear to the sky.

"He's warning all the crow people in the area to be alert for a bad human. A white man," *says the grandmother.*

Her granddaughter looks confused and asks:

"How do you know it's a white man?"

The Grandmother responds:

"The only bad men I know of, besides the Magua, are the white men. It must be the white men coming to see Gchi Zôgemô (the Great Chief)" *says the old woman.*

The old lady continues:

"I've heard the English kill the crow people."

"Why would they kill them?"

"Who knows," *says the Grandmother.*

Grandmother continues:

"The crow people remember. I've heard that wherever an English settler travels, crows announce the arrival of the English to other crows beforehand. Therefore, the Penagok know that a non-Indian has come onto their land.

The granddaughter appears impressed.

"Is that true?" *asks Great Heart*

"Yes. It is also true for bear," *responds Scorching Tail.*

"That it is," *agrees Fire Eyes.*

Noses twitch at the arrival of the dark wool wearing Puritans followed by their sharp clipped voices.

"Yes, I can smell them now," *the old woman notes, her nose scrunched up as she looks over and scrutinizes the white men.*

"I've heard these white men like to wallow in their own sweat and stink," *the grandmother added.*

"My nose now knows that what is said about them is true. They stink like a skunk!"

"I can smell them, too" *the Granddaughter says.*

"Sour on the nose like rancid meat."

The granddaughter grimaces.

"Come, let us move from here," *the Grandmother urged her granddaughter.*

In the distance Walderne, Paine and Coffin appear with a Penagok guide who, also disgusted by the scent, walks well ahead of them. The travel from Dover to Penagok had been hard going, causing all to sweat. The guide had jumped in a brook to clean off the sweat, but the Puritans refused to follow suit.

"It is not good for your health to swim in cold water," *they said to the guide.*

The guide responded:

"It is not good for your health to not do so. Also, you are letting all the game in the forest know you are here. That is one of the reasons why we smear bear's grease on our skins: to smell as the animal people."

The guide's charges will have none of it.

"Indians stink like bears," *Paine notes.*

The Guide is not impressed by the scent of the Puritans, either. During the summer, the sun is unrelenting, the days hot and humid. The Penagok guide had done his best to stay downwind from his charges.

"Nine months of winter; a month of rain, a month of mud, and a month where you wander across the face of the sun," *Coffin notes sourly.*

"What use is land like this?" *Paine asks, scuffing through the sandy soil.*

"Only runty pines grow here."

"And sand," *says Paine.*

"Why would we want to settle here? The land appears useless," *complains Coffin.*

"That's because you've yet to see the river beyond the palisade. The land below the bluff is fat. It will yield abundant crops," *replies Walderne.*

"Will the authorities at Boston allow settlement at Penagok? Doesn't New Hampshire claim jurisdiction here?" *asked Paine.*

"Both claim jurisdiction but remember Boston sent two expeditions up the Morôdemak to find its source and lay out its boundaries. New Hampshire has not done the same. Boston's claim to the land is therefore legal. That's why I suggested we submit our petition to Boston. Besides New Hampshire won't protect settlers at Penagok, but Boston, wanting to maintain a presence this far upriver, will protect settlers," *said Walderne.*

At this point a crow swoops down close to the party, landing nearby to begin squawking at the men.

"Bloody crows! First thing I'd do is exterminate the lot of them!" *says Paine as he kicks a stone at one.*

"Go! Get lost!" *shouts Coffin.*

The crow relents and darts toward the top of a nearby pine. From its perch it calls out to other crows that join in. The resulting raucus from their screeching becomes deafening. Walderne and his men reach the Penagok palisade from the south east, careful to avoid the above-ground cemetery located just east of the palisade.

"During the winter when the ground is solid the Indians locate their dead atop wooden frames. Eventually they bury the dead in the ground. For the Indians, above ground burial grounds and graveyards are places of medicine. Be careful not to enter them. They don't like anyone intruding their places of medicine."

Soon Walderne, Coffin, Paine and their guide reach the rim of the falling bank.

"A good location for a palisade," *Coffin comments, his eyes scanning the horizon where the Penagok's totem mountain, Gôwizawajo, rises in the distance.*

The Abenaki guide explains to them:

"This place is known by two names: 'Place of the Falling Bank' because the sandy soil gives way beneath your feet, and also 'At the Bend in the River' because of the crookedness of the river here that nearly bends back on itself."

"The soil is very fat and good for crops," *remarks Walderne, as he takes off his hat and wipes his brow.*

Coffin and Paine are impressed by the sight they see below and beyond them.

"It is beautiful and looks bountiful," *says Coffin.*

"Aye," *agrees Paine.*

"Now I see why you covet this land," *adds Coffin.*

"The Indians have fields all up and down this river as well as on the islands in the middle of the river," *remarks Walderne.*

Coffin and Paine were impressed.

"How long have these Indians lived here at Penagok?" *asked Paine.*

Walderne considers the question.

"I suppose for thousands of years. Some of the ministers, Reverand Eliot in particular, think these savages are the descendants of one of the lost tribes of Israel."

"Truly?" *asks Coffin.*

Walderne quickly responds:

"I didn't say I believed it."

Coffin shakes his head.

It was Walderne's intention to settle on this land himself if Boston would really allow it. The group heads to the palisade entrance where a Penagok delegation waits to bring them to the council lodge. Inside the lodge, a number of elderly and middle aged men sit around the periphery of the walls on mats covering the ground. Toward the back of the lodge, seated on a bear fur behind the fire pit in the place of honor is the Great Chief, Passaconaway. The men are all chiefs. The chief of the Wiwninibesaki, the Bemijijoasek, the Bigwaki, the Nashua and others. They have all come to hear their chief speak with Walderne.

Passaconaway is no fool. He's been one of the major powerbrokers in the northeast since before the Pilgrims landed at Patuxet. He knows that Walderne is a powerful man, one who has influence with the authorities at Boston. To beat such a man at his own game, Passaconaway must be like the crow that, after the blue jay scares all other birds away with his imitation of a bird of prey, then scares away the blue jay. The Great Chief also knows that if he wants to prevent Penagok from being taken by Boston, he must make Walderne desire something more than land. For that reason, he invited the chiefs who make up the confederation he founded over forty winters ago.

The make up of the assemblage is not lost on Walderne as he recognizes some of the chiefs from near Oyster River. As he and his companion take their place on the mats, they are offered pine needle tea and corn meal fried in bear fat which is then sweetened with maple syrup.

"The Great Chief welcomes you," *begins the translator.*

 "He trusts that your journey was a good one."

"Very good, kchi wliwni," *responds Walderne, thanking the Great Chief in Abenaki, the language of the Penagok.*

Passaconaway is the quintessential diplomat. He never comes directly to the point, especially in dealings with the English. After polite conversation about each other's welfare and those of family, the crops and the weather, Passaconaway broaches his real reason for asking Walderne to Penagok. The bear council members listen as Passaconaway relates his conversation with Walderne.

I told Walderne:

"You've been a trusted friend to the Penagok peoples for almost twenty winters. During this time our peoples have mutually benefited from the friendship."

Walderne listened intently to my words. I continued:

"In light of this friendship I've discussed with the council and we've agreed to make you an offer. The Penagok Confederation invites you to build a trading station here at the Confederation capitol."

I stopped to measure Walderne's response. His face showed me that he was pleased by my words. I continued:

"We are aware that Englishmen would like to trade directly with us, as well."

Walderne's eyebrows rise. It was clear at that moment to Passaconaway that Walderne hadn't thought of that.

"Clever blue jay outwitted himself. But I am a bear and can outwit you!" *I thought to myself regarding Walderne.*

Passaconaway continues relating his conversation with Walderne:

"This is why we invite you first, our good friend."

Passaconaway smiles benignly at Walderne and then continues:

"We fear, though we know you'd never let it happen since you are our good friend and you would lose the exclusive right to trade with us if a settlement happened here, that if Boston were to ever send settlers to Penagok that such a settlement would change our trading arrangements. You would no longer have profit since there would be too much competition. A fur trading post here at Penagok would also be advantageous for the Wiwninibesaki, Bemijoasek, Bigwaki and others who now must travel far to Dover to trade."

I sized up Walderne's response to my speech. It was clear from his eager face and shifting eyes that Walderne was very interested in my proposal. But I also knew that Walderne was no fool. He was clever as a bear searching for food. I imagined that he realized that his request from the Boston English chiefs had been found discovered by me.

"Of course Passaconaway was correct," *says Fire Eyes.*

Walderne ruminated on the proposal, finally concluding:

"'I'll accept the Penagok proposal and for now will not push the settlement petition to be reviewed by the General Court next year. The Boston authorities weren't really excited about the prospect of considering settlement at Penagok anyway with Mason grant friends in

London potentially stirring things up with the king. No, I will wait and try again later at a more fortuitous time.'"

Walderne glances towards Coffin who nods agreement with his business partner Walderne. Never mind the other petitioners who had desired settlement at Penagok. Walderne's needs are first in his mind. The others can fend for themselves.

"I accept your generous offer," Walderne said to me.

I smiled and thought to myself:

"He'll just bide his time, while we will be as the crow to the blue jay."

I offered Walderne the pipe.

 I knew Walderne would not give up his desire for settlement at Penagok. But as with the crow screeching to his fellow crows, I have warned my people of what is coming.

By 1663 Walderne and Peter Coffin will set up a fur trading post at Penagok, not more than a few yards from a Penagok fort as well as the site of Passaconaway's summer lodge at Sewell's Island.

My people believe that when we die, we go beyond the White Mountains. There are many stories related to the White Mountains. One story is that long ago, there was a great flood. During that time the Land of the Dawn was flooded and all the people and animal people upon grandmother land were drowned. Only one Medôlinôwinno (person of medicine) and his wife, who had seen the flood in a dream sent to them by the Great Spirit, escaped by fleeing to the White Mountains. They carried a rabbit with them as they escaped. After many days, the Medôlinôwinno sent the rabbit away. When the rabbit did not return, the Medôlinôwinno and his wife knew it was safe and so they descended the mountains. It is said by some that it is from these people that we are all descended.

(b)

When I died, my desire was to ascend the mountains and from there to join the Great Spirit. The Great Spirit in a dream told me that if I obeyed and allowed the white man to live in peace, I would be rewarded by attending the Great Council with the Great Spirit. The Great Spirit also revealed to me that if I obeyed him, then before I died a glimpse into the future of my people would be revealed to me.

Eyes twinkled as starlight on the members of the great council led by the bears.

8

PAWTUCKET

Death

Is the beginning life;

Life

The beginning of death.

Fear only

That while alive

You will not be aware

of life.

(a)

Fire Eyes, his eyes twinkling like Orion, looks toward the human plane and says:

"The Great Chief is dying. He knows it."

"Is he fearful?" *asks Great Heart.*

"No. Not for himself, but for his people," *says Fire Eyes.*

"Why?"

"Because he will no longer be there to protect them," *answers Fire Eyes.*

Fire Eyes adds:

"He trusts his son, Waolinasad, but not the English settlers."

Scorching Tail says: "With good reason."

Fire Eyes also adds: "Nor does he trust Kancamagus whom he believes to be a firebrand who will tip the scale."

Great Heart asks:

"How do you mean?"

Gray Ears says:

"Kancamagus appears peaceful, but his anger is boiling over like a tea kettle. Eventually he and others will explode."

Fire Eyes says:

"That's right and Passaconaway believes Kancamagus will lead the rebellion against the English settlers."

Great Heart considers for a moment and says:

"At that point, the peace will be gone."

Scorching Tail says:

"The Shifting Shape of Peace."

Fire Eyes:

"Yes. Exactly. The Shapeshifter's Peace will be no more."

The Bear Council members fade as Passaconaway comes into view.

I was dying. This I knew. We die a little every day: death of dreams; death of fear; death of schemes... the number of little deaths we all die each day is unlimited. Our physical death is also inevitable, but not to be feared. Physical death is the beginning of another life, a life in the stars from where we all came.

I was not afraid. The only fear that I knew lived in my heart and was for my people. I did not want my people to die. For that reason alone did I adhere to the admonition of the Great Spirit and allow death to my pride and subsequently the English to grow so many that they began to take over our land.

Already the land was changing from that which I'd known as a boy. Now that we Penagok were so few the forests around us grew and grew, retaking land, which our ancestors had forested. Planting fields became overgrown with weeds, as did the forest floors. Our practice had been to set fire to the forest's floors around the villages so that all the undergrowth which would otherwise encroach on our paths would be burned away. If we hadn't done this hunting would be affected and my people would starve.

Scorching Tail notes:

"The Penagok were gardeners, yet those who came later would claim that it was the English settlers who 'tamed the wilderness and it was glad for it.'"

As I looked around me in my later years, many of the villages that had stood since the beginning time, like Beskeodanak (Franklin, NH), which had been abandoned due to so many deaths, had once again been taken over by woods and it looked a wilderness. The land was like no one lived there any longer. I felt sad in my heart. We had once cultivated the land so that we rarely had want. Now it was all gone like a leaf in the wind.

"For hundreds of generations people had lived at Penagok. Rarely was the land empty of fields or people," *said Fire Eyes.*

More painful things happened. The English settlers once again mistreated my son, Waolinasad. In the year the English called 1659 my son was forced by circumstances beyond his control to sell Wickasaukee Island in order to set free his brother, Nanomocomuck. Nanomocomuck had co-signed for a Penagok man who later defaulted on his debt. Nanomocomuck was then thrown into jail for non-payment of debt. It broke my heart.

Fire Eyes explains:

"Nanomocomuck had become surety to John Tinker for another Indian. The total debt was 45 pounds."

As the winters passed, the settlers grew and grew, while my people continued to die and suffer. My people were once a proud and strong people who were now growing more and more dependant on the setters for survival on land that had once been theirs. As winters passed my people took to drinking strong waters: whiskey and rum. They took to gambling and gradually lost more and more of their dignity and self-respect. As I looked in their eyes I knew and felt their pain. Many, like my son, became debtors to the English settlers and in the process lost their lands, which the English happily took from them. The Massachusetts Bay law was on their side, not on the side of the Penagok.

"You agreed to come under our laws," my people were told.

"You must follow our laws or be put in jail."

When my people were put in jail they had to pay their captors and for their captivity. The cells were no larger than the size of a Englishman's body, while we Penagok were taller and larger. My people would also be chained to the wall and have to pay the price for each link in the chain. The jailers also did not provide food; our people had to bring it. In some cases, a person who was unpopular would linger in jail and eventually die from starvation. No matter to the Massachusetts Bay officials: we were Indians and our deaths did not matter to them.

During these times I remembered those gone. I wanted to join them. I remembered my sister, Blue Wing, saying as she lay dying, that she saw light. Light everywhere. There was no darkness. It proved to me that her spirit had entered Ktakoswôdi, the "Great Spirit Road" and that she would become one of the stars who shone. So, too, were my wife, my friend Gray Moose and all who came before me. All were now stars, stars that lit the night sky.

I wanted to join the Great Spirit's Council. To join the Great Council that was held by the bears. I had to wait until the Great Spirit allowed me entrance.

The bear council members nodded their heads in agreement.

(b)

The Great Creator revealed to me in a dream what was to become of my people if they did not walk the path of peace. What I saw in my dreams froze my heart like ice on the winter Wiwninibesaki. Now that my wife and friend, Gray Moose, were gone, my one solace was my son, Waolinasad. He shared my vision of peace.

"I will address the people at Pawtucket Falls," I said to my son, Waolinasad.

"I must urge them to keep the peace."

My son, Waolinasad, agreed:

"I will follow your path, father" he said. "I will maintain your peace," he promised, but I knew that I had to address my people myself.

Fire Eyes says:

"Passaconaway spoke to his people as he decided he would do. He went to Pawtucket and at the falls addressed them. His people strained to hear his words over the noise of the falls. On hand were several Puritan ministers from Boston."

Wôwôbadenak

I told my people:

"Listen and hear the words of your father. I am an old oak that has withstood the storms of more than a hundred winters. Leaves and branches have been stripped from me by the winds and frosts. My eyes are dim. My limbs totter and must soon fall! But when young and sturdy, when my bow, which no young man of the Penagoks could bend, when my arrow would pierce a deer at an hundred yards. I could bury my hatchet in a sapling to the eye. No wigwam had so many furs; no pole so many scalps as Passaconaway's! In those days I delighted in war. The whoop of the Penagoks was heard upon the Mohawk and no voice so loud as Passaconaway's! The scalps upon the pole of my wigwam told the story of Mohawk suffering."

"Then the English came and they seized our lands; I sat me down at Penagok. The English followed upon my footsteps. I made war upon them, but they fought with fire and thunder. My young men were swept down before me, when no one was near them. I tried medicine against them, but the English still increased and prevailed over me and mine. I gave place to them and retired to my beautiful island of Natigok (Natticook). I that can make the dry leaf turn green and live again; I that can take the rattlesnake in my palm as I would a worm, without harm; I who have had communion with the Great Spirit dreaming and awake; I am powerless before the Pale Faces.

"The oak will soon break before the whirlwind. It shivers and shakes even now; soon its trunk will be prostrate and the ant and worm will sport upon it. Then think, my children, of what I say; I commune with the Great Spirit. He whispers me now. "Tell your people, Peace, Peace, is the only hope of your race. I have given fire and thunder to the pale faces for weapons. I have made them plentier than the leaves of the forest, and still shall they increase! These meadows they shall turn with the plow. These forests shall fall by the ax. The pale faces shall live upon your hunting grounds, and make their villages upon your fishing places!' The Great Spirit says this, and it must be so! We are few and powerless before them! We must bend before the storm! The wind blows hard! The old oak trembles! Its branches are gone! Its sap is frozen! It bends! It falls! Peace, Peace, with the white men, is the command of the Great Spirit, and the wish, the last wish, of Passaconaway."

After my speech I left Pawtucket and headed back to Penagok to wait for death. But the Great Spirit was not ready for me.

(c)

I waited at Penagok through the winter. When the snows melted I realized that though my bones were old as dry oak branches, I'd survived into spring. I sent a messenger out and prepared a message to Boston. If I was to live longer, I wanted to return to my family's planting grounds at Natigok. In hopes to reclaim that land I petitioned Boston.

Fire Eyes continues his tale.

"On April 9, 1662, the Great Chief of the Penagok, Passaconaway, petitioned the General Court of Massachusetts for a piece of land. After some deliberation, his request was granted and Passaconaway was granted land north of the Souhegan River."

"I don't understand," *said Great Heart.*

"Wasn't the land still tilled and cared for by Passaconaway and the Penagok peoples?"

"Yes, but the English claimed that by the 1645 treaty with Massachusetts Bay Colony that the Penagok had given up their lands in order to come under the protection of Boston."

Scorching Tail said: "In other words, the land was theirs not the Indians."

Fire Eyes stated:

"The land, which would be north of Horseshoe Pond in present day Litchfield, was one and a half miles wide and three miles long and extended along both sides of the Morôdemak River. Included in the grant were two river islands known for a time as Nunnehaha and Minnewawa and later as Reed's Island. These islands are located in the northern section of Merrimack, New Hampshire."

Among the men who surveyed the land was Jonathon Danforth, the Chief Surveyor for Massachusetts Bay Colony and brother to the Deputy Govenor of the colony, Thomas Danforth.

The petition stated:

> To the honerd John Endecot Esqr together with the rest of the honerd General Court now Assembled in Boston the petition of papisseconnewa in behalf of himself as also of many other Indians who now for a longe time o'r selves o'r progenators seated upon a tract of land called Naticot and is now in the possession of Mr. William Brenton

of Rode Island marchant; and is confirmed to the said Mr. Brenton to him his heir and assigns according to the Laws of this Jurisdiction, by reason of which tracte of land being taken up as a foresaid, and thereby yr pore petitionir with many oth (ers is) in an onsetled condition and must be forced in a short time to remove to some other place.

The Humble request of yr petitionr is that this honerd Courte wolde pleas to grante vnto vs a parcell of land for or comfortable cituation; to be stated for or Injoyment; as also for the comfort of oths after vs; as also that this honerd Court wold pleas to take in to yr serious and grave consideration the condition and also the requeste of yr pore Supliant and to a poynte two or three persons as a Committee to Ar (range wi) th sum one or two Indians to vew and determine of some place and to Lay out the same, not further to trouble this honerd Assembly, humbly cravinge an expected answer this present sesion I shall re main yr humble Servante

Wherein yu Shall commande

PAPISSECONEWA.

Boston: 8:3 mo 1662.

The petition was, in effect, the Great Chief's hope that the English would be generous enough to allow him to die on a piece of what was heretofore his own land. He made the request not knowing whether or not his wish would be fulfilled. Eventually, a year after his initial request for land, the Great Chief's petition was granted and the islands were included. The grant stated:

> The order of the upon is as follows, Viz: In answer to the petition of Papisseconneway, this Court Judgeth it meete to grant said Papisseconneway and his men or associates about Naticot, above Mr. Brenton's lands (Litchfield) where it is free, a mile and a half on either side Merrimack River in breadth, three miles on either side in length provided he nor they do not alienate any part of this grant without leave and license from this Court first obtained.

> According to order of Honerd General Court, there is laid out unto the Indians, Passaconaway and his associates, the inhabitants of Naticott, Three miles square, or so much (eather) as containes it in the fiture of a Romboides upon Merrimack River; beginning at the head of Mr. Brenton's lands of Naticott, on the east side of the River, and then it jointh to his line, which line runs halfe a point North West of the East, it lyeth one mile and one half wide on side of ye River and somewhat

152

better, and runnes three miles up the River, the northern line on the east side of ther River is bounded by a brook, called by the Indians Suskayquetuck (Great Cohos Brook) right against the falls in the River called Pokechous, the line on both sides of the River are parallels; the side line of the east side of the River runs halfe a point eastward of the NNE and the side line of the west side of the River runs Northeast by North all of which is sufficiently bounded and marked with an I, also there is two small islands in the River, part of which the lower and line crosses. One of them Papiesseconneway had lived upon and planted a long time, a small patch of Intervale land on the west side of the River adjacent and a little below ye islands, by estimation about 40 acres which jointh their land to Souhegan River, which the Indians have planted (much of it) a long time and considering that there is very little good land in that which is now laid out to them the Indians do earnestly request this Honerd Court to grant these two small islands and ye patch of Intervale as it is bounded by the hills.

Laid out by Parker and Danforth, Surveyors, 27, 3ʳᵈ Mo. 1663

It was with no small surprise to Passaconaway when he received the news of the land grant. He'd given up hope and hadn't expected, after a year, to receive anything, especially islands. Islands were a favored site for the Penagok. During the heat of summer islands were cool places to be and the breeze coming off the river blew away the swarms of mosquitoes that haunted the banks of the rivers. It was a surprise that the English would give up such favored sites as islands. Passaconaway was also surprised that the General Court ordered him to pay the bill for surveying the grant! He would have not been surprised; however, to learn that after his death, the whole tract of land reverted to the government of Massachusetts Bay Colony, and was granted in 1729 to John Richardson, Joseph Blanchard and others.

(c)

"That Sachem once to Dover came,

From Pennacook, when eve was setting in;

With plumes his locks were dressed, his eyes shot flame,

He struck his massy club with dreadful din,

SHAPESHIFTED PEACE

That oft had made the ranks of battle thin,

Around his copper neck terrific hung

A tied-together, bear and catamount skin,

The curious fish bones o'er his bosom swung

And thrice the Sachem danced and thrice the Sachem sung.

"Strange man was he! 'Twas said, he oft pursued

The sable bear, and slew him in his den,

That oft he howled through many a pathless wood,

And many a tangled wild, and poisonous fen,

That ne'er was trod by other mortal men.

The craggy ledge for rattle-snakes he sought,

And choked them one by one, and then

O'ertook the tall gray moose, as quick as thought,

And the mountain cat he chased, and chasing caught.

"A wondrous sight! For o'er 'Siogee's ice,

With brindled wolves all harnessed three and three,

High seated on a sledge, made in a trice,

On Mount Agiocochook, of hickory,

He lashed and reeled, and sung right jollily;

And once upon a car of flaming fire,

The dreadful Indian shook with fear to see

The king of Pennacook, his chief, his sire,

Ride flaming up towards heaven, than any mountain higher![13]

Farmer and Moore: Historical Collections, vol. II, 83-92, 1831.

As with all things, there is an ending. My ending was very near and I waited for it at Natigok. One night, the Great Spirit's voice spoke into my ear, answering my prayer by telling me that I was to join the Great Spirit's Council soon.

There were few people left. Except for my children, grandchildren and great-grandchildren, all of my friends and family had taken the trail to the stars long ago. I brought my family together one last time and prepared them for my death.

"The Great Spirit has told me that I am soon to join the Great Council," I told them.

"We must prepare for the journey."

(d)

As the time neared for me to travel the Spirit Road to join my ancestors, I thought back over my long life and considered all that had happened during my life. I felt regret. Regret not because I was dying and would soon enter the land of dreams; but regret that I'd been unable to change the hearts of those who came to settle on our lands. Regret that I did not choose the right path to peace and that the path to peace I had walked with the settlers had become a shapesfhifted peace.

My people were weary; afraid. I worried, too, for my son Waolinasad, who now followed my path to peace. He was a good human being with a kind heart and one who sought after peace. But, he would, I could foresee, a tool for the settlers to use to carve out their own path. Where were my people to walk on the path?

I felt sad for the English settlers. They were leaving behind everything they knew in their lands to start a new life. But they grew more and more stubborn and refused to treat us as equals. We respected them for being sons and daughters of the Great Spirit who had just as much right to life as we had. But the English settlers did not feel the same regard for our lives. We did not admire their culture, their food, their great weapons because they would not respect our culture, food, beliefs or right to the land of our ancestos that were held in trust to our descendants. I knew these people had left their homeland to have freedom and liberty, something they often spoke about; yet they strove to deny us the very same things. I regretted that I could not change the hearts of the English settlers toward us and was not able to get them to let their hearts speak to us instead of their greed.

Fire Eyes began:

"All Penagok had heard of the Very-Little-One-of-He-Who-Like's-to-Sleep-So-Well's request to the Great Spirit that he be allowed to attend the Great Council in the Happy Hunting Grounds. All Penagok had heard that the Great Spirit Kchi Nwaskw who from time to time descended from the above land and alighted atop Agiocochook when he visited earth had granted the request. Agiocochook was chief among the White Mountains. The White Mountains was sacred land. The Penagok, the Bemijijoasek, the Wiwninibesaki, the Bigwaki and others had long hunted and trapped in the notches and dales, but dared not go above the tree line where the spirits lived. Only those people who worked with medicine, the Medôlinôwinnoak, ever went there to commune with the Great Spirit. The greatest of these Medôlinôwinno-ak was the Great Chief Babiwseso-Ogawinno."

Fire Eyes took a breath and continued:

"The day the Great Chief left the Penagok was in the middle of summer. It had been hot and humid and the white pine trees were sticky with sweat. On this day that the Great Spirit acceded to the Great Chief's wish to join the Great Council that was being brought together by the Great Spirit. In order to join the Great Council; however, the body of the Great Chief had to leave his people forever. The Penagok people were all very sad for they felt a family member was leaving them behind. The Great Chief had been old when even their great-grandparents were young. He had lived for more than five generations of the Penagok and had led them through all their trials and tribulations. The people felt the Great Chief would endure longer than even the ancient white pines. In truth, they all felt scared, as though they were losing their spiritual and temporal protector. The Great Chief urged us to remain at peace and to follow his son, Waolinasad, who had promised to follow the path of peace."

"'Remember' the Great Chief urged:

"'Follow the path of peace. If you take up your arrows and tomahawks against the English you will be destroyed. Follow the path of peace' he urged.

"As the Great Chief's voice trailed off, summer suddenly became winter. A great toboggan was brought to him. After the toboggan was prepared a great cloud of fire appeared. The Great Spirit had sent it down. Out of the fiery cloud appeared twenty four gigantic white wolves."

"'Don't be afraid' the Great Chief urged."

"'Hitch them to the sleds. They will take me to the Great Council fire.'"

"The twenty four wolves were then attached to the sled. The Great Chief, wrapped in his bearskin robe with a bear claw necklace around his neck, mounted the sled."

"'Kchi wlwni' he said, thanking his people."

"'Wli nanawalmezi' – 'Take care of youself' he said as the toboggan began to climb into the cloud. The wolves sped up into the sky, flying above the Morôdemak, over the quick frozen Wiwninibesaki Lake and up toward the White Mountains."

"As Passaconaway, the wolves' team and toboggon flew into the sky the Great Chief screamed with joy. He was young again! As we looked to where the Great Chief went we saw in the furthest reach of our eye's vision bone white Agiocochook suddenly standing out boldly against the backdrop of a blue jay feather sky. We saw the Great Chief driven up the slopes of the Hidden One by the team of two dozen wolves pulling him on the toboggan soar into the sky above Agiocochook. As it rose above Agiocochook the toboggan burst into flames as the Great Chief ascended into the above land."

The protector of the Penagok was dead.

****

York, Maine. President of the Province of Maine, Thomas Danforth and his younger brother, Jonathon who was the chief surveyor for the Massachusetts Bay Colony, are seated at a gate leg table in front of the keeping room's fireplace. Thomas, Jonathon and their brother, Samuel had arrived with their father, Reverend Nicholas Danforth in 1634 from Suffolk, England and originally settled at Cambridge. Their brother, Samuel, a Harvard graduate, had been invited in 1641 by Reverend Thomas Welde to join with Reverend John Eliot to become colleague pastor of the Roxbury Church. Samuel had accepted and after ordaining in 1650 served the Roxbury Congregation until his death.

Betty Lamp, c. 17th century

Thomas is speaking with his brother, Jonathon:

"Passaconaway died about 12 years ago. His son, Waolinasad, became chief in 1674."

Jonathon asks:

"By chief, you mean sagamore or sachem?"

Thomas answers:

"The Penagoks used the word 'Sagamore.'"

Jonathon appears puzzled:

"What's the difference?"

Thomas ponders for a moment before responding:

"As I understand it, the Penagok, unlike the Wampanoag, chose their chiefs; those here are hereditary."

Jonathon is confused:

"So one is hereditary the other isn't?"

Thomas appears perplexed and says:

"Perhaps."

Thomas answers:

"Passaconaway has been pliant to our desires but I doubt this fellow Kancamagus who Eliot refers to as John Hawkins who may well succeed Wonalancet, will be as pliant."

"He seems to possess a less amiable nature. Then again, the old witch Passaconaway was of a more conciliatory nature only because he feared we'd destroy his people."

"Truly?"

"Yes. I imagine the old Child of the Bear is now in hell with the rest of the witches," *the dough faced Thomas answered.*

Jonathon, who had personally met Passaconaway when he led the survey team that measured the Litchfield land that had been granted to the old chief before he died was sympathetic to Indians and didn't share his brother's sour attitude toward the "heathens." Jonathon advocated peaceful relations and lawful acquisition of land not the skillful maneuvering around the truth when agreeing to "rent" land.

"I had heard that he had become a Christian," *Jonathon ventured.*

"Christian? I should think not," *Thomas laughed.*

"I suppose Reverend Eliot believes he converted the old witch. Passaconaway may have thought he was a Christian but I doubt the veracity of the claims. At most Passaconaway realized it was useful to be Christian. Besides which, he could become a Praying Indian but certainly not 'Christian.' I do doubt he became a Praying Indian. He was a very politic man."

Scorching Tail says:

"So, he's smarter than I gave him credit for."

Bear Council members nod in agreement.

Thomas continues:

 "It's well to be remembered about these heathens that what they voice by the mouth isn't necessarily echoed in their heart and soul."

"Likewise for the Puritans," *notes Scorching Tail.*

"What they say about the Penagok is true also about the Puritans, in that regard," *agrees Fire Eyes.*

Jonathon says:

"You doubt Reverend Eliot's appraisal of the old chief Passaconaway then?"

Thomas appeared to ponder the idea, then responds:

"I don't doubt the good Reverend's appraisal that he believed Passaconaway said he believed; what I doubt was Passaconaway's conversion."

"When I met with Wonalancet he told me that when Passaconaway died he was led by a team of gigantic wolves to the summit of Agiocochook where he was spirited to heaven in a fiery cloud," *Jonathon said, adding fish oil to the smoking betty lamp that hung off the mantle.*

Thomas laughed at the suggestion.

"I doubt anything of the sort. Certainly I believe that he descended into a fiery cloud to hell to be judged as all his people will be."

Thomas looked out his window toward the gray Atlantic swells.

"No, Jonathon, I rather think, though, that our days of peace are coming to an end."

Jonathon asked:

"Why?"

Thomas looked at him and at the fire:

"Witch or not, Passaconaway did keep the peace even when he had opportunity to take another road."

Jonathon looked concerned and said:

"Well, I should think they have good reason to want war. It surprised me that Wonalancet (Waolinasad) kept the peace after that Dover fiasco in 1676 when Walderne orchestrated that sham fight between Indians and then separated them."

Thomas interrupted:

"We had to do it. The good ones had to be separated from the bad."

"Yes. The good went free but the bad were either put to death or enslaved. That very action caused all Indians to distrust the word of the English. It's amazing to me that Major Walderne hasn't been killed, yet. When I saw Kanacamagus he nearly spat when someone mentioned Walderne," *Jonathon said.*

There was a long silence. Thomas realized the truth of what his brother said, but what was done was done. Thomas hadn't had a hand in putting together that affair. Even though Thomas hadn't approved of the plan it was a fait accompli by the time he became aware of the incident.

Thomas stared into the fire and said:

"Passaconaway's son Wonalancet is growing old."

Jonathon asked:

"How old is he?"

Thomas answered:

"Who knows? Some say he was 100 years of age."

Jonathon appeared surprised.

"What do you think?"

Thomas thought long and hard and then said:

"I'd say at least 50, his father was 110."

Jonathon was visibly impressed.

"110?!"

"110."

Jonathon says:

"I know of very few Englishmen who have reached that age."

"Nor I."

They both seemed to reflect for a moment.

Thomas continued:

"Once the son is gone and the grandson, Kancamagus assumes the chieftainship I imagine our relations with the Penagok will be of another kind."

He paused for a moment and added:

"Another kind entirely."

Jonathon asked:

"How do you mean?"

Thomas asked:

"What do I mean?"

The fire cracked and popped, sending a cinder across the wide pine board floor. Jonathon moved his foot put out the fire and glanced over at his brother:

"It won't be as simple to put out the fire that will consume the land once Kancamagus is chief."

Jonathon said:

"I thought he had already become chief. Isn't he leading some of those who want war against the English?"

Thomas responded:

"That is true. But there are many who still look to Waolinasad."

Jonathon said:

"And Waolinasad is for peace?"

Thomas answered:

"Yes."

He then said:

"Our peace. The Puritan Peace. It is because of us that these Indians are alive. Without us they'd all be dead. We are giving them some light. A chance to know God. They are fortunate that we came."

Scorching Tail grumbled.

"Sure. Lucky for them."

Thomas added:

"Only the future will show if we were right or not."

Within a few short years the relationship did change. In 1689 Dover was attacked. The leader of the attack was Kancamagus who believed the only way to deal with the English was through blood. Major Walderne and many other settlers paid with their own blood that day. War had come and the Great Chief Babiwseso-Ogawinno's peace was dead.

Coda

Charter of New England

King James I

The Charter of New England : 1620

JAMES, by the Grace of God, King of England, Scotland, France and Ireland, Defender of the Faith, &c. to all whom these Presents shall come, Greeting, Whereas, upon the humble Petition of divers of our well disposed Subjects, that intended to make several Plantations in the Parts of America, between the Degrees of thirty-ffoure and ffourty-five; We according to our princely Inclination, favouring much their worthy Disposition, in Hope thereby to advance the in Largement of Christian Religion, to the Glory of God Almighty, as also by that Meanes to streatch out the Bounds of our Dominions, and to replenish those Deserts with People governed by Lawes and Magistrates, for the peaceable Commerce of all, that in time to come shall have occasion to traffique into those Territoryes, granted unto Sir Thomas Gates, Sir George Somers, Knights, Thomas Hanson, and Raleigh Gilbert, Esquires, and of their Associates, for the more speedy Accomplishment thereof, by our Letters-Pattent, bearing Date the Tenth Day of Aprill, in the Fourth Year of our Reign of England, France and Ireland, and of Scotland the ffourtieth, free Liberty to divide themselves into two several Collonyes; the one called the first Collonye, to be undertaken and advanced by certain Knights, Gentlemen, and Merchants, in and about our Cyty of London; the other called the Second Collonye, to be undertaken and advanced by certaine Knights, Gentlemen, and Merchants, and their associates, in and about our Citties of Bristol, Exon, and our Towne of Plymouth, and other Places, as in and by our said Letters-Pattents, amongst other Things more att large it doth and may appears. And whereas, since that Time, upon the humble Petition of the said Adventurers and Planters of the said first Collonye, We have been graciously pleased to make them one distinct and entire Body by themselves, giving unto them their distinct Lymitts and Bounds, and have upon their like humble Request, granted unto them divers Liberties, Priveliges, Enlargements, and Immunityes, as in and by our severall Letters-Patents it doth and may more at large appears. Now forasmuch as We have been in like Manner humbly petitioned unto by our trusty and well beloved Servant, Sir fferdinando Gorges, Knight, Captain of our ffort and Island by Plymouth, and by certain the principal Knights and Gentlemen Adventurers of the said Second Collonye, and by divers other Persons of Quality, who now intend to be their Associates, divers of which have been at great and extraordinary Charge, and sustained many Losses in seeking and discovering a Place fitt and convenient to lay the Foundation of a hopeful Plantation, and have divers Years past by God's Assistance, and their own endeavours, taken actual Possession of the Continent hereafter mentioned, in our Name and to our Use, as Sovereign Lord thereof, and have settled already some of our People in Places agreeable to their Desires in those Parts, and in Confidence of prosperous Success therein, by the Continuance of God's Devine Blessing, and our Royall Permission, have resolved in a more plentifull and effectual Manner to prosecute the same, and to that Purpose and Intent have desired of Us, for their better Encouragement and Satisfaction herein, and that they may avoide all Confusion, Questions, or Differences between themselves, and those of the said first Collonye, We would likewise be graciously pleased to make certaine Adventurers, intending to erect and. establish fishery, Trade, and Plantacion, within the Territoryes, Precincts, and Lymitts of the said second Colony, and their Successors, one several distinct and entire Body, and to grant unto them, such Estate, Liberties, Priveliges, Enlargements, and Immunityes there, as in these our Letters-Pattents hereafter particularly expressed and declared. And for asmuch as We have been certainly given to understand by divers of our good Subjects, that have for these many Years past frequented those Coasts and Territoryes, between the Degrees of Fourty and Fourty-Eight, that there is noe other the Subjects of any Christian King or State, by any Authority from their Soveraignes, Lords, or Princes, actually in Possession of any of the said Lands or Precincts, whereby any Right, Claim, Interest, or Title, may, might, or ought by that Meanes accrue, belong, or appertaine unto them, or any of them. And also for that We have been further given certainly to knowe, that within these late Yeares there hath by God's Visitation reigned a wonderfull Plague, together with many horrible Slaugthers, and Murthers, committed amoungst the Sauages and brutish People there, heertofore inhabiting, in a Manner to the utter Destruction, Deuastacion, and Depopulacion of that whole Territorye, so that there is not left for many Leagues together in a Manner, any that doe claime or challenge any Kind of Interests therein, nor any other Superiour Lord or Souveraigne to make Claime "hereunto, whereby We in our Judgment are persuaded and satisfied that the appointed Time is come in which Almighty God in his great Goodness and Bountie towards Us and our People, hath thought fitt and determined, that those large and goodly Territoryes, deserted as it were by their naturall Inhabitants, should be possessed and enjoyed by such of our Subjects and People as heertofore have and hereafter shall by his Mercie and Favour, and by his Powerfull Arme, be directed and conducted thither. In Contemplacion and serious Consideracion whereof, Wee have thougt it fitt according to our Kingly Duty, soe much as in Us lyeth, to second and followe God's sacred Will, rendering reverend Thanks to his Divine Majestie for his gracious favour in laying open and revealing the same unto us, before any other Christian Prince or State, by which Meanes without Offence, and as We trust to his Glory, Wee may with Boldness goe on to the settling of soe hopefull a Work, which tendeth to the reducing and Conversion of such Sauages as remaine wandering in Desolacion and Distress, to Civil Societie and Christian Religion, to the Inlargement of our own Dominions, and the Aduancement of the Fortunes of such of our good Subjects as shall willingly intresse themselves in the said Imployment, to whom We cannot but give singular Commendations for their soe worthy Intention and Enterprize; Wee therefore, of our especiall Grace, mere Motion, and certaine Knowledge, by the Aduice of the Lords and others of our Priuy Councell have for Us, our Heyrs and Successors, graunted, ordained, and established, and in and by these Presents, Do for Us, our Heirs and Successors, grant, ordaine and establish, that all that Circuit, Continent, Precincts, and Limitts in America, lying and being in Breadth from Fourty Degrees of Northerly Latitude, from the Equnoctiall Line, to Fourty-eight Degrees of the said Northerly Latitude, and in length by all the Breadth aforesaid throughout the Maine Land, from Sea to Sea, with all the Seas, Rivers, Islands, Creekes, Inletts, Ports, and Havens, within the Degrees, Precincts and Limitts of the said Latitude and Longitude, shall be the Limitts; and Bounds, and Precints of the second Collony: And to the End that the said Territoryes may forever hereafter be more particularly and certainly known and distinguished, our Will and Pleasure is, that the sa.ne shall from henceforth be nominated, termed, and called by the Name of New-England, in America; and by that Name of New-England in America, the said Circuit, Precinct, Limitt, Continent, Islands, and Places in America, aforesaid, We do by these Presents, for Us, our Heyrs and Successors, name, call, erect, found and establish, and by that Name to have Continuance for ever.

And for the better Plantacion, ruling, and governing of the aforesaid New-England, in America, We will, ordaine, constitute, assigne, limits and appoint, and for Us, our Heyrs and Successors, Wee, by the Advice of the Lords and others of the said priuie Councill, do by these Presents ordaine, constitute, limett, and appoint, that from henceforth, there shall be for ever hereafter, in our Towne of Plymouth, in the County of Devon, one Body politicque and corporate, which shall have perpetuall Succession, which shall consist of the Number of fourtie Persons, and no more, which shall be, and shall be called and knowne by the Name the Councill established at Plymouth, in the County of Devon for the planting, ruling, ordering, and governing of New-England, in America; and for that Purpose Wee have, at and by the Nomination and Request of the said Petitioners, granted, ordained, established, and confirmed; and by these Presents, for Us, our Heyres and Successors, doe grant, ordaine, establish, and confirme, our right trusty and right well beloved Cosins and Councillors Lodovick, Duke of Lenox, Lord Steward of our Houshold, George Lord Marquess Buckingham, our High Admiral of England, James Marquess Hamilton, William Earle of Pembrocke, Lord Chamberlaine of our Houshold, Thomas Earl of Arundel, and our right trusty and right well beloved Cosin, William Earl of hathe, and right trusty and right well beloved Cosin and Councellor, Henry Earle of Southampton, and our right trusty and right well beloved Cousins, William Earle of Salisbury, and Robert Earle of Warwick, and our right trusty and right well beloved John Viscount Haddington, and our right trusty and well beloved Councellor Edward Lord Zouch, Lord Warden of our Cincque Ports, and our trusty and well beloved Edmond Lord Sheffield, Edward Lord Gorges, and our well beloved Sir Edward Seymour, Knight and Barronett, Sir Robert Manselle, Sir Edward Zouch, our Knight Marshall, Sir Dudley Diggs, Sir Thomas Roe, Sir fferdinando Gorges, Sir Francis Popham, Sir John Brook, Sir Thomas Gates, Sir Richard Hawkins, Sir Richard Edgcombe, Sir Allen Apsley, Sir Warwick Hale, Sir Richard Catchmay, Sir John Bourchier, Sir Nathaniel Rich, Sir Edward Giles, Sir Giles Mompesson, and Sir Thomas Wroth, Knights; and our well beloved Matthew Sutcliffe, Dean of Exeter, Robert Heath, Esq; Recorder of our Cittie of London, Henry Bourchier, John Drake, Rawleigh Gilbert, George Chudley, Thomas Hamon, and John Argall, Esquires, to be and in and by these Presents; We do appoint them to be the first modern and present Councill established at Plymouth, in the County of Devon, for the planting, ruling, ordering, and governing of New-England, in America; and that they, and the Suruiuours of them, and such as the Suruluours and Suruinor of them shall, from tyme to tyme elect, and chuse, to make up the aforesaid Number of fourtie Persons, when, and as often as any of them, or any of their Successors shall happen to decease, or to be removed from being of the said Councill, shall be in, and by these Presents, incorporated to have a perpetual Succession for ever, in Deed, Fact, and Name, and shall be one Bodye corporate and politicque; and that those, and such said Persons, and their Successors, and such as shall be elected and chosen to succeed them as aforesaid, shall be, and by these Presents are, and be incorporated, named, and called by the Name of the Councill established at Plymouth, in the County of Devon, for the planting, ruling, and governing of New-England, in America; and them the said Duke of Lenox, Marquess Buckingham, Marquess Hamilton, Earle of Pembroke, Earle of Arundell, Earle of hathe, Earle of Southampton, Earle of Salisbury, Earle of Warwick, Viscount Haddington, Lord Zouch, Lord Sheffleld, Lord Gorges, Sir Edward Seymour, Sir Robert Mansell, Sir Edward Zouch, Sir Dudley Diggs, Sir Thomas Roe, Sir fferdinando

Gorges, Sir ffrancis Popham, Sir John Brooks, Sir Thomas Gates, Sir Richard Hawkins, Sir Richard Edgcombe, Sir Allen Apsley, Sir Warwick Heale, Sir Richard Catchmay, Sir John Bourchier, Sir Nathaniell Rich, Sir Edward Giles, Sir Giles Mompesson, Sir Thomas Wroth, Knights; Matthew Suttcliffe, Robert Heath, Henry Bourchier, John Drake, Rawleigh Gilbert, George Chudley, Thomas Haymon, and John Argall, Esqrs. and their successors, one Body corporate and politick, in Deed and Name, by the Name of the Councell established att Plymouth, in the County of Devon for the planting, ruling, and governing of New-England, in America. Wee do by these Presents, for Us, our Heyres and Successors, really and fully incorporate, erect, ordaine. name, constitute, and establish, and that by the same Name of the said Councill, they and their Successors for ever hereafter be incorporated, named, and called, and shall by the same Name have perpetual Succession. And further, Wee do hereby for Us, our Heires and Successors, grant unto the said Councill established aft Plymouth, that they and their Successors, by the same Name, be and shall be, and shall continue Persons able and capable in the Law, from time to time, and shall by that Name, of Councill aforesaid, have full Power and Authority, and lawful Capacity and Habilily, as well to purchase, take, hold, receive, enjoy, and to have, and their Successors for ever, any Manors, Lands, Tenements, Rents, Royalties, Privileges, Immunities, Reversions, Annuities, Hereditaments, Goods, and Chattles whatsoever, of or from Us, our Heirs, and Successors, and of or from any other Person or Persons whatsoever, as well in and within this our Realme, of England, as in and within any other Place or Places whatsoever or wheresoever; and the same Manors, Lands, Tenements, and Hereditaments, Goods or Chattles, or any of them, by the same Name to alien and sell, or to do, execute, ordaine and performe all other Matters and Things whatsoever to the said Incorporation and Plantation concerning and-belonging.

And further, our Will and Pleasure is, that the said Councill, for the time being, and their Successors, shall have full Power and lawful authority, by the Name aforesaid, to sue, and be sued; implead, and to be impleaded; answer, and to be answered, unto all Manner of Courts and Places that now are, or hereafter shall be, within this our Realme and elsewhere, as well temporal as spiritual, in all Manner of Suits and Matters whatsoever, and of what Nature or Kinde soever such Suite or Action be or shall be. And our Will and Pleasure is, that the said flourty Persons, or the greater Number of them, shall and may, from time to time, and at any time hereafter, at their owne Will and Pleasure, according to the Laws, Ordinances, and Orders of or by them, or by the greater Part of them, hereafter in Manner and forme in these Presents mentioned, to be agreed upon, to elect and choose amongst themselves one of the said dourty Persons for the Time being, to be President of the said Councill, which President soe elected and chosen, Wee will, shall continue and be President of the said Council for so long a Time as by the Orders of the said Councill, from time to time to be made, as hereafter is mentioned, shall be thought fitt, and no longer; unto which President, or in his Absence, to any such Person as by the Order of the said Councill shall be thereunto appointed, Wee do give Authority to give Order for the warning of the said Council, and summoning the Company to their Meetings. And our Will and Pleasure is, that from time to time, when and so often as any of the Councill shall happen to decease, or to be removed from being of the said Councell, that then, and so often, the Survivors of them the said Councill, and no other, or the greater Number of them, who then shall be from time to time left and remaininge, and who shall, or the greater Number of which that shall be assembled at a public Court or Meeting to be held for the said Company, shall elect and choose one or more other Person or Persons to be of the said Councill, and which from time to time shall be of the said Councill, so that the Number of Bounty Persons of the said Councill may from time to time be supplied: Provided always that as well the Persons herein named to be of the said Councill, as every other Councellor hereafter to be elected, shall be prevented Lord Chancellor of England, or to the Lord High Treasurer of England, or to the Lord Chamberlaine of the Household of Us, our Heires and Successors for the Time being, to take his and their Oath and Oathes of a Councellor and Councellors to Us, our Heirs and Successors, for the said Company and Collonye in New-England.

And further, Wee will and grant by these Presents, for Us, our Heires and Successors, unto the said Councill and their Successors, that they and their Successors shall have and enjoy for ever a Common Seale, to be engraver according to their Discretions; and that it shall be lawfull for them to appoint whatever Seale or Seales, they shall think most meete and necessary, either for their Use, as they are one united Body incorporate here, or for the publick of their Gouvernour and Ministers of New-England aforesaid, whereby the Incorporation may or shall scale any Manner of Instrument touching the same Corporation, and the Manors, Lands, Tenements, Rents, Reversions, Annuities, Hereditaments, Goods, Chattles, Affaires, and any other Things belonging unto, or in any wise appertaininge, touching, or concerning the said Councill and their Successors, or concerning the said Corporation and plantation in and by these our Letters-Patents as aforesaid founded, erected, and established.

And Wee do further by these Presents, for Us, our Heires and Successors, grant unto the said Councill and their Successors, that it shall and may be lawfull to and for the said Councill, and their Successors for the Time being, in their discretions, from time to time to admits such and so many Person and Persons to be made free and enabled to trade traffick unto, within, and in New-England aforesaid, and unto every Part and Parcell thereof, or to have, possess, or enjoy, any Lands or Hereditaments in New-England aforesaid, as they shall think fitt, according to the Laws, Orders, Constitutions, and Ordinances, by the said Councill and their Successors from time to time to be made and established by Virtue of, and according to the true Intent of these Presents, and under such Conditions, Reservations, and agreements as the said Councill shall set downe, order and direct, and not otherwise. And further, of our especiall Grace, certaine Knowlege, and mere Motion, for Us, our Heires and Successors, Wee do by these Presents give and grant full Power and Authority to the said Councill and their Successors, that the said Councill for the Time being, or the greater Part of them, shall and may, from time to time, nominate, make, constitute, ordaine, and confirms by such Name or Names, Style or Styles, as to them shall seeme Good; and likewise to revoke, discharge, change, and alter, as well all and singular, Governors, Officers, and Ministers, which hereafter-shall be by them thought fill and needful to be made or used, as well to attend the Business of the said Company here, as for the Government of the said Collony and Plantation, and also to make, ordaine, and establish all Manner of Orders, Laws, Directions, Instructions, Forms, and Ceremonies of Government and Magistracy fitt and necessary for and concerning the Government of the said Collony and Plantation, so always as the same be not contrary to the Laws and Statutes of this our Realme of England, and the same att all Times hereafter to abrogate, revoke, or change, not only within the Precincts of the said Collony, but also upon the Seas in going and coming to and from the said Collony, as they in their good Discretions shall thinke to be fittest for the good of the Adenturers and Inhabitants there.

And Wee do further of our especiall Grace, certaine Knowledge, and mere Motion, grant, declare, and ordain, that such principall Governor, as from time to time shall be authorized and appointed in Manner and Forme in these Presents heretofore expressed, shall haue full Power and Authority to use and exercise marshall Laws in Cases of Rebellion, Insurrection and Mutiny in as large and ample Manner as our Lieutenants in our Counties within our Realme of England have or ought to have by Force of their Commission of Lieutenancy. And for as much as it shall be necessary for all our lovinge Subjects as shall inhabit within the said Precincts of New-England aforesaid, to determine to live together in the Feare and true Worship of Allmighty God, Christian Peace, and civil Quietness, each with other, whereby every one may with more Safety, Pleasure, and Profist, enjoye that whereunto they shall attaine with great Pain and Perill, Wee, for Us, our Heires and Successors, are likewise pleased and contented, and by these Presents do give and grant unto the said Council and their Successors, and to such Governors, Officers, and Ministers, as shall be by the said Councill constituted and appointed according to the Natures and Limitts of their Offices and Places respectively, that they shall and may, from time to time for ever heerafter, within the said Precincts of New-England, or in the Way by the Seas thither, and from thence have full and absolute Power and Authority to correct, punish, pardon, governe, and rule all such the Subjects of Us, our Heires and Successors, as shall from time to time adventure themselves in any Voyage thither, or that shall aft any Time heerafter inhabit in the Precincts or Territories of the said Collony as aforesaid, according to such Laws, Orders, Ordinances, Directions, and Instructions as by the said Councill aforesaid shall be established; and in Defect thereof, in Cases of Necessity, according to the good Discretions of the said Governors and Officers respectively, as well in Cases capital and criminal, as civill, both marine and others, so allways as the said Statutes, Ordinances, and Proceedings, as near as conveniently may be, agreeable to the Laws, Statutes, Government and Policie of this our Realme of England. And furthermore, if any Person or Persons,-Adventurers or Planters of the said Collony, or any other, aft any Time or Times heereafter, shall transport any Moneys, Goods, or Merchandizes, out of any of our Kingdoms, with a Pretence or Purpose to land, sell, or otherwise dispose of the same within the Limitts and Bounds of the said Collony, and yet nevertheless being att Sea, or after he hath landed within any Part of the said Collony shall carry the same into any other fforaigne Country with a Purpose there to sell and dispose thereof, that then all the Goods and Chattles of the said Person or Persons so offending and transported, together with the Ship or Vessell wherein such Transportation was made, shall be forfeited to Us, our Heires and Successors.

And Wee do further of our especial Grace, certaine Knowledge, and meere Motion for Us, our Heirs and Successors for and in Respect of the Considerations aforesaid, and for divers other good Causes and Considerations, us thereunto especially moving, and by the Advice of the Lords and Others of our said Privy Councill have absolutely giuen, granted, and confirmed, and do by these Presents absolutely give, grant, and confirm unto the said Councill, called the Counceil established att

Plymouth in the County of Devon for the planting, ruling, and governing of New-England in America, and unto their Successors for ever, all the aforesaid Lands and Grounds, Continent, Precinct, Place, Places and Territoryes, viz, the aforesaid Part of America, lying, and being in Breadth from ffourty Degrees of Northerly Latitude from the Equinoctiall Line, to ffourty-eight Degrees of the said Northerly Latitude inclusively, and in Length of, and within all the Breadth aforesaid, throughout the Maine Land from Sea to Sea, together also, with the Firme Lands, Soyles, Grounds Havens, Ports, Rivers, Waters, Fishings, Mines, and Mineralls, as well Royall Mines of Gold and Silver, as other Mine and Mineralls, precious Stones, Quarries, and all, and singular other Comodities, Jurisdictions, Royalties, Priveliges, Franchises, and Preheminences, both within the same Tract of Land upon the Maine, and also within the said Islands and Seas adjoining: Provided always, that the said Islands, or any of the Premises herein before mentioned, and by these Presents intended and meant to be granted, be not actually possessed or inhabited by any other Christian Prince or Estate, nor he within the Bounds, Limitts, or Territoryes, of that Southern Collony Heretofore by us granted to be planted by diverse of our loving Subjects in the South Parts, to have and to hold, possess and enjoy, all, and singular, the aforesaid Continent, Lands, Territoryes, Islands, Hereditaments and Precincts, Sea Waters, Fishings, with all, and all Manner their Commodities, Royalties, Liberties, Preheminences and Profitts, that shall arise from thence, with all and singular. their Appertenances, and every Part and Parcell thereof, and of them, to and unto the said Councell and their Successors and Assignes for ever, to the sole only and proper Use, Benefit and Behooffe of them the said Council and their Successors and Assignes for ever, to be holden of Us, our Heires, and Successors, as of our Manor of East-Greenwich, in our County of Kent, in free and common Soccage and not in in Capite, nor by Knight's Service; yielding and paying therefore to Us, our Heires, our Successors, the fifth Part, of the Ores of Gold and Silver, which from time to time, and aft all times hereafter, shall happen to be found, gotten, had, and obtained, in or within any the said Lands, Limitts, Territoryes, and Precincts, or in or within any Part or Parcell thereof, for, or in Respect of all, and all Manner of Dutys, Demands, and Services whatsoever, to be done, made, or paid to Us, our Heires, and Successors.

And Wee do further of our especiall Grace, certaine Knowledge and meere Motion, for Us, and our Heires, and Successors, give and grant to the said Councell, and their Successors for ever by these Presents, that it shall be lawfull and free for them and their Assignes, att all and every time and times hereafter, out of our Realmes or Dominions whatsoever, to take, load, carry, and transport in, and into their Voyages, and for, and towards the said Plantation in New-England, all such and so many of our loveing Subjects, or any other Strangers that will become our loving Subjects, and live under our Allegiance, as shall willingly accompany them in the said Voyages and Plantation, with Shipping, Armour, Weapons, Ordinances, Munition, Shott, Victuals, and all Manner of Cloathing, Implements, Furniture, Beasts, Cattle, Horses, Mares, and all other Things necessary for the said Plantation, and for their Use and Defence, and for Trade with the People there, and in passing and returning to and fro, without paving or yielding, any Custom or Subsidie either inwards or outwards, to Us, our Heires, or Successors, for the same, for the Space of seven Years, from the Day of the Date of these Presents, provided, that none of the said Persons be such as shall be hereafter by special Name restrained by Us, our Heire, or Successors.

And for their further Encouragement, of our especial Grace and Favor, Wee do by these Presents for Us, our Heires, and Successors, yield and grant, to and with the said Councill and their Successors, and every of them, their Factors and Assignes, that they and every of them, shall be free and quits from all Subsidies and Customes in NewEngland for the Space of seven Years, and from all Taxes and Impositions for the Space of twenty and one Yeares, upon all Goods and Merchandizes aft any time or times hereafter, either upon Importation thither, or Exportation from thence into our Realme of England, or into any our Dominions by the said Councill and their Successors their Deputies, Factors, and Assignes, or any of them, except only the five Pounds per Cent. due for Custome upon all such Goods and Merchandizes, as shall be brot and imported into our Realme of England, or any other of our Dominions, according to the ancient Trade of Marchants; which five Pounds per Cent. only being paid, it shall be thenceforth lawful and free for the said Adventurers, the same Goods and Merchandize to export and carry out of our said Dominions into fforraigne Parts, without any Custom, Tax, or other Duty to be paid to Us, our Heires, or Successors, or to any other Officers or Ministers of Us, our Heires, or Successors; provided, that the said Goods and Merchandizes be shipped out within thirteene Months after theire first Landing within any Part of those Dominions.

And further our Will and Pleasure is, and Wee do by these Presents charge, comand, warrant, and authorize the said Councill, and their Successors, or the major Part of them, which shall be present and assembled for that Purpose, shall from time to time under their comon

Seale, distribute, convey, assigne, and sett over, such particular Portions of Lands, Tenements, and Hereditaments, as are by these Presents, formerly granted unto each our loveing Subjects, naturally borne or Denisons, or others, as well Adventurers as Planters, as by the said Company upon a Comission of Survey and. Distribution, executed and returned for that Purpose, shall be named, appointed, and allowed, wherein our Will and Pleasure is, that Respect be had as well to the Proportion of the Adventurers, as to the special Service, Hazard, Exploit, or Meritt of any Person so to be recompensed, advanced, or rewarded, and wee do also, for Us, our Heires, and Successors, grant to the said Councell and their Successors and to all and every such Governours, other Officers, or Ministers, as by the said Councill shall be appointed to have Power and Authority of Government and Command in and over the said Collony and Plantation, that they and every of them, shall, and lawfully may, from time to time, and aft all Times hereafter for ever, for their severall Defence and Safety, encounter, expulse, repel, and resist by Force of Arms, as well by Sea as by Land, and all Ways and Meanes whatsoever, all such Person and Persons, as without the speciall Licence of the said Councell and their Successors, or the greater Part of them, shall attempt to inhabitt within the said severall Precincts and Limitts of the said Collony and Plantation. And also all, and every such Person or Persons whatsoever, as shall enterprise or attempt att any time hereafter Destruction, Invasion, Detriment, or Annovance to the said Collony and Plantation; and that it shall be lawfull for the said Councill, and their Successors, and every of them, from Time to Time, and att all Times heereafter, and they shall have full Power and Authority, to take and surprize by all Ways and Means whatsoever, all and every such Person and Persons whatsoever, with their Ships, Goods, and other Furniture, trafficking in any Harbour, Creeke, or Place, within the Limitts and Precintes of the said Collony and Plantations, and not being allowed by the said Councill to be adventurers or Planters of the said Collony. And of our further Royall Favor, Wee have granted, and for Us, our Heires, and Successors, Wee do grant unto the said Councill and their Successors, that the said Territoryes, Lands, Rivers, and Places aforesaid, or any of them, shall not be visited, frequented, or traded unto, by any other of our Subjects, or the Subjects of Us, our Heires, or Successors, either from any the Ports and Havens belonging or appertayning, or which shall belong or appertayne unto Us, our Heires, or Successors, or to any forraigne State, Prince, or Pottentate whatsoever: And therefore, Wee do hereby for Us, our Heires, and Successors, charge, command, prohibit and forbid all the Subjects of Us, our Heires, and Successors, of what Degree and Quality soever, they be, that none of them, directly, or indirectly, presume to vissitt, frequent, trade, or adventure to traffick into, or from the said Territoryes, Lands, Rivers, and Places aforesaid, or any of them other than the said Councill and their Successors, Factors, Deputys, and Assignes, unless it be with the License and Consent of the said Councill and Company first had and obtained in Writing, under the comon Seal, upon Pain of our Indignation and Imprisonment of their Bodys during the Pleasure of Us, our Heires or Successors, and the Forfeiture and Loss both of theire Ships and Goods, wheresoever they shall be found either within any of our Kingdomes or Dominions, or any other Place or Places out of our Dominions.

And for the better effecting of our said Pleasure heerein Wee do heereby for Us, our Heires and Successors, give and grant full Power and Authority unto the said Councill, and their Successors for the time being, that they by themselves, their Factors, Deputyes, or Assignes, shall and may from time to time, and at all times heereafter, attach, arrest, take, and seize all and all Manner of Ship and Ships, Goods, Wares, and Merchandizes whatsoever, which shall be bro't from or carried to the Places before mentioned, or any of them, contrary to our Will and Pleasure, before in these Presents expressed. The Moyety or one halfe of all which Forfeitures Wee do hereby for Us, our Heires and Successors, give and grant unto the said Councill, and their Successors to their own proper Use without Accompt, and the other Moyety, or halfe Part thereof, Wee will shall be and remaine to the Use of Us, our Heires and Successors. And we likewise have condiscended and granted, and by these Presents, for Us, our Heires and Successors, do condiscend, and grant to and with the said Councill and their Successors, that Wee, our Heires or Successors, shall not or will not give and grant any Lybertye, License, or Authority to any Person or Persons whatsoever, to saile, trade, or trafficke unto the aforesaid parts of New-England, without the good Will and Likinge of the said Councill, or the greater Part of them for the Time Hinge, let any their Courts to be assembled. And Wee do for us, our Heires and Successors, give and grant unto the said Councill, and their Successors, that whensoever, or so often as any Custome or Subsidie shall growe due or payable unto Us, our Heires or Successors, according to the Limitation and Appointment aforesaid by Reason of any Goods, Wares, Merchandizes, to be shipped out, or any Returne to be made of any Goods, Wares, or Merchandizes, unto or from New-England, or any the Lands Territoryes aforesaid, that then so often, and in such Case the ffarmers, Customers, and Officers of our Customes of England and Ireland, and every of them, for the Time being, upon Request made unto them by the said Councill, their Successors, Factors, or Assignes, and upon convenient Security to be given in that Behalfe, shall give and allowe unto the said Councill and their Successors, and to all Person and Persons free of the said Company as aforesaid, six Months Time for the Payment of the one halfe of all such Custome and Subsidie, as shall be due, and payable unto Us, our Heires and Successors for the same, for which these our Letterspattent, or the Duplicate, or the Enrolrnent thereof, shall be Onto our said Officers a sufficient Warrant and Discharge. Nevertheless, our Will and Pleasure is, that if any of the said Goods, Wares, and Merchandizes, which be, or shall be, aft any Time heereafter, ended and exported out of any of our Realmes aforesaid, and shall be shipped with a Purpose not to be carried to New-England aforesaid, that then such Payment, Duty, Custome, Imposition, or Forfieture, shall be paid and belong to Us, our Heires and Successors, for the said Goods, Wares, and Merchandices, so fraudulently sought to be transported, as if this our Grant had not been made nor granted: And Wee do for Us, our Heires and Successors, give and grant unto the said Councill and theire Successors for ever, by these Presents, that the said President of the said Company, or his Deputy for the Time being, or any two others of the said Councill, for the said Collony in New-England, for the Time beinge, shall and may, and aft all Times heereafter, and from time to time, have full Power and Authority, to minister and give the Oath and Oaths of Allegiance and Supremacy, or either of them, to all and every Person and Persons, which shall aft any Time and Times heereafter, goe or pass to the said Collony in New-England. And further, that it shall be likewise-be lawful for the said President, or his Deputy for the Time being, or any two others of the said Councill for the said Collony of New-England for the Time being, from time to time, and aft all Times heerafter, to minister such a formal Oath, as by their Discretion shall be reasonably devised, as well unto any Person and Persons imployed or to be imployed in, for, or touching the said Plantation, for their honest, faithfull, and just Discharge of their Service, in all such Matters as shall be committed unto them for the Good and Benefist of the said Company, Collony, and Plantation, as also unto such other Person or Persons, as the said President or his Deputy, with two others of the said Councill, shall thinke meete for the Examination or clearing of the Truth in any Cause whatsoever, concerning the said Plantation, or any Business from thence proceeding, or "hereunto belonging.

And to the End that now lewd or ill-disposed Persons, Saylors, Soldiers, Artificers, Labourers, Husbandmen, or others, which shall receive Wages, Apparel, or other Entertainment from the said Councill, or contract and agree with the said Councill to goe, and to serve, and to be imployed, in the said Plantation, in the Collony in NewEngland, do afterwards withdraw, hide, and conceale themselves, or refuse to go thither, after they have been so entertained and agreed withall; and that no Persons which shall be sent and imployed in the said Plantation, of the said Collony in New-England, upon the Charge of the said Councill, doe misbehave themselves by mutinous Seditions, or other notorious Misdemeanors, or which shall be imployed, or sent abroad by the Governour of New England or his Deputy, with any Shipp or Pinnace, for Provision for the said Collony, or for some Discovery, or other Business or Affaires concerninge the same, doe from thence either treacherously come back againe, or returne into the Realme of Englande by Stealth, or without Licence of the Governour of the said Collonv in New-England for the Time being, or be sent hither as Misdoers or Oflendors; and that none of those Persons after theire Returne from thence, being questioned by the said Councill heere, for such their Misdemeanors and Offences, do, by insolent and contemptuous Carriage in the Presence of the said Councill shew little Respect and Reverence, either to the Place or Authority in which we have placed and appointed them and others, for the clearing of their Lewdness and Misdemeanors committed in New-England, divulge vile and scandalous Reports of the Country of New-England, or of the Government or Estate of the said Plantation and Collonv, to bring the said Voyages and Plantation into Disgrace and Contempt, by Meanes whereof, not only the Adventurers and Planters already engaged in the said Plantation may be exceedingly abused and hindered, and a great number of our loveing and well-disposed Subjects, otherways well affected and inclined to joine and adventure in so noble a Christian and worthy Action may be discouraged from the same, but also the Enterprize itself may be overthrowne, which cannot miscarry without some Dishonour to Us and our Kingdome: Wee, therefore, for preventing so great and enormous Abuses and Misdemeanors, Do, by these Presents for Us, our Heires, and Successors, give and grant unto the said President or his Deputy, or such other Person or Persons, as by the Orders of the said Councill shall be appointed by Warrant under his or their Hand or Hands, to send for, or cause to-be apprehended, all and every such Person and Persons, who shall be noted, or accused, or found at any time or times hereafter to offend or misbehave themselves in any the Affaires before mentioned and expressed; and upon the Examination of any such Offender or Offenders, and just Proofe made by Oathe taken before the said Councill, of any such notorious Misdemeanours by them comitted as aforesaid, and also upon any insolent, contemptuous, or irreverent Carriage or Misbehaviour, to or against the said Councill, to be shewed or used by any such Person or Persons so called, convened, and appearing before them as aforesaid, that in all such Cases, our said Councill, or any two or more of them for the Time being, shall and may have full Power and Authority, either heere to bind them over with good Sureties for their good Behaviour, and further therein to proceed, to all Intents and Purposes as it is used in other like Cases within our Realme of England, or else at their Discretions to remand and send back the said offenders, or any of them, to the said Collony of New-England, there to be proceeded against and punished as the Governour's Deputy or Councill there for the Time being, shall think meete, or otherwise according to such Laws and Ordinances as are, and shall be, in Use there, for the well ordering and good Government of the said Collony.

And our Will and Pleasure is, and Wee do hereby declare to all Christian Kings, Princes, and States, that if any Person or Persons which shall hereafter be of the said Collony or Plantation, or any other by License or Appointment of the said Councill, or their Successors, or otherwise, shall at any time or times heereafter, rob or spoil, by Sea or by Land, or do any Hurt, Violence, or unlawfull Hostillity to any of the Subjects of Us, our Heires, or Successors, or any of the Subjects of any King, Prince, Ruler, or Governour, or State, being then in League and Amity with Us, our Heires and Successors, and that upon such Injury, or upon just Complaint of such Prince, Ruler, Governour, or State, or their Subjects, Wee, our Heires, or Successors shall make open Proclamation within any of the Ports of our Realme of England commodious for that Purpose, that the Person or Persons having committed any such Robbery or Spoile, shall within the Term limited by such a Proclamation, make full Restitution or Satisfaction of all such Injuries done, so as the said Princes or other, so complaining, may hold themselves fully satisfied and contented. And if that the said Person or Persons having committed such Robery or Spoile, shall not make or cause to be made Satisfaction accordingly within such Terme so to be limited, that then it shall be lawful for Us, our Heires, and Successors, to put the said Person or Persons our of our Allegiance and Protection; and that it shall be lawful and free for all Princes to prosecute with Hostillity the said Offenders and every of them, their, and every of their Procurers, Aidors, Abettors, and Comforters in that Behalfe. Also, Wee do for Us, our Heires, and Successors, declare by these Presents, that all and every the Persons, beinge our Subjects, which shall goe and inhabitt within the said Collony and Plantation, and every of their Children and Posterity, which shall happen to be born within the Limitts thereof, shall have and enjoy all Liberties, and ffranchizes, and Immunities of free Denizens and naturall Subjects within any of our other Dominions, to all Intents and Purposes, as if they had been abidinge and born within this our Kingdome of England, or any other our Dominions.

And lastly, because the principall Effect which we can desire or expect of this Action, is the Conversion and Reduction of the People in those Parts unto the true Worship of God and Christian Religion, in which Respect, Wee would be loath that any Person should be permitted to pass that Wee suspected to affect the Superstition of the Chh of Rome, Wee do hereby declare that it is our Will and Pleasure that none be permitted to pass, in any Voyage from time to time to be made into the said Country, but such as shall first have taken the Oathe of Supremacy; for which Purpose, Wee do by these Presents give full Power and Authority to the President of the said Councill, to tender and exhibit the said Oath to all such Persons as shall at any time be sent and imployed in the said Voyage. And Wee also for us, our Heires and Successors, do covenant and grant to and with the Councill, and their Successors, by these Presents, that if the Councill for the time being, and their Successors, or any of them, shall at any time or times heereafter, upon any Doubt which they shall conceive concerning the Strength or Validity in Law of this our present Grant, or be desirous to have the same renewed and confirmed by Us, our Heires and Successors, with Amendment of such Imperfections and Defects as shall appear fitt and necessary to the said Councill, or their Successors, to be reformed and amended on the Behalfe of Us, our Heires and Successors, and for the furthering of the Plantation and Government, or the Increase, continuing, and flourishing thereof, that then, upon the humble Petition of the said Councill for the time being, and their Successors, to us, our Heires and Successors, Wee, our Heires and Successors, shall and will forthwith make and pass under the Great Seall of England, to the said Councill and theire Successors, such further and better Assurance, of all and singular the Lands, Grounds, Royalties, Privileges, and Premisses aforesaid granted, or intended to be granted, according to our true Intent and Meaneing in these our Letters-patents, signified, declared, or mentioned, as by the learned Councill of Us, our Heires, and Successors, and of the said Company and theire Successors shall, in that Behalfe, be reasonably devised or advised. And further our Will and Pleasure is, that in all Questions and Doubts, that shall arise upon any Difficulty of Instruction or Interpretation of any Thing contained in these our Letters-pattents, the same shall be taken and Interpreted in most ample and beneficial Manner, for the said Council and theire Successors, and every Member thereof. And Wee do further for Us, our Heires and Successors, charge and comand all and singular Admirals, Vice-Admirals, Generals, Commanders, Captaines, Justices of Peace, Majors,

Sheriffs, Bailiffs Constables, Customers, Comptrollers, Waiters, Searchers, and all the Officers of Us, our Heires and Successors, whatsoever to be from time to time, and att all times heereafter, in all Things aiding, helping, and assisting unto the said Councill, and their Successors, and unto every of them, upon Request and Requests by them to be made, in all Matters and Things, for the furtherance and Accomplishment of all or any the Matters and Things by Us, in and by these our Letters-pattents, given, granted, and provided, or by Us meant or intended to be given, granted, and provided, as they our said Officers, and the Officers of Us, our Heires and Successors, do tender our Pleasure, and will avoid the contrary att their Perills. And Wee also do by these Presents, ratifye and confirm unto the said Councill and their Successors, all Priveliges, Franchises, Liberties, Immunities granted in our said former Letters-patents, and not in these our Letters-patents revoked, altered, changed or abridged, altho' Expressed, Mentioned, &c.

In Witness, &c.

Witnes our selfe at Westminster, the Third Day of November, in the Eighteenth Yeare of our Reign over England, &c.

Par Breve de Privato Sigillo, &c.

First Charter of Massachusetts

King Charles I

First Charter of Massachusetts
March 4, 1629

CHARLES, BY THE, GRACE, OF GOD, Kinge of England, Scotland, Fraunce, and Ireland, Defendor of the Fayth, &c. To all to whome theis Presents shall come Greeting. WHEREAS, our most Deare and Royall Father, Kinge James, of blessed Memory, by his Highnes Letters-patents bearing Date at Westminster the third Day of November, in the eighteenth Yeare of His Raigne, HATH given and graunted vnto the Councell established at Plymouth, in the County of Devon, for the planting, ruling, ordering, and governing of Newe England in America, and to their Successors and Assignes for ever. all that Parte of America, lyeing and being in Bredth, from Forty Degrees of Northerly Latitude from the Equinoctiall Lyne, to forty eight Degrees Of the saide Northerly Latitude inclusively, and in Length, of and within all the Breadth aforesaid, throughout the Maine Landes from Sea to Sea; together also with all the Firme Landes, Soyles, Groundes, Havens, Portes, Rivers, Waters, Fishing, Mynes, anal Myneralls, as well Royall Mynes of Gould and Silver, as other Mynes ind Mvneralls, precious Stones, Quarries, and all and singular other Comodities, Jurisdiccons, Royalties, Priviledges, Franchesies, and Prehemynences, both within the said Tract of Land vpon the Mayne, and also within the Islandes and Seas adjoining: PROVIDED alwayes, That the saide Islandes, or any the Premisses by the said Letters-patents intended and meant to be graunted, were not then actuallie possessed or inhabited, by any other Christian Prince or State, nor within the Boundes, Lymitts, or Territories of the Southerne Colony, then before graunted by our saide Deare Father, to be planted by divers of his loveing Subiects in the South Partes. TO HAVE and to houlde, possess, and enjoy all and singular the aforesaid Continent, Landes Territories, Islandes, Hereditaments, and Precincts, Seas, Waters, Fishings, with all, and all manner their Comodities, Royalties, Liberties, Prehemynences, and Proffits that should from thenceforth arise from thence, with all and.singuler their Appurtenances, and every Parte and Parcell thereof, vnto the saide Councell and their Successors and Assignes for ever, to the sole and proper Vse, Benefitt, and Behoofe of them the saide Councell, and their Successors and Asignes for ever: To be houlden of our saide most Deare and Royall Father, his Heires and Successors, as of his Mannor of East Greenewich in the County of Kent, in free and comon Soccage, and not in Capite nor by Knight's Service: YEILDINGE and paying therefore to the saide late Kinge, his heires and Successors, the fifte Parte of the Oare of Gould and Silver, which should from tyme to tyme, and at all Tymes then after happen to be found, gotten, had, and obteyned in, att, or within any of the saide Landes, Lymitts, Territories, and Precincts, or in or within any Parte or Parcell thereof, for or in Respect of all and all Manner of Duties, Demaunds anr Services whatsoever, to be don, made, or paide to our saide Dear Father the late Kinge his Heires and Successors, as in and by the saide Letters-patents (amongst sundrie and other Clauses, Powers, Priviledges, and Grauntes therein conteyned), more at large appeareth:

AND WHEREAS, the saide Councell established at Plymouth, in the County of Devon, for the plantinge, ruling, ordering, and governing of Newe England in America, have by their Deede, indented vnder their Comon Seale, bearing Date the nyneteenth Day of March last past, in the third Yeare of our Raigne, given, graunted, bargained, soulde, enfeofled, aliened, and confirmed to Sir Henry Rosewell, Sir John Young, Knightes, Thomas Southcott, John Humphrey, John Endecott, and Symon Whetcombe, their Heires and Assignes, and their Associats for ever, all that Parte of Newe England in America aforesaid, which lyes and extendes betweene a greate River there comonlie called Monomack alias Merriemack, and a certen other River there, called Charles River, being in the Bottome of a certayne Bay there, comonlie called Massachusetts, alias Mattachusetts, alias Massatusetts Bay, and also all and singuler those Landes and Hereditaments whatsoever, lyeing within the Space of three English Myles on the South Parte of the said Charles River, or of any, or everie Parte thereof; and also, all and singuler the Landes and Hereditaments whatsoever, lyeing and being within the Space of three English Myles to the Southward of the Southermost Parte of the saide Bay called Massachusetts, alias Mattachusetts, alias Massatusets Bay; and also, all those Landes and Hereditaments whatsoever, which lye, and be within the space of three English Myles to the Northward of the said River called Monomack, alias Merrymack, or to the Northward of any and every Parte thereof, and all Landes and Hereditaments whatsoever, lyeing within the Lymitts aforesaide, North and South in Latitude and breath, and in Length and Longitude, of and within all the Bredth aforesaide, throughout the Mayne Landes there, from the Atlantick and Westerne Sea and Ocean on the East Parte, to the South Sea on the West Parte; and all Landes and Groundes, Place and Places, Soyles, Woodes and Wood Groundes, Havens, Portes, Rivers, Waters, Fishings, and Hereditaments whatsoever, lyeing within the said Boundes and Lymitts, and everie Parte and Parcell thereof; and also, all Islandes lyeing in America aforesaide, in the saide Seas or either of them on the Westerne or Eastern Coastes or Partes of the said Tractes of Lande, by the saide Indenture mencoed to be given, graunted, bargained, sould, enfeofled, aliened, and confirmed, or any of them; and also, all Mynes and Myneralls, as well Royall Mynes of Gould and Silver, as other Mynes and Myneralls whatsoeuer, in the saide Lands and Premisses, or any Parte thereof; and all Jurisdiccons, Rights, Royalties, Liberties, Freedomes, Ymmunities, Priviledges, Franchises, Preheminences, and Comodities whatsoever, which they, the said Councell established at Plymouth, in the County of Devon, for the planting, ruling, ordering, and governing of Newe England in America, then had, or might vse, exercise, or enjoy, in or within the saide Landes and Premisses by the saide Indenture mencoed to be given, graunted, bargained, sould, enfeoffed, and confirmed, or in or within any Parte or Parcell thereof:

To HAVE and to hould, the saide Parte of Newe England in America, which lyes and extendes and is abutted as aforesaide, and every Parte and Parcell thereof; and all the saide Islandes, Rivers, Portes, Havens, Waters, Fishings, Mynes, and Myneralls, Jurisdiccons, Franchises, Royalties, Liberties, Priviledges, Comodities, Hereditaments, and Premisses whatsoever, with the Appurtenances vnto the saide Sir Henry Rosewell, Sir John Younge, Thomas Southcott, John Humfrey, John Endecott, and Simon Whetcombe, their Heires and Assignes, and their Associatts, to the onlie proper and absolute vse and Behoofe of the said Sir Henry Rosawell, Sir John Younge, Thomas Southcott, John Humfrey, John Endecott, and Simon Whettcombe, their Heires and Assignes, and their Associatts forevermore; TO BE HOULDEN of Vs. our Heires and Successors, as of our Mannor of Eastgreenwich, in the County of Kent, in free and comon Soccage, and not in Capite, nor by Knightes Service; YEILDING and payeing therefore vnto Vs. our Heires and Successors, the fifte Parte of the Oare of Goulde and Silver, which shall from Tyme to Tyme, and at all Tymes hereafter, happen to be founde, gotten, had, and obteyned in any of the saide Landes, within the saide Lymitts, or in or witllin any Parte thereof, for, and in Satisfaccon of all manner Duties, Demaundes, and Services whatsoever to be done, made, or paid to Vs. our Heires or Successors, as in and by the said recited Indenture more at large maie appeare.

NOWE Knowe Yee, that Wee, at the humble Suite and Peticon of the saide Sir Henry Rosewell, Sir John Younge, Thomas Southcott, John Humfrey, John Endecott, and Simon Whetcombe, and of others whome they have associated vnto them, HAVE, for divers good Causes and consideracons, vs moveing, graunted and confirmed, and by theis Presents of our especiall Grace, certen Knowledge, and meere mocon, doe graunt and confirme vnto the saide Sir Henry Rosewell, Sir John Younge, Thomas Southcott, John Humfrey, John Endecott, and Simon

Whetcombe, and to their Associatts hereafter named; (videlicet) Sir Richard Saltonstall, Knight, Isaack Johnson, Samuel Aldersey, John Ven, Mathew Cradock, George Harwood, Increase Nowell, Richard Perry, Richard Bellingham, Nathaniell Wright, Samuel Vassall, Theophilus Eaton, Thomas Goffe, Thomas Adams, John Browne, Samuell Browne, Thomas Hutchins, William Vassall, William Pinchion, and George Foxcrofte, their Heires and Assignes, all the saide Parte of Newe England in America, lyeing and extending betweene the Boundes and Lvmytts in the said recited Indenture expressed, and all Landes and Groundes, Place and Places, Soyles, Woods and Wood Groundes, Havens, Portes, Rivers, Waters, Mynes, Mineralls, Jurisdiccons, Rightes, Royalties, Liberties, Freedomes, Immunities, Priviledges, Franchises, Preheminences, Hereditaments, and Comodities whatsoever, to them the saide Sir Henry Rosewell, Sir John Younge, Thomas Southcott, John Humfrey, John Endecott, and Simon Whetcombe, theire Heires and Assignes, and to their Associatts, by the saide recited Indenture, given, graunted, bargayned, solde, enfeoffed, aliened, and confirmed, or mencoed or intended thereby to be given, graunted, bargayned, sold, enfeoffed, aliened, anal confirmed: To HAVE, and to hould, the saide Parte of Newe England in America, and other the Premisses hereby mencoed to be graunted and confirmed, and every Parte and Parcell thereof with the Appurtenuces, to the saide Sir Henry Rosewell, Sir John Younge, Sir Richard Saltonstall, Thomas southcott, John Humfrey, John Endecott, Simon Whetcombe, Isaack Johnson, Richard Pery, Richard Bellingham, Nathaniell Wright, Samuell Vassall, Theophilus Eaton, Thomas Gode, Thomas Adams, John Browne, Samuel Bromine, Thomas Hutchins, Samuel Aldersey, John Ven, Mathewe Cradock, George Harwood, Increase Nowell, William Vassall, William Pinchion, and George Foxcrofte, their Heires and Assignes forever, to their onlie proper and absolute Vse and Behoofe for evermore; To be holden of Vs. our Heires and Successors, as of our Mannor of Eastgreenewich aforesaid, in free and comon Socage, and not in Capite, nor by Knights Service; AND ALSO YEILDING and paying therefore to Vs. our Heires and Successors, the fifte parte onlie of all Oare of Gould and Silver, which from tyme to tyme, and aft all tymes hereafter shalbe there gotten, had, or obteyned for all Services, Exaccons and Demaundes whatsoever, according to the Tenure and Reservacon in the said recited Indenture expressed.

AND FURTHER, knowe yee, that of our more especiall Grace, certen Knowledg, and meere mocon, Wee have given and graunted, and by theis Presents, doe for Vs. our Heires and Successors, give and graunte onto the saide Sir Henry Rosewell, Sir John Younge. Sir Richard

Saltonstall, Thomas Southcott, John Humfrey, John Endecott, Symon Whetcombe, Isaack Johnson, Samuell Aldersey, John Ven, Mathewe Cradock, George Harwood, Increase Nowell, Richard Pery, Richard Bellingham, Nathaniel Wright, Samuell Vassall, Theophilus Eaton, Thomas Gode, Thomas Adams, John Browne, Samuell Browne, Thomas Hutchins, William Vassall, William Pinchion, and George Foxcrofte, their Heires and Assignes, all that Parte of Newe England in America, which lyes and extendes betweene a great River there, comonlie called Monomack River, alias Merrimack River, and a certen other River there, called Charles River, being in the Bottome of a certen Bay there, comonlie called Massachusetts, alias Mattachusetts, alias Massatusetts Bay; and also all and singuler those Landes and Hereditaments whatsoever, lying within the Space of Three Englishe Myles on the South Parte of the said River, called Charles River, or of any or every Parte thereof; and also all and singuler the Landes and Hereditaments whatsoever, lying and being within the Space of Three Englishe Miles to the southward of the southermost Parte of the said Baye, called Massachusetts, alias Mattachusetts, alias Massatusets Bay: And also all those Landes and Hereditaments whatsoever, which lye and be within the Space of Three English Myles to the Northward of the saide River, called Monomack, alias Merrymack, or to the Norward of any and every Parte thereof, and all Landes and Hereditaments whatsoever, lyeing within the Lymitts aforesaide, North and South, in Latitude and Bredth, and in Length and Longitude, of and within all the Bredth aforesaide, throughout the mayne Landes there, from the Atlantick and Westerne Sea and Ocean on the East Parte, to the South Sea on the West Parte; and all Landes and Groundes, Place and Places, Soyles, Woodes, and Wood Groundes, Havens, Portes, Rivers, Waters, and Hereditaments whatsoever, lyeing within the said Boundes and Lymytts, and every Parte and Parcell thereof; and also all Islandes in America aforesaide, in the saide Seas, or either of them, on the Westerne or Easterne Coastes, or Partes of the saide Tracts of Landes hereby mencoed to be given and graunted, or any of them; and all Mynes and Mynerals as well Royal mynes of Gold and Silver and other mynes and mynerals, whatsoever, in the said Landes and Premisses, or any parte thereof, and free Libertie of fishing in or within any the Rivers or Waters within the Boundes and Lymytts aforesaid, and the Seas therevnto adjoining; and all Fishes, Royal Fishes, Whales, Balan, Sturgions, and other Fishes of what Kinde or Nature soever, that shall at any time hereafter be taken in or within the saide Seas or Waters, or any of them, by the said Sir Henry Rosewell, Sir John Younge, Sir Richard Saltonstall, Thomas Southcott, John Humfrey, John Endecott, Simon Whetcombe, Isaack Johnson, Samuell Aldersey, John Ven, Mathewe Cradock, Greorge Harwood,

Increase Noell, Richard Pery, Richard Bellingham, Nathaniell Wright, Samuell Vassell, Theophilus Eaton, Thomas Goffe, Thomas Adams, John Browne, Samuell Browner, Thomas Hutchins, William Vassall, William Pinchion, and George Foxcrofte, their Heires and Assignes, or by any other person or persons whatsoever there inhabiting, by them, or any of them, to be appointed to fishe therein.

PROVIDED alwayes, That yf the said Landes, Islandes, or any other the Prernisses herein before menconed, and by theis presents, intended and meant to be graunted, were at the tyme of the graunting of the saide former Letters patents, dated the Third Day of November, in the Eighteenth Yeare of our said deare Fathers Raigne aforesaide, actuallie possessed or inhabited by any other Christian Prince or State, or were within the Boundes, Lymytts or Territories of that Southerne Colony, then before graunted by our said late Father, to be planted by divers of his loveing Subiects in the south partes of America, That then this present Graunt shall not extend to any such partes or parcells thereof, soe formerly inhabited, or lyeing within the Boundes of the Southerne Plantacon as aforesaide, but as to those partes or parcells soe possessed or inhabited by such Christian Prince or State, or being within the Bounders aforesaide shal be vtterlie voyd, theis presents or any Thinge therein conteyned to the contrarie notwithstanding. To HAVE and hould, possesse and enioye the saide partes of New England in America, which lye, extend, and are abutted as aforesaide,and every parse and parcell thereof; and all the Islandes, Rivers, Portes, Havens, Waters, Fishings, Fishes, Mynes, Myneralls, Jurisdiccons, Franchises, Royalties, Liberties, Priviledges, Comodities, and Premisses whatsoever, with the Appurtenances, vnto the said Sir Henry Rosewell, Sir John Younge, Sir Richard Saltonstall, Thomas Southcott, John Humfrey, John Endecott, Simon Whetcombe, Isaack Johnson, Samuell Aldersey, John yen, Mathewe Cradock, George Harwood, Increase Noweil, Richard Perry, Richard Bellingham, Nathaniell Wright, Samuell Vassall, Theophilus Eaton, Thomas Gofle, Thomas Adams, John Browne, Samuell Browne, Thomas Hutchins, William Vassall, William Pinchion, and George Foxeroft, their Heires and Assignes forever, to the onlie proper and absolute Vse and Behoufe of the said Sir Henry Rosewell, Sir John Younge, Sir Richard Saltonstall, Thomas Southcott, John Humfrey, John Endecott, Simon Whetcombe, Isaac Johnson, Samuell Aldersey, John Ven, Mathewe Cradocke, George Harwood, Increase Noweil, Richard Pery, Richard Bellingham, Nathaniell Wright, Samuell Vassall, Theophilus Eaton, Thomas Goffe, Thomas Adams, John Browne, Samuell Browne, Thomas Hutchins, William Vassall, William Pinchion, and George Foxcroft, their Heires and Assignes forevermore: To BE

HOLDEN of Vs. our Heires and Successors, as of our Manor of Eastgreenwich in ouF Countie of Kent, within our Realme of England, in free and comon Soccage, and not in Capite, nor by Knights Service; and also yeilding and paying therefore, to Vs. our Heires and Sucessors, the fifte Parte onlie of all Oare of Gould and Silver, which from tyme to tyme, and at all tymes hereafter, shal be there gotten, had, or obteyned, for all Services, Exaccons, and Demaundes whatsoever; PROVIDED alwaies, and our expresse Will and Meaninge is, that onlie one fifte Parte of the Gould and Silver Oare above mencoed, in the whole, and noe more be reserved or payeable vnto Vs. our Heires and Successors, by Collour or Vertue of theis Presents, the double Reservacons or rentals aforesaid or any Thing herein conteyned notwithstanding. AND FORASMUCH, as the good and prosperous Successe of the Plantacon of the saide Partes of Newe-England aforesaide intended by the said Sir Henry Rosewell, Sir John Younge, Sir Richard Saltonstall, Thomas Southcott, John Humfrey, John Endecott, Simon Whetcombe, Isaack Johnson, Samuell Aldersey John Ven, Mathew Cradock, George Harwood, Increase Noell, Richard Pery, Richard Bellingham, Nathaniell Wright, Samuell Vassall, Theophilus Eaton, Thomas Goffe, Thomas Adams, John Browne, Samuell Browne, Thomas Hutchins, William Vassall, William Pinchion, and George Foxcrofte, to be speedily sett vpon, cannot but cheifly depend, next vnder the Blessing of Almightie God, and the support of our Royall Authoritie vpon the good Government of the same, To the Ende that the Affaires and Buyssinesses which from tyme to tyme shall happen and arise concerning the saide Landes, and the Plantation of the same maie be the better mannaged and ordered, WEE HAVE FURTHER hereby of our especial Grace, certain Knowledge and mere Mocon, Given, graunted and confirmed, and for Vs. our Heires and Successors, doe give, graunt, and confirme vnto our said trustie and welbeloved subjects Sir Henry Rosewell, Sir John Younge, Sir Richard Saltonstall, Thomas Southcott, John Humfrey, John Endicott, Simon Whetcombe, Isaack Johnson, Samuell Aldersey, John yen, Mathewe Cradock, George Harwood, Increase Nowell, Richard Pery, Richard Bellingham, Nathaniell Wright, Samuell Vassall, Theophilus Eaton, Thomas Goffe, Thomas Adams, John Browne, Samuell Browne, Thomas Hutchins, William Vassall, William Pinchion, and George Foxcrofte: AND for Vs. our Heires and Successors, Wee will and ordeyne, That the saide Sir Henry Rosewell, Sir John Young, Sir Richard Saltonstall, Thomas Southcott, John Humfrey, John Endicott, Svmon Whetcombe, Isaack Johnson, Samuell Aldersey, John Ven, Mathewe Cradock, George Harwood, Increase Noell, Richard Pery, Richard Bellingham, Nathaniell Wright, Samuell Vassall, Theophilus Eaton, Thomas Goffe, Thomas Adams, John Browne, Samuell Browne,

Thomas Hutchins, William Vassall, William Pinchion, and George Foxcrofte, and all such others as shall hereafter be admitted and made free of the Company and Society hereafter mencoed, shall from tyme to tyme, and att all tymes forever hereafter be, by Vertue of theis presents, one Body corporate and politique in Fact and Name, by the Name of the Governor and Company of the Mattachusetts Bay in Newe-England, and them by the Name of the Governour and Company of the Mattachusetts Bay in Newe-England, one Bodie politique and corporate, in Deede, Fact, and Name; Wee doe for vs. our Heires and Successors, make, ordoyne, constitute, and confirme by theis Presents, and that by that name they shall have perpetuall Succession, and that by the same Name they and their Successors shall and maie be capeable and enabled aswell to implead, and to be impleaded, and to prosecute, demaund, and aunswere, and be aunsweared veto, in all and singuler Suites, Causes, Quarrells, and Accons, of what kinde or nature soever. And also to have, take, possesse, acquire, and purchase any Landes, Tenements, or Hereditaments, or any Goodes or Chattells, and the same to lease, graunte, demise, alien, bargaine, sell, and dispose of, as other our liege People of this our Realme of England, or any other corporacon or Body politique of the same may lawfully doe.

AND FURTHER, That the said Governour and Companye, and their Successors, maie have forever one comon Seale, to be vsed in all Causes and Occasions of the said Company, and the same Seale may alter, chaunge, breake, and newe make, from tyme to tyme, at their pleasures. And our Will and Pleasure is, and Wee doe hereby for Vs. our Heires and Successors, ordeyne and graunte, That from henceforth for ever, there shalbe one Governor, one Deputy Governor, and eighteene Assistants of the same Company, to be from tyme to tyme constituted, elected and chosen out of the Freemen of the saide Company, for the tyme being, in such Manner and Forme as hereafter in theis Presents is expressed, which said Officers shall applie themselves to take Care for the best disposeing and ordering of the generall buysines and Affaires of, for, and concerning the said Landes and Premisses hereby mencoed, to be graunted, and the Plantacion thereof, and the Government of the People there. AND FOR the better Execucon of our Royall Pleasure and Graunte in this Behalf, WEE doe, by theis presents, for Vs. our Heires and Successors, nominate, ordeyne, make, & constitute; our welbeloved the saide Mathewe Cradocke, to be the first and present Governor of the said Company, and the saide Thomas Goffe, to be Deputy Governor of the saide Company, and the saide Sir Richard Saltonstall, Isaack Johnson, Samuell Aldersey, John Ven, John Humfrey, John Endecott, Simon Whetcombe, Increase Nowell, Richard Pery, Nathaniell Wright,

Samuell Vassall, Theophilus Eaton, Thomas Adams, Thomas Hutchins, John Browne, George Foxcrofte, William Vassall, and William Pinchion, to be the present Assistants of the saide Company, to continue in the saide several Offices respectivelie for such tyme, and in such manner, as in and by theis Presents is hereafter declared and appointed.

AND FURTHER, Wee will, and by theis Presents, for Vs. our Heires and Successors, doe ordoyne and graunte, That the Governor of the saide Company for the tyme being, or in his Absence by Occasion of Sicknes or otherwise, the Deputie Governor for the tyme being, shall have Authoritie from tyme to tyme vpon all Occasions, to give order for the assembling of the saide Company, and calling them together to consult and advise of the Bussinesses and Affaires of the saide Company, and that the said Governor, Deputie Governor, and Assistants of the saide Company, for the tyme being, shall or maie once every Moneth, or oftener at their Pleasures, assemble and houlde and keepe a Courte or Assemblie of themselves, for the better ordering and directing of their Affaires, and that any seaven or more persons of the Assistants, togither with the Governor, or Deputie Governor soe assembled, shalbe saide, taken, held, and reputed to be, and shalbe a full and sufficient Courte or Assemblie of the said Company, for the handling, ordering, and dispatching of all such Buysinesses and Occurrents as shall from tyme to tyme happen, touching or concerning the said Company or Plantacon; and that there shall or maie be held and kept by the Governor, or Deputie Governor of the said Company, and seaven or more of the said Assistants for the tyme being, vpon every last Wednesday in Hillary, Easter, Trinity, and Michas Termes respectivelie forever, one grease generall and solempe assemblie, which foure generall assemblies shalbe stiled and called the foure grease and generall Courts of the saide Company; IN all and every, or any of which saide grease and generall Courts soe assembled, WEE DOE for Vs. our Heires and Successors, give and graunte to the said Governor and Company, and their Successors, That the Governor, or in his absence, the Deputie Governor of the saide Company for the tyme being, and such of the Assistants and Freeman of the saide Company as shalbe present, or the greater nomber of them so assembled, whereof the Governor or Deputie Governor and six of the Assistants at the least to be seaven shall have full Power and authoritie to choose, nominate, and appointe, such and soe many others as they shall thinke fitt, and that shall be willing to accept the same, to be free of the said Company and Body, and them into the same to admits; and to elect and constitute such Officers as they shall thinke fitt and requisite, for the ordering, mannaging, and dispatching of the Affaires of the saide Govenor and

Company, and their Successors; And to make Lawes and Ordinnces for the Good and Welfare of the saide Company, and for the Government and ordering of the saide Landes and Plantacon, and the People inhabiting and to inhabite the same, as to them from tyme to tyme shalbe thought meete, soe as such Lawes and Ordinances be not contrarie or repugnant to the Lawes and Statuts of this our Reaime of England. AND, our Will and Pleasure is, and Wee doe hereby for Vs, our Heires and Successors, establish and ordeyne, That yearely once in the yeare, for ever hereafter, namely, the last Wednesdav in Easter Tearme, yearely, the Governor, Deputy-Governor, and Assistants of the saide Company and all other officers of the saide Company shalbe in the Generall Court or Assembly to be held for that Day or Tyme, newly chosen for the Yeare ensueing by such greater parse of the said Company, for the Tyme being, then and there present, as is aforesaide. AND, yf it shall happen the present governor, Deputy Governor, and assistants, by theis presents appointed, or such as shall hereafter be newly chosen into their Roomes, or any of them, or any other of the officers to be appointed for the said Companv, to dye, or to be removed from his or their severall Offices or Places before the saide generall Day of Eleccon (whome Wee doe hereby declare for any Misdemeanor or Defect to be removeable by the Governor, Deputie Governor, Assistants, and Company, or such greater Parte of them in any of the publique Courts to be assembled as is aforesaid) That then, and in every such Case, it shall and male be lawfull, to and for the Governor, Deputie Governor, Assistants, and Company aforesaide, or such greater Parte of them soe to be assembled as is aforesaide, in any of their Assemblies, to proceade to a new Eleccon of one or more others of their Company in the Roome or Place, Roomes or Places of such Officer or Officers soe dyeing or removed according to their Discrecons, And, Mediately vpon and after such Eleccon and Eleccons made of such Governor, Deputie Governor, Assistant or Assistants, or any other officer of the saide Company, in Manner and Forme aforesaid, the Authoritie, Office, and Power, before given to the former Governor, Deputie Governor, or other Officer and Officers soe removed, in whose Steade and Place newe shabe soe chosen, shall as to him and them, and everie of them, cease and determine

PROVIDED alsoe, and our Will and Pleasure is, That aswell such as are by theis Presents appointed to be the present Governor, Deputie Governor, and Assistants of the said Company, as those that shall Succeed them, and all other Officers to be appointed and chosen as aforesaid, shall, before they undertake the Execucon of their saide Offices and Places respectivelie, take their Corporal Oathes for the due and faithfull Performance of their Duties in their severall Offices and Places, before such Person or Persons as are bv theis Presents hereunder appointed to take and receive the same; That is to sale, the saide Mathewe Cradock, whoe is hereby nominated and appointed the present Governor of the saide Company, shall take the saide Oathes before one or more of the Masters of our Courte of Chauncery for the Tyme being, vnto which Master or Masters of the Chauncery, Wee doe by theis Presents give full Power and Authoritie to take and administer the said Oathe to the said Governor accordinglie: And after the saide Governor shalbe soe sworne, then the said Deputy Governor and Assistants, before by theis Presents nominated and appointed, shall take the said severall Oathes to their Offices and Places respectivelie belonging, before the said Mathew Cradock, the present Governor, soe formerlie sworne as aforesaide. And every such person as shallbe at the Tvme of the annuall Eleccon, or otherwise, vpon Death or Removeall, be appointed to be the newe Governor of the said Company, shall take the Oathes to that Place belonging, before the Deputy Governor, or two of the Assistants of the said Company at the least, for the Tyme being: And the newe elected Deputie Governor and Assistants, and all other officers to be hereafter chosen as aforesaide from Tyme to Tyme, to take the Oathes to their places respectivelie belonging, before the Governor of the said Company for the Tyme being, vnto which said Governor, Deputie Governor, and assistants, Wee doe by theis Presents Dive full Power and Authoritie to give and administer the said Oathes respectively, according to our true Meaning herein before declared, without any Comission or further Warrant to be had and obteyned of our Vs. our Heires or Successors, in that Behalf. AND, Wee doe further, of our especial Grace, certen Knowledge, and meere mocon, for Vs. our Heires and Successors, give and graunte to the said Governor and Company, and their Successors for ever by theis Presents, That it shalbe lawfull and free for them and their Assignes, at all and every Tyme and Tymes hereafter, out of any our Realmes or Domynions whatsoever, to take, leade, carry, and transport, for in and into their Voyages, and for and towardes the said Plantacon in Newe England, all such and soe many of our loving Subjects, or any other strangers that will become our loving Subjects, and live under our Allegiance, as shall willinglie accompany them in the same Voyages and Plantacon; and also Shippmg, Armour, Weapons, Ordinance, Municon, Powder, Shott, Come, Victualls, and all Manner of Clothing, Implements, Furniture, Beastes, Cattle, Horses, Mares, Merchandizes, and all other Thinges necessarie for the saide Plantacon, and for their Vse and Defence, and for Trade with the People there, and in passing and returning to and fro, any Lawe or Statute to the contrarie hereof in any wise notwithstanding;

and without payeing or yeilding any Custome or Subsidie, either inward
or outward, to Vs. our Heires or Successors, for the same, by the Space
of seaven Yeares from the Day of the Date of theis Presents. PROVIDED,
that none of the saide Persons be such as shalbe hereafter by especiall
Name restrayned by Vs. our Heires or Successors. AND, for their further
Encouragement, of our especiall Grace and Favor, Wee doe by theis
Presents, for Vs. our Heires and Successors, yeild and graunt to the
saide Governor and Company, and their Successors, and every of them,
their Factors and Assignes, That they and every of them shalbe free and
quits from all Taxes, Subsidies, and Customes, in Newe England, for the
like Space of seaven Yeares, and from all Taxes and Imposicons for the
Space of twenty and one Yeares, vpon all Goodes and Merchandizes at
any Tyme or Tymes hereafter, either vpon Importacon thither, or
Exportacon from thence into our Realme of England, or into any other
our Domynions by the said Governor and Company, and their
Successors, their Deputies, Factors, and Assignes, or any of them;
EXCEPT onlie the five Pounds per Centum due for Custome vpon all
such Goodes and Merchandizes as after the saide seaven Yeares shalbe
expired, shalbe brought or imported into our Realme of England, or any
other of our Dominions, according to the auncient Trade of Merchants,
which five Poundes per Centum onlie being paide, it shall be
thenceforth lawfull and free for the said Adventurers, the same Goodes
and Merchandizes to export and carry out of our said Domynions into
forraine Partes, without any Custome, Tax or other Dutie to be paid to
Vs. our Heires or Successors, or to any other Officers or Ministers of Vs.
our Heires and Successors. PROVIDED, that the said Goodes and
Merchandizes be shipped out within thirteene Monethes, after their
first Landing within any Parte of the saide Domynions.

AND, Wee doe for Vs. our Heires and Successors, give and graunte vnto
the saide Governor and Company, and their Successors, That
whensoever, or soe often as any Custome or Subsedie shall growe due
or payeable vnto Vs our Heires, or Successors, according to the
Lymittacon and Appointment aforesaide, by Reason of any Goodes,
Wares, or Merchandizes to be shipped out, or any Retorne to be made
of any Goodes, Wares, or Merchandize vnto or from the said Partes of
Newe England hereby moncoed to be graunted as aforesaid, or any the
Landes or Territories aforesaide, That then, and soe often, and in such
Case, the Farmors, Customers, and Officers of our Customes of England
and Ireland, and everie of them for the Tyme being, vpon Request made
to them by the saide Governor and Company, or their Successors,
Factors. or Assignes, and vpon convenient Security to be given in that
Behalf, shall give and allowe vnto the said Governor and Company, and

their Successors, and to all and everie Person and Persons free of that Company, as aforesaide, six Monethes Tyme for the Payement of the one halfe of all such Custome and Subsidy as shalbe due and payeable unto Vs. our Heires and Successors, for the same; for which theis our Letters patent, or the Duplicate, or the inrollemt thereof, shalbe vnto our saide Officers a sufficient Warrant and Discharge. NEVERTHELESS, our Will and Pleasure is, That yf any of the saide Goodes, Wares, and Merchandize, which be, or shalbe at any Tyme hereafter landed or exported out of any of our Realmes aforesaide, and shalbe shipped with a Purpose not to be carried to the Partes of Newe England aforesaide, but to some other place, That then such Payment, Dutie, Custome, Imposicon, or Forfeyfure, shalbe paid, or belonge to Vs. our Heires and Successors, for the said Goodes, Wares, and Merchandize, soe fraudulently sought to be transported, as yf tllis our Graunte had not been made nor graunted. AND, Wee doe further will, and by theis Presents, for Vs. our Heires and Successors, firmlie enioine and comaunde, as well the Treasorer, Chauncellor and Barons of the Exchequer, of Vs. our Heires and Successors, as also all and singuler the Customers, Farmors, and Collectors of the Customes, Subsidies, and Imposts' and other the Officers and Ministers of Vs our Heires and Successors whatsoever, for the Tyme Being, That they and every of them, vpon the strewing forth vnto them of theis Letters patents, or the Duplicate or exemplificacon of the same, without any other Writt or Warrant vvhatsoever from Vs. our Heires or Successors, to be obteyned or sued forth, doe and shall make full, whole, entire, and due Allowance, and cleare Discharge vnto the saide Governor and Company, and their Successors, of all Customes, Subsidies, Imposicons, Taxes and Duties whatsoever, that shall or maie be claymed by Vs. our Heires and Successors, of or from the said Governor and Company, and their Successors, for or by Reason of the said Goodes, Chattels, Wares, Merchandizes, and Premises to be exported out of our saide Domynions, or any of them, into any Parte of the saide Landes or Premises hereby mencoed, to be given, graunted, and confirmed, or for, or by Reason of any of the saide Goodes, Chattells, Wares, or Merchandizes to be imported from the said Landes and Premises hereby mencoed, to be given, graunted, and confirmed into any of our saide Dominions, or any Parte thereof as aforesaide, excepting onlie the saide five Poundes per Centum hereby reserved and payeable after the Expiracon of the saide Terme of seaven Yeares as aforesaid, and not before: And theis our Letters-patents, or the Inrollment, Duplicate, or Exemplificacon of the same shalbe for ever hereafter, from time to tyme, as well to the Treasorer, Chauncellor and Barons of the Exchequer of Vs. our Heires and Successors, as to all and singuler the

Customers, Farmors, and Collectors of the Customes, Subsidies, and Imposts of Vs. our Heires and Successors, and all Searchers, and other the Officers and Ministers whatsoever of Vs. our Heires and Successors, for the Time being, a sufficient Warrant and Discharge in this Behalf.

AND, further our Will and Pleasure is, and Wee doe hereby for Vs' bur Heires and Successors, ordeyne and declare, and graunte to the saide Governor and Company, and their Successors, That all and every the Subiects of Vs. our Heires or Successors, which shall goe to and inhabite within the saide Landes and Premisses hereby mencoed to be graunted, and every of their Children which shall happen to be borne there, or on the Seas in goeing thither, or returning from thence, shall have and enjoy all liberties and Immunities of free and naturall Subiects within any of the Domynions of Vs. our Heires or Successors, to all Intents, Construccons, and Purposes whatsoever, as yf they and everie of them were borne within the Realme of England. And that the Governor and Deputie Governor of the said Company for the Tyme being, or either of them, and any two or more of such of the saide Assistants as shalbe therevnto appointed by the saide Governor and Companv at any of their Courts or Assemblies to be held as aforesaide. shall and male at all Tymes, and from tyme to tyme hereafter, have full Power and Authoritie to minister and give the Oathe and Oathes of Supremacie and Allegiance, or either of them, to all and everie Person and Persons, which shall at any Tyme or Tymes hereafter goe or passe to the Landes and Premisses hereby mencoed to be graunted to inhabite in the same. AND, Wee doe of our further Grace, certen Knowledg and meere Mocon, give and graunte to the saide Governor and Companv, and their Successors, That it shall and male be lawfull, to and for the Governor or Deputie Governor, and such of the Assistants and Freemen of the said Company for the Tyme being as shalbe assembled in any of their generall Courts aforesaide, or in any other Courtes to be specially sumoned and assembled for that Purpose, or the greater Parte of them (whereof the Governor or Deputie Governor, and six of the Assistants to be alwaies seaven) from tyme to tome, to make, ordeine, and establishe all Manner of wholesome and reasonable Orders, Lawes, Statutes, and Ordilmces, Direccons, and Instruccons, not contrairie to the Lawes of this our Realme of England, aswell for selling of the Formes and Ceremonies of Governmt and Magistracy fitt and necessary for the said Plantacon, find the Inhabitants there, and for nameing and setting of all sorts of Officers, both superior and inferior, which they shall finde needefull for that Governement and Plantacon, and the distinguishing and setting forth of the severall duties, Powers, and Lymytts of every such Office and Place, and the Formes of such Oathes warrantable by the Lawes and Statutes of this our Realme of England, as shalbe respectivelie ministred vnto them for the Execucon of the said severall Offices and Places; as also, for the disposing and ordering of the Eleccons of such of the said Officers as shalbe annuall, and of such others as shalbe to succeede in Case of Death or Remove all and ministering the said Oathes to the newe elected Officers, and for Imposicons of lawfull Fynes, Mulcts, Imprisonment, or other lawfull Correccon, according to the Course of other Corporacons in this our Realme of England, and for the directing, ruling, and disposeing of all other Matters and Thinges, whereby our said People, Inhabitants there, may be soe religiously, peaceablie, and civilly governed, as their good Life and orderlie Conversacon, male wynn and incite the Natives of Country, to the Knowledg and Obedience of the onlie true God and Saulor of Mankinde, and the Christian Fayth, which in our Royall Intencon, and the Adventurers free Profession, is the principall Ende of this Plantacion. WILLING, comaunding, and requiring, and by theis Presents for Vs. our Heiress Successors, ordoyning and appointing, that all such Orders, Lawes, Statuts and Ordinnces, Instruccons and Direccons, as shalbe soe made by the Governor, or Deputie Governor of the said Company, and such of the Assistants and Freemen as aforesaide, and published in Writing, under their comon Seale, shalbe carefullie and duke observed, kept, performed, and putt in Execucon, according to the true Intent and Meaning of the same; and theis our Letters-patents, or the Duplicate or exemplificacon thereof, shalbe to all and everie such Officers,-superior and inferior, from Tyme to Tyme, for the putting of the same Orders, Lawes, Statutes, and Ordinuces, Instruccons, and Direccons, in due Execucon against Vs. our Heires and Successors, a sufficient Warrant and Discharge.

AND WEE DOE further, for Vs. our Heires and Successors, give and graunt to the said Governor and Company, and their Successors bv theis Presents, that all and everie such Chiefe Comaunders, Captaines, Governors, and other Officers and Ministers, as by the said Orders, Lawes, Statuts, Ordinnces, Instruccons, or Direccons of the said Governor and Company for the Tyme being, shalbe from Tyme to Tyme hereafter vmploied either in the Government of the saide Inhabitants and Plantacon, or in the Waye by Sea thither, or from thence, according to the Natures and Lymitts of their Offices and Places respectively, shall from Tyme to Tyme hereafter for ever, within the Precincts and Partes of Newe England hereby mencoed to be graunted and confirmed, or in the Wale by Sea thither, or from thence, have full and Absolute Power and Authoritie to correct, punishe, pardon, governe, and rule all such the Subiects of Vs. our Heires and Successors, as shall from Tyme to

Tyme adventure themselves in any Voyadge thither or from thence, or that shall at any Tyme hereafter, inhabite within the Precincts and Partes of Newe England aforesaid, according to the Orders, Lawes, Ordinnces, Instruccons, and Direccons aforesaid, not being repugnant to the Lawes and Statutes of our Realme of England as aforesaid. AND WEE DOE further, for Vs. our Heires and Successors, give and graunte to the said Governor and Company, and their Successors, by theis Presents, that it shall and male be lawfull, to and for the Chiefe Comaunders, Governors, and officers of the said Company for the Time being, who shalbe resident in the said Parte of Newe England in America, by theis presents graunted, and others there inhabiting by their Appointment and Direccon, from Tyme to Tvme, and at ail Tymes hereafter for their speciall Defence and Safety, to incounter, expulse, repell, and resist by Force of Armes, aswell by Sea as by Lande, and by all fitting Waies and Meanes whatsoever, all such Person and Persons, as shall at any Tyme hereafter, attempt or enterprise the Destruccon, Invasion, Detriment, or Annoyaunce to the said Plantation or Inhabitants, and to take and surprise by all Waies and Meanes whatsoever, all and every such Person and Persons, with their Shippes, Armour, Municons and other Goodes, as shall in hostile manner invade or attempt the defeating of the said Plantacon, or the Hurt of the said Company and Inhabitants: NEVERTHELESS, our Will and Pleasure is, and Wee doe hereby declare to all Christian Kinges, Princes and States, that yf any Person or Persons which shall hereafter be of the said Company or Plantacon or anv other by Lycense or Appointment of the said Governor and Cmpany for the Tyme being, shall at any Tyme or Tymes hereafter, robb or spoyle, by Sea or by Land, or doe any Hurt, Violence, or vnlawful Hostilitie to any of the Subjects of Vs. our Heires or Successors, or any of the Subjects of any Prince or State, being then in League and Amytie with Vs. our Heires and Successors, and that upon such injury don and vpon iust Complaint of such Prince or State or their Subjects, WEE, our Heires and Successors shall make open Proclamacon within any of the Partes within our Realme of England, comodious for that purpose, that the Person or Persons haveing comitted any such Roberie or Spoyle, shall within the Terme lymytted by such a Proclamacon, make full Restitucon or Satisfaccon of all such Iniureis don, soe as the said Princes or others so complayning, maie hould themselves fullie satisfied and contented; and that yf the said Person or Persons, haveing comitted such Robbery or Spoile, shall not make, or cause to be made Satisfaccon accordinglie, within such Tyme soe to be lymytted, that then it shalbe lawfull for Vs. our Heires and Successors, to putt the said Person or Persons out of our Allegiance and Proteccon, and that it shalbe lawfull and free for all Princes to prosecute with Hostilitie, the said Offendors, and every of them, their and every of their Procurers, Ayders, Abettors, and Comforters in that Behalf: PROVIDED also, and our expresse Will and Pleasure is, And Wee doe by theis Presents for Vs. our Heires and Successors ordeyne and appoint That theis Presents shall not in any manner envre, or be taken to abridge, barr, or hinder any of our loving subjects whatsoever, to vse and exercise the Trade of Fishing vpon that Coast of New England in America, by theis Presents mencoed to be graunted. But that they, and every, or any of them shall have full and free Power and Liberty to continue and vse their said Trade of Fishing vpon the said Coast, in any the Seas therevnto adioyning, or any Armes of the Seas or Saltwater Rivers where they have byn wont to fishe, and to build and sett vp vpon the Landes by theis Presents graunted, such Wharfes, Stages, and Workehouses as shalbe necessarie for the salting, drying, keeping, and packing vp of their Fish, to be taken or gotten vpon that Coast; and to cutt down, and take such Trees and other Materialls there groweing, or being, or shalbe needefull for that Purpose, and for all other necessarie Easements, Helpes, and Advantage concerning their said Trade of Fishing there, in such Manner and Forme as they have byn heretofore at any tyme accustomed to doe, without making any wilfull Waste or Spoyle, any Thing in theis Presents conteyned to the contrarie notwithstanding. AND WEE DOE further, for Vs. our Heires and Successors, ordeyne and graunte to the said Governor and Company, and their Successors by theis Presents that theis our Letters-patents shalbe firme, good, effectuall, and availeable in all Thinges, and to all Intents and Construccons of Lawe, according to our true Meaning herein before declared, and shalbe construed, reputed, and adjudged in all Cases most favourablie on the Behalf, and for the Benefist and Behoofe of the saide Governor and Company and their Successors: ALTHOUGH expresse mencon of the true yearely Value or certenty of the Premisses or any of them; or of any other Guiftes or Grauntes, by Vs. or any of our Progenitors or Predecessors to the foresaid Governor or Company before this tyme made, in theis-Presents is not made; or any Statute, Acte, Ordinnce, Provision, Proclamacon, or Restrainte to the contrarie thereof, heretofore had, made, published, ordeyned, or provided, or any other Matter, Cause, or Thinge whatsoever to the contrarie thereof in any wise notwithstanding.

IN WITNES whereof, Wee have caused theis our Letters to be made Patents.

WITNES ourself, at Westminster, the fourth day of March, in the fourth Yeare of our Raigne.

Per Breve de Privato Sigillo, Wolseley.

Praedictus Matthaeus Cradocke Juratus est de Fide et Obedientia Regi et Successoribus suis, et de Debita Executione Officii Guberatoris Juxta Tenorem Praesentium, 18° Martii, 1628. Coram me Carolo Casare Milite in Cancellaria Mro.

CHAR.CAESAR. The Great Seal of England appendant by a parti-coloured silk string.

Abenaki-English Glossary

Alnôbak	Abenaki
Asenikiwakw	Stone giants; the first people
Babiwseso	He is very small; Child (Papoeis)
Babiwseso Ogawinno	Passaconaway - "Very-Little-One-of-He-Who-Likes-to-Sleep-so-Well" – i.e. "Child-of-the-Bear"
Benôko/Benôkok	Downhill; a downslope
Benôkoi	A falling hill
Benôkoiak	Falling hill persons
Benôkoik	Falling Hill person; a Penacook (Penagok) Indian
Benômkahla	Sand falls
Bezo	Wild Cat - bobcat
Bittôllo	Much Tail – cougar
Gchi Nwaskw	Great Spirit
Gchi Zôgamô	Great Chief
Inglizmônak	Englishmen
Magua	Mohawk; "Man Eaters"
Maji Nwaskw	Bad Spirit
Medôlinôwinno	Person of Medicine; person who works with medicine
Medôlinôwinnoak	Persons of Medicine; people who work with medicine
Nawawas	The Creator; the One who Comes Among us
Nwaskw	Spirit; spirit protector
Nwaskwomak	Spirits; spirit protectors
Ogawinno	"The one who likes to sleep so much (respectful name of the Bear) Totem of the Abenaki bear clan
ôtsôzig	A pass; notch (in the mountains)
Ozigwaôn	Arrowhead
Penagok/Benôko/Benôkok	Downhill; a downslope; Penacook, Pennacook.
Sagamô	Chief; Sagamore
Waolinasad	Wonalancet
Wigwô	Wigwam
Wigwôk	Wigwams

Native American Place Names in New England

Ômanosek	Ammonoosuc River (Fishing Place)
Adelahiganek	Weirs, NH (Barring-the-Way-Instrument)
Agiocochook	Mt. Washington (Place of the Great Storm Spirit)
Amariscoggin	Androscoggin (Rock Shelter Place)
Amerascoggin	Androscoggin (Rock Shelter Place)
Ameriscoggin	Androscoggin (Rock Shelter Place)
Annahooksett	Hooksett, NH (Place of the Beautiful Forest)
Asepihtegw	Ossippee River (River Alongside)
Bagôntegw	Contoocook River (Butternut River)
Bemiawassok	Pemigewasset River (Bemi-grease; awassok-bears-Bears Grease River)
Bemijijoasek/Pemijoaswek	Pemigewasset River (Swift Current)
Beskeodanak/P'skeodanak	Franklin, NH (Beske: Branch of a river or Forked: Odanak – Settlement - i.e. Forked Settlement) **NOTE:** Conjecture - no proof ever called this name by Abenaki
Bigwaki	Echoing Land - Pigwacket
Gawasiwajo/Gôwizawajo	Mt. Kearsarge (Rough Mountain)
Gchi (Kchi) Senisizokw	Great Stone Face (possible Abenaki name for Old Man of the Mountains)
Gwenitegw	Connecticut River (Long River)
Gôdag Wajo/Gôdagwjo	Mt. Washington (Hidden Mountain)
Gôwizawajo	Mt. Kearsarge (Rough Mountain)
Kôdaakwajo	Mt. Washington (Hidden Mountain)
Ktsipontegok	Bellows Falls (Great Falls)
Massabeskik	Lake Massabesic (Large Lake)
Massasecum	Lake Massasecum (Great Narrow Lake)
Menonadenak	Mt. Monadnock (Stands Alone)
Molôdemak	Merrimack River (Deep Water)
Morôdemak	Merrimack River (Deep Water) Ancient Abenaki word
Nôwijoanek	Salmon Falls River (Long Rapids)
Namaskik	Manchester; (At the Fishing Place)
Naumkeag	Salem, MA
Passaguanik	Piscataquog River (Landing Place at the Sand Bar on the Fork of the river-Pass-bar, river bottom rising; agua-landing; Nik- fork of the river)

Patuxet	Plymouth, MA
Pawtucket	Lowell, MA
Penakok/Penagok/	
Penagok/Penegok	Concord (At the Place of the Falling Bank), Penacook; Pennacook
P'enegokw	At the Falling Bank
Pennaquiauke	At the Crooked Place
Pesgatakwa	Piscataqua River (Dark River)
Senikok	Suncook (At the Rocks)
Seninebik	Sunapee (Stony Waters)
Shawmut	Boston, MA
Wajo	Mountain
Waumbek	Mt Washington (White Rocks)
Wôbiadenak	The White Mountains
Wawobadenik	The White Mountains
Wôwôbadenak	The White Mountains
Winnepiscogee	Lake Winnipesaukee (Land Around Lakes)
Winnepiseogee	Lake Winnipesaukee (Land Around Lakes)
Winnimsquam	Lake Winnisquam (Where the Salmon Waters Flow out; Winn - outlet)
Wiwinijoanek	Dover (Water Flows Around It)
Wiwninebesaki	Lake Winnipesaukee (Land Around Lakes)
Wôbanaki	Northern New England, Southern Quebec (Dawnland)
Zawakwtegok	Saco River
Zobagw	Atlantic Ocean

About the Author

Stephen W.F. Berwick, a descendant of northern New England and Quebec's Native American peoples as well as French and English settlers, was born in Laconia, New Hampshire in 1962. In his life and work Stephen strives to open minds and hearts, believing as Buddha did that "In the sky, there is no distinction of east and west; people create distinctions out of their own minds and then believe them to be true." Stephen, who speaks Japanese, Mandarin Chinese, and French and is also conversant in Swedish, Indonesian and Thai, has traveled widely throughout Northeast and Southeast Asia. A practicing Buddhist since 1981, Stephen underwent ordination as a Buddhist monk in 2004. His preceptor, the Venerable Luang Po Chan Kusalo, one of Thailand's foremost theologians, consented to Stephen's ordination only after considerable persuasion, allowing him

Stephen W.F. Berwick

to become the first Westerner in 600 years to ordain at Chiangmai's Wat Chedi Luang, a temple famous as the former home of the Emerald Buddha. Upon returning to New Hampshire Stephen began publishing Asia-Link Journal with the goal of promoting cultural understanding, respect and peace. Stephen also wrote a biography about a Korean-American woman entitled "From Ch'ongnyangni to Northfield" which was published by the Korean Cultural Service as well as two biographies about Vietnamese refugees, which were published as part of the anthology "Voices of the Vietnamese Boat People." Stephen has received a number of awards for his poetry and was named International Poet of Merit in 1995 by the International Poetry Association as well as nominated as the Association's 1995 Poet of the Year for his poem "Exile," a poem that embodies the spirit of America's immigrants. In February 2011 Stephen's book "Land of the Shapeshifter" was published. The book employs interpretive short stories based on historical events as a guide to the world of Passaconaway and his descendants to explore the land the Abenaki call "N'dakinna" – "Our Land." In April 2011 "Shapeshifter's Peace – Passaconaway's Path to Peace" was published, the first in a series of seven historical fiction books about the effects of European settlement on the Abenaki peoples of New Hampshire with the hope of promoting understanding of America's past as well as respect and peace amongst all peoples. In July 2011 "In the Shadow of Agiocochook – Stories from the Land of the Shapeshifter" was published.

Stephen W.F. Berwick books:

Land of the Shapeshifter

Shapeshifter's Peace – Passaconaway's Path to Peace

In the Shadow of Agiocochook – Stories from the Land of the Shapeshifter

COMING IN SPRING 2012

Deep Water; Falling Bank: *More stories from the Land of the Shapeshifter*

COMING IN AUTUMN 2012

The Shifting Shape Of Peace: *Wonalancet follows the Shapeshifter's Path to Peace*

Stephen's books are available from:
Amazon.com
Barnes & Noble
parisburg.com
and other internet book sellers and retailers